CONTENTS

THE DEMICHELLIS CASE

Francisco Marín

Translated from the Spanish
By
Marta Sprague

FRANCISCO MARÍN

In memory of my parents, and for my son, Luca.

FRANCISCO MARÍN

1

Under the watchful eye of the judge, presiding over the courtroom adorned in his judicial robe, the jury foreman opened the envelope and extracted the court record containing the findings of fact and, consequently, the verdict. On the other side of the courtroom, in front of the nine members of the jury, stood the legal representative of the prosecution and the defense attorney, also dressed in their respective black robes, the indispensable vestments for the ritual of justice.

Raúl Ballesteros had spent half of his 45 years practicing law. While he'd managed to accumulate reasonable prestige in addition to a considerable fortune, he still worked duty shifts as a court appointed legal counsel because of a vague sense of social responsibility, despite the fact that the emolument for this work couldn't begin to compare with the earnings received from his paying clients. He often asked himself why he continued to sign up for these shifts, employing a portion of his time to represent crooks and delinquents in exchange for a nominal fee, instead of exclusively defending criminals who were able to pay his inflated rates.

He entertained no romantic notions about his chosen profession. He was a criminal defense attorney specializing in criminal law, and nearly every client who came to his office in need of services was guilty of some crime. The image of the defenseless man that had been falsely or unjustly accused (and even convicted), which was so widespread in the United States among the African American population, was a rarity when practicing law in the courts of Spain. Yet he was about to hear the verdict in precisely one of those extraordinary cases in which his client had been tried as a defendant for felony murder, and Raúl Ballesteros was convinced of his innocence—to the point that a skeptical lawyer could be. In some measure, this case had revived long-buried feelings dating back to the beginning of his career, when he had dreamed of becoming a champion defender of justice.

One way in which Spaniards did resemble Americans, Ballesteros mused, was with the institution of the jury trial, whose jurisdiction extended to judicial proceedings for criminal homicide. It was the ultimate in democracy and political demagoguery. Back in the 4th century BC, Plato posited that just as steering a ship or practicing medicine required specific knowledge, the ability to govern and exercise justice also required sufficient knowledge not available to all people. Therefore, he concluded, rulers should be philosophers. Would someone have their tooth pulled by a person picked by lot from the voter registry? Would someone have their vehicle fixed by a person chosen at random? Surely in both cases, any reasonable person would prefer an experienced dentist or mechanic. And yet, it appears justice can be doled out by anyone. Our society randomly chooses nine people whose knowledge of court procedures likely comes from watching a television series. We casually explain the principle of the presumption of innocence to them (in case they hadn't figured it out from watching the series), and with that, they decide whether to convict or acquit someone of committing murder.

Yes, this was the type of case coveted by every criminal attorney, defending an innocent client. But Raúl would have preferred that the decision be made by the objectivity, legal expertise, and impartiality of a judge, as opposed to the malleability, biases, and impressions of nine people who are presumably of good will. In order to establish a guilty verdict in Spain, there must be agreement by seven members of the jury, while five votes are enough to determine a verdict of not guilty. The mathematical probabilities swing in favor of innocence. The law also demands that there be clear and convincing evidence to substantiate the conviction. *But in fact,* Ballesteros thought, *there is no evidence here. Just a series of circumstances that point to the accused.* He looked at his client who sat on the bench with his fingers interlocked and a blank expression on his face. The jury foreman had not looked at him which, per the attorney's experience, did not bode well for the defendant. Despite spending seven and a half months in pretrial detention and having submitted himself to a detox program, the long-term use of every type of drug had left its mark on Eduardo Ribas' face, which projected a permanently clenched grimace and a tic that made him blink without rhyme or reason. A hair analysis, performed at the insistence of his attorney in order to claim mitigating circumstances in the event that it became necessary, had detected the presence of cocaine, heroin, cannabis, amphetamines and MDMA in his system.

Still, Ballesteros reminded himself, there was no clear and convincing evidence. Throughout the spring of 2012, three home robberies had been reported in a subdivision in the area of Cap Martinet, in the suburbs of Ibiza. The development was a cluster of semi-detached townhomes built with little or no zoning that had erupted like a rash of cement blocks strewn on the hillside of a mountain range with gentle slopes. According to the investigation by the Spanish Civil Guard, the perpetrator was a man acting alone, and the modus operandi of the thief did not vary. He climbed up to the second floor balcony of the homes at dawn, after making sure no interior lights were visible and the neighbors were asleep, and forced the lock on the door. The front door of the townhomes was reinforced with a deadbolt, but the upstairs door was easy to open. The thief chose homes occupied by women who lived alone. It was assumed he purposefully targeted them to minimize his risk. Once inside the home, he quietly approached the bedroom and sprayed the sleeping victim's face with chloroform. The possibility this would backfire was minimal since, even if the woman awoke, it only took a few seconds to produce the expected sleep effect once she'd inhaled the anesthetic substance. The rest was a walk in the park. The perpetrator knew that, at least for an hour, the woman would remain anesthetized and he could open drawers and closets at will. He primarily stole money and jewelry, objects that were easy to transport. The following morning, the victims would awaken with a severe headache that only worsened when they discovered that someone had ransacked their home during the night.

On May 3rd, 2012, the corpse of a 30-year-old woman who worked as a nurse at Can Misses Hospital was discovered by her sister. Her lifeless body had been found in her residence, a country home located at km 3 of Carretera San Josep. The nurse had not shown up to work that day, nor had she called to explain her absence. Calls to her landline had gone unanswered, her cell phone message indicated it was off or out of the service area, and neither her parents, co-workers nor friends knew why she was absent, so the victim's sister had gone to her home. After ringing the doorbell repeatedly with no response, she entered with her duplicate key. As soon as she crossed the threshold to the living room, she realized something was wrong. Chaos reigned. The drawers were dislodged and their contents were strewn all over the floor forming a hodgepodge of objects: CDs, DVDs, various receipts, clips, chewing gum packages, an old wallet, a stapler, pens. She headed to the upper floor and called out to her sister as she walked up the stairs. No response. She found her sister's body in the first floor bedroom, lying on her bed.

Although the country home where this most recent victim was found was six kilometers from the housing development at Cap Martinet, the Civil Guard's Judicial Police Unit suspected that the perpetrator of this homicide was the same individual who had committed the Cap Martinet robberies during the previous month. The method used to enter the home by the assailant had been almost identical, forcing open the locked door. The autopsy had revealed chloroform remains in the victim's body, and the cause of death had been asphyxia by strangulation. The time of death was between 3:00 and 4:00 p.m. on the 2nd of May. The house had been ransacked. After a detailed analysis by the judicial police team, three types of fingerprints had been found besides those of the victim. However, a comparison of those fingerprints with police records found no match. Logically, the fingerprints might belong to family or friends.

On May 5th, 2012, at 11:45 p.m., Eduardo Ribas was riding his motorcycle in the Cap Martinet area, heading toward Ibiza. He was wearing a parka, scarf, and gloves, in addition to a helmet with the plastic visor lowered, to protect his face from the cold evening air. He took the last turn out of the housing development, toward the avenue that led to the exiting rotunda. At that moment, he noticed an unusual appearance at the edge of the roundabout: flashing yellow lights that signaled the unmistakable presence of law enforcement. He hit the brakes and turned off the motorcycle lights as he swung around toward the opposite end of the street. From their position, barely 100 meters away, the Civil Guard officers had spotted the motorcycle and its sudden change of direction. They yelled at him to halt while two officers got into their antiquated Nissan Patrol car to initiate pursuit. Eduardo Ribas ignored the police shouts ordering him to stop and went full throttle. He was aware that he was driving a 125cc scooter that wouldn't go faster than 90 km per hour. His only option was to zigzag through the labyrinthine streets that made up the suburban development and hope the police would lose him. He turned right at the first corner at full speed, loosened his hand on the throttle, and lightly pressed the rear brake handle. For an instant, the bluish flurry of lights emanating from the hood of the police vehicle stopped following him. Dew had covered the asphalt and, when he hit the brakes, the rear tire skidded to one side. Startled, Eduardo let go of the brake handle and accelerated again. The scooter swerved toward the other side. For a brief moment he thought he was in control of the bike, a momentary pipe dream of victory just before he felt it slide to the ground, his knee crashing against the pavement. Eduardo saw himself falling in slow motion for a few seconds and experienced a flash of disparate thoughts: the first thing that came to mind was that he had screwed up; then he thought he should try to protect his back to avoid crashing into some obstacle. And he also suddenly realized he had no drugs with him, in the event that he was arrested. Eduardo stayed motionless next to a parked car, then got on his feet quickly and tried to run. He felt a sharp pain in his knee as his leg suddenly buckled, preventing his escape.

He leaned on a parked car and saw the police SUV turn the corner toward him, flooding the street with flashes of blue light. The car's brakes screeched and stopped two meters before reaching the bike that was laying in the middle of the road. The headlights were shining on Eduardo who, either in a show of goodwill or defeat, raised his hands in surrender. Both doors of the Nissan Patrol opened, and an officer climbed out of each one. One of them was holding a gun with both hands, pointing it at the fugitive.

2

Ballesteros was having dinner with his childhood friend, Paco Marín, at a place known as signature cuisine restaurant. Their table was next to a window with a view of distant lights and boats in the Ibizan harbor. He was bringing a forkful of monkfish up to his mouth when his on-duty cell phone rang. He took it out of his trouser pocket and looked at the screen before answering.

"Shit! It's the Civil Guard office!"

"Don't answer," advised Paco.

"Oh yeah, right. Goddammit! Being on call means I have to accept the consequences. Of course, it might be nothing."

He pressed the button to answer the call.

"Hello? … And this can't wait until first thing tomorrow? … Alright, I'll be there in 45 minutes."

"At least you should finish your dinner," said Paco, with a tone somewhere between a statement and question.

"Yeah, but we've had a bit of wine. I don't know if I'm in any condition to assist someone who's been arrested. It's not normal to have to go at this hour. Normally, I have an eight-hour window in which to appear, but I'd rather get it over with."

"Does it pay anything?"

"The truth is I often ask myself why I sign on for this. Financially, it's not worthwhile. And legally, I don't contribute much. It's always the same. They catch a guy doing something: dealing, stealing, whatever. If there's evidence, he's guilty. If not, he's acquitted. My job is minimal."

"And on top of that, your dinners are interrupted…."

"Right. But sometimes we don't ask ourselves why we do things. For example, why do you have art exhibits? I understand you like to paint although I don't understand your paintings or your painting style. But exhibits? What for? It's not like you need the money. Is it so you can listen to compliments and satisfy your ego or to feel like more of an artist?"

"Alright look, you don't have to get angry because the cops ruined dinner," said Paco. "We were talking about you and your duty shift cases, and ended up talking about me and painting. Yes, I suppose there's some vanity involved in the exhibits. The interesting thing is, given the life I lead, I don't really need the money. Ultimately, my hobbies are painting, reading, and watching the occasional movie or football game. You don't need a huge fortune to dedicate yourself to that."

Ballesteros mopped up a little sauce with a piece of bread and, before putting it in his mouth, he responded.

"Here we go again, Paco! It's so easy for you to watch from the sidelines! Yes, reading may be cheap, even free if you get your books from the library; and canvas, oil or acrylic paints are available to almost anyone, but you're forgetting an essential factor: time. If your bills weren't covered, you'd have to do what most people do or, these days, what most people who *can* do, and that's work. You'd have to stop getting up at nine, going to the gym, having breakfast on the terrace of your little bungalow, and then deciding if you feel like painting or reading or going for a walk today. Shit, Paco, give me a break! If one day you feel like you want to unplug, you just take off to Bali or New York or the middle of nowhere, and that's okay. Or if you don't want to go to bed alone, you hire a model who works extra hours at night. You don't attach any value to those things because you're able to do them. Sure, you like to paint and read, but when you have a couple million in the bank, money seems less important."

"You're right, maybe I got carried away. But so did you. Besides, I hardly travel anymore and since I've been with Tanya I haven't associated with what you call the 'models who work extra hours', which, by the way, I've done only twice in my life. And suddenly, I have a reputation!" Paco replied defensively.

Ballesteros enjoyed the ritual of dining on Fridays with his childhood friend. They met every other week. On alternate Fridays, Ballesteros spent the weekend with his daughter, Julieta, per the terms of his divorce agreement. He and Paco had gone to school together in Ibiza and had shared an apartment in Barcelona while they studied law. By that time, Paco was already more interested in painting than in jurisprudence, but his parents thought a law career would offer more opportunities than Fine Arts. Unlike Ballesteros, Paco had not been a good student, and after two and a half years dedicated to *il dolce far niente*, he stopped kidding himself and his parents and abandoned the career. That summer, he started working as a waiter in a restaurant on the beachfront. The job was exhausting. His workday was 12 hours long and he had no days off. There was always something to do in the restaurant and it always had to be done right away. They started serving food at one in the afternoon in order to adapt to the schedules of various English and German tourists that flooded the island and had not adapted to the Spanish timetable. Paco was in charge of serving drinks. He rushed from one side of the restaurant to the other carrying orders on his tray, pretending not to see the many customers that were trying to get his attention with their gestures and increasingly irritated voices. By evening, after the last of the pesky people had left the locale, he still had to sweep, wash the floor, and fill the cold storage unit so the drinks were cold the following morning.

In October, when the summer season was over, Paco began preparing to take a judicial assistant exam. He passed the exam the following year and, after months of waiting, was assigned to a body of justices of the peace in Linyola, in the province of Lleida. He worked from nine to two and earned enough income to get by without any extravagances, but was still able to afford small vices like beer and cigarettes. After his experience in the hospitality industry, he found it incredible that he could make a living working five hours a day, with weekends and holidays off and nine personal days a year. What a deal! He rented a two-room apartment for a moderate price and used one of the rooms as a studio. It was a comfortable and solitary life. He spent his afternoons painting, and in the evening went out for a beer at one of the two bars in town. Where this tranquil and routine life might have led him would remain a mystery due to the occurrence of an unexpected event. On the morning of February 4th, 1998, while routinely checking his lottery ticket (in preparation for tossing it in the garbage), he stared in disbelief at the amazing coincidence between the numbers in the newspaper and the ones on his ticket. He left the café without finishing his coffee, walking to the nearby kiosk at a fast pace. It had been a year and a half since he'd started his new job. Paco bought three different newspapers and sat down at a nearby bench. All three newspapers showed the same winning combination of lottery numbers. There was only one winning ticket and the accumulated jackpot had grown to four billion pesetas which, in 2002, translated to a little more than 24 million euros. His heart jumped. A whirlwind of ideas swarmed in his head. He had occasionally fantasized about an imaginary lottery prize and the direction his life might take. His wish list included a country home with a pool, or a penthouse, travel on the Orient Express, exploring Asia, Africa, and America and, last but not least, hiring someone to clean the house and wash and iron his clothes. Paco liked order and cleanliness, and having a clean house provided a feeling of satisfaction despite the unpleasantness of the task. He enjoyed cooking and shopping at the grocer and didn't mind washing and hanging his clothes to dry, but he hated cleaning house and ironing. Yes, hiring a cleaning lady to come to his future country home or penthouse to perform domestic tasks was nothing to sneeze at.

He decided not to share the news of his good fortune with anyone; not his friends, his two sisters, or most certainly, his coworkers. Obviously, he'd have to explain why he was leaving his civil servant position with a nine-to-two workday, but he'd think of something. Besides, he didn't have any close friends, or any other kind of friends really, in Linyola.

Paco spent that afternoon feeling uneasy. After the euphoria came the anxiety. What if someone mugged him and stole his ticket? It was a remote possibility. Nobody knew he had it. A more plausible hypothesis was that after he deposited it in the bank, the manager would be tempted to keep it for himself. The following morning, he went to the court office before it opened and made a couple copies of the lottery ticket, on which he had previously made a small mark with a red pen. He went to the only Caixa Bank in town and, after a brief meeting with the branch manager to whom he expressed his request that no news of his fortune become known, he deposited the ticket at the bank.

'It usually takes a few days to receive payment,' the manager had said. 'Of course, my experience has been with much smaller prizes. I don't know how long it will take to receive this amount, but as soon as we get it we will let you know. If you need any kind of advance or a credit card, just let me know.'

'Well, for now I don't need anything.' Paco had responded. 'I'm still considering my options. Maybe I'll keep working for a while, so I have time to think about it.'

"I have to leave, it's getting late," said Ballesteros, resting the palms of his hands on the tablecloth to gesture that he was getting up. "I suppose I'll spend a minimum of an hour at police headquarters, so we'll have to leave our drink to next Friday. Give my regards to Tanya."

"I will," said Paco. "Go on then, I know you're in a hurry. I'll get the check."

"I'd expect nothing less," Ballesteros replied. "But next Friday it's my turn. You know I don't like to be a kept man."

"Fine. And we're not going to argue about it either—that would be rude."

3

The taxi dropped Ballesteros off at the entrance to the Civil Guard's headquarters in Santa Eulalia. He walked through the door into a small room where he encountered an officer dressed in the standard olive-green uniform, sitting behind a brown desk.

"Can I help you?" asked the uniformed young man. Ballesteros had not met him before. His voice had that particularly authoritative tone employed by some officers in law enforcement to remind the public of who is in charge and who is not. Ballesteros knew from experience that all this bravado toward the general public would transform into deference and subservience when addressing a judge in a courtroom. That same manner, incidentally, was adopted by attorneys, advocates, and most members of the public when standing before a judge, thereby contributing to the arrogance of the judiciary class. Undoubtedly, the Civil Guard as a whole, had begrudgingly toned down their authoritarian attitude of decades past until it resembled a forced courtesy. But there were still some for whom the uniform provided a power trip, which they manifested by treating the public to a dose of arrogance and contempt.

"I'm the on-duty court appointed counsel. I was informed there is a prisoner who requires legal assistance."

"Yes, there is a prisoner. My orders from Sergeant Ferrando indicate you should speak with him first, before you meet with the perp."

The officer accompanied Ballesteros to the sergeant's office at the end of a short corridor. It was a small office: the walls were lined with shelves stacked with yellowing papers pertaining to matters that likely expired years ago. The Civil Guard sergeant, dressed in plain clothes, was seated behind a desk. He wore a beige suit, his forearms rested on the desktop. Ballesteros recognized him and knew he hadn't been at this post long. The transfer of Civil Guards, national policemen, and all types of governmental civil servants was normal in Ibiza. They arrived at the island on a mandatory assignment, and later, after a position freeze of one or two years when a list of available transfers was released, they returned to the Peninsula where their families and friends lived. Only a small percentage settled on the island permanently.

The sergeant was thirty-something years old and thin, with black hair speckled gray at the temples. If there was a face that could define a pissed off look, this officer would be its perfect illustration.

"You are Raúl Ballesteros."

"Correct. And you are Sergeant Ferrando."

"Do you know why we called you?"

"I only know there is a prisoner here, and apparently, you couldn't wait until 9:00 o'clock tomorrow morning," Ballesteros replied.

"Yes, this is a serious matter. Have you heard about the nurse who was killed a few days ago?"

"I read something about it in the newspaper."

"Well, we arrested the alleged offender … and he wants to confess."

"He told you he killed her or you're assuming he wants to confess his guilt?"

"He implied it."

"I want to assume he has not made any statements in my absence."

"That's right, we have not taken his statement. It would be best if we don't complicate this case too much," said Ferrando. "If he confesses, we can all go home and the world will have one less son of a bitch to deal with. I already asked them to bring him in."

Ballesteros got up without saying a word. He was used to police officers trying to convince him of a client's guilt.

Didn't they know that he was obligated to defend clients equally whether they were innocent or guilty? Didn't they know that the purpose of the preliminary investigation and trial was to determine guilt or innocence? They really were a bunch of ball-busters.

Ballesteros sat on a bench against the wall next to the door to Sergeant Ferrando's office watching the cuffed suspect approached, accompanied by an officer. Eduardo Ribas was a scrawny, nervous looking man who blinked incessantly. His face carried a thin layer of sweat and his eyes had the impatient expression of an addict who hadn't had a fix in a while.

"Are you feeling alright?" asked Ballesteros.

"I want this to be over already," Eduardo Ribas mumbled.

4

The trial began on the morning of January 10, 2013, at 9:00 a.m., in the courtroom of the Provincial Court in Palma, where jury trials take place. A storm bearing high winds and heavy precipitation had encompassed the entirety of the Balearic Islands, and Ballesteros had traveled by plane the night before from Ibiza to Mallorca to avoid getting up at dawn and to sidestep possible delays or flight cancellations.

Through the large windows of the courtroom, he contemplated the dense mass of water raining down on Palma. He thought back on the interrogation Eduardo Ribas had been subjected to by the officers that had arrested him. After informing him of the rights available to a detained person and asking his name, address, and additional personal information, the incriminating questions began.

"Have you ever been to the Siesta housing development in the Cap Martinet area?" asked the Civil Guard sergeant modulating his voice.

"Yeah."

"How many times?"

"I don't remember exactly, two, maybe three." Eduardo Ribas stumbled over his words, as if he was anxious.

"What were you doing in that housing complex?"

"I went in to rob a couple houses."

"Did you enter a cottage located at Km 3 on Carretera San Josep on the 3rd of May at about 2:00 or 3:00 o'clock?"

"Yeah."

"That is not how you ask a question!" Ballesteros interrupted loudly.

It was becoming crystal clear to Ballesteros that this interrogation was being orchestrated, and that the sergeant was manipulating his client by asking leading questions because he was more interested in finding his client guilty (and subsequently scoring points with his superiors and the media) than getting at the truth. He was also aware that these law enforcement officers were resorting to deception to obtain a confession or find contradictions in Ribas' statements, even if it meant turning a blind eye to constitutional requirements. Sergeant Ferrando glared at the attorney with a dark expression.

"What do you mean by that, Ballesteros?" he asked in a scornful and menacing tone. The attorney felt sudden rage at this man who, in theory, was in charge of ensuring compliance with the law. However, he knew that in the interest of his client, his best approach would be to control the urge to tell this arrogant cop to go to hell, and he exercised restraint.

"You are leading this man's statement." Ballesteros responded in a calm voice, gesturing to Eduardo Ribas who was sitting next to him. "You should be asking him what he did on such and such day and not whether on this day at that time he entered a house, so that he just answers yes."

"Your client is an adult, and my questions are quite clear. He can answer yes, no, or I don't know."

"He knows what's at stake and what his rights are," said Ballesteros softly, addressing his client. "He doesn't have to make a statement now, nor is he required to confess if he has done anything illegal. He won't get a prize for confessing to a crime. It might be a mitigating factor, at best, but what is guaranteed is certain conviction."

"I'm tired. I just wanna finish already and sleep," said Ribas.

"I don't think this is a good idea. Are you sure you want to make a statement here, now, instead of tomorrow in front of a judge, after you've rested?" insisted Ballesteros speaking directly to Eduardo Ribas, who had a blank expression on his face, as if he was disconnected from what was being discussed in the Civil Guard's office.

"No!" Eduardo shouted loudly, "I said I wanna make a

statement! If you're not gonna listen to what I say, then I want another lawyer!"

"Look," said Sergeant Ferrando in a terse voice while gesturing forced patience, "your client seems to know his rights. We read them to him, and you have just reminded him of them. You cannot stop him from making a statement if he wants to."

"Then let's get on with it," said Ballesteros with a look of deep resignation and fatigue on his face. He also wanted to finish this and return home to sleep.

The rest of the statement turned out to be a load of nonsense and Ballesteros felt that, despite his years of experience, he had not been shrewd, and he'd been outplayed like a rookie. Maybe his mental acuity had not been at one hundred percent because of the wine he drank at dinner with Paco, but that wasn't an excuse. He should have tried harder to stop his client from making a statement, or withdrawn from the case. Eduardo Ribas admitted having been at the deceased woman's home at the approximate time of death and anesthetizing her with chloroform. He confessed to perpetrating more robberies in other homes in the Cap Martinet area. When the sergeant asked if he remembered having strangled the victim, Eduardo Ribas stated that he did not remember. The following day, they appeared at the preliminary hearing and the presiding judge imposed a pretrial detention of the prisoner and ordered a search and seizure of his home where they found items that had been stolen from some of the homes in the Siesta housing development. They did not find any object that could be identified as belonging to the deceased nurse. Still, there was enough circumstantial evidence to incriminate him.

5

A month and a half later, Eduardo Ribas had contacted Ballesteros from the prison in Ibiza.

"It was all a trap!" he said in a manic tone. Presumably he had not used drugs for a month, yet he seemed more agitated than the day he was arrested.

"What are you talking about?" asked Ballesteros.

"I wasn't in that dead lady's house. All that stuff happened at three in the afternoon and I only went in at night, when people were sleeping. That copper told me if I confessed he'd give me drugs, and I needed something badly. But I didn't know he was gonna pin a murder on me."

"Shit! You're telling me this now?" Ballesteros surmised it was pointless to say *'I warned you not to make a statement'* to his client. The confession was a done deal, and now they needed to be pragmatic. "Let's take this one step at a time: was anything you confessed true, or did you make everything up so they would give you drugs for saying what they wanted?"

"The part about the burglaries was true, but I always broke in at night and in Cap Martinet. I wouldn't have gone in during the day. And I dunno where that dead lady's house is. I wouldn't even recognize the other women I robbed. All I did was spray them with chloroform, robbed 'em, and left. At that time of day when she was killed—near Carretera Sant Josep—that wasn't me."

"Do you remember what you did on May 2nd around 3 or 4 in the afternoon?"

"I dunno … I was probably stoned or sleeping it off."

"Did you see anyone else at about that time, before or after?"

"I dunno. I can't remember."

"Okay, relax. We haven't gone to trial yet." Now Balles-teros' mind *was* at one hundred percent. He could see the situation clearly and was acutely aware that all the cards were not in their favor.

"Obviously, Sergeant Ferrando is going to deny that he offered you drugs in exchange for your statement, and the matter of the burglaries is set in stone. Apart from your confession, there are the items they found in your house. But let's see if we can't save you from the homicide charge. I think that, given the way things are, it would be best if you told the whole truth. We could also allege that you confessed to the robberies under duress, but I expect that would be useless. Besides, there's the fact that you were arrested in that area."

"Yeah, sure. I don't care if I have to do time for the burglaries, but they can't pin that dead lady on me! How much time could I do for the ... the ... murder?"

"Technically, you haven't been accused of murder. It's manslaughter. Murder requires payment or premeditation or malice. The version maintained by the prosecution is that you broke in to steal, something went wrong, and you killed the girl. You could end up with 10-15 years."

"Look, I needed drugs. That's why I told the cops what they wanted to hear."

"Right. You don't need to explain it to me. There are others guiltier than you for your confession, though I don't think we can prove that."

6

Ballesteros studied the members of the jury, five women and four men, while attempting to calculate the possibilities of obtaining a favorable verdict. He had to undo some damage if he wanted his client to have the slightest chance of being acquitted. Only one woman appeared to be under thirty years old; most of the jury members were older than forty, and one looked about sixty. He was discouraged. He thought it would be difficult for these nine people to concede more credibility to the accused, a drug-addicted thief, than to a sergeant of the Civil Guard. He would have preferred a younger jury, one more inclined to be dubious about members of the police force. He needed five jury members to vote in favor of his client's innocence. It would be hard enough to convince just five.

The trial was brief. The principal witnesses for the prosecution were the officers that arrested Eduardo Ribas and the forensic pathologist. Ballesteros had called the suspect to testify, and he had acknowledged having perpetrated the burglaries at the Siesta housing complex, but he denied having killed the nurse and maintained that he had not even been in the area where she lived. The suspect explained the contradiction between his current testimony and his previous statement to the officers and the judge at the preliminary hearing; a statement given because of the promise made by Sergeant Ferrando to provide him with drugs in exchange for his confession of guilt. Given this testimony, the prosecutor called on Sergeant Ferrando as a witness who, with a look of righteous indignation, denied having offered the suspect drugs and reiterated that all of the suspect's constitutional rights had been protected, including the presence of an attorney.

The trial resumed in the early afternoon, after a forty-five minutes recess for lunch. The prosecution succinctly presented the evidence against the accused: the suspect had acknowledged having committed the robberies, therefore, the only verdict available to the jury on this count was guilty.

"Regarding the homicide of Ms. Ana López Demichellis," argued the prosecutor while addressing the members of the jury, "which the suspect before you denies having committed, you must take into account that for crimes in which only the victim and perpetrator are present, the determination is based on circumstantial evidence. In this case, as in many others, there was no eyewitness who saw the suspect commit the homicide; however, there is overwhelming evidence that points to Eduardo Ribas' guilt. First, we have the confession which Mr. Ribas himself gave to the Civil Guard officers and to the judge in front of his attorney, who is also present here today and who later attempted to discredit the confession by fabricating a bizarre story about the defendant having been subjected to some sort of blackmail which, in turn, was refuted by the sergeant who performed the interrogation. Obviously, the Civil Guard's version is more credible than that of the accused, as the officer has no personal interest in the matter other than enforcing the law. Second, the method used to break into the victim's home was identical to the one used in the burglaries which Mr. Ribas acknowledges having committed. Third, traces of chloroform were found on the victim's body, which was the substance used by Mr. Ribas to anesthetize his victims while committing the robberies. Jurors, you may ask: why would he acknowledge having committed the burglaries and deny having killed Ms. López Demichellis? The answer is simple. He could not deny the burglaries. He was arrested a couple of nights after the homicide in the Siesta complex. A backpack containing an electric lock pick, a spray gun with chloroform, and a mask to avoid inhaling the substance himself was found close to the scene of the arrest. Results from the search and seizure conducted at Mr. Ribas' home found items stolen in the robberies. The suspect has not denied the robberies because he has no other option than to acknow-

ledge them, or his entire statement would have been unbelievable. But he does deny the homicide because, in addition to the
likelihood of a substantially longer prison sentence, he believes
that since no one saw him commit the crime he cannot be convicted. As I have stated, Spanish law includes the principle of the
presumption of innocence, but this presumption of innocence
can be discarded even when there is no eyewitness. If we required an eyewitness for every crime committed, most criminals would be on the street. Moreover, I suggest to you that we
would give rise to an increase in crime. In summary, based on
the overwhelming evidence which indicates that the only person who could have committed this homicide is Mr. Ribas, I have
no choice but to request that you deliver a verdict of guilty."

Ballesteros looked up from his notes on the table and
turned his gaze directly to the jury box where the nine men and
women sat in anticipation. Ballesteros had only taken part in
four jury trials and he had won them all. He knew he had to
clearly and succinctly explain the facts that favored his client
without getting tangled up in legal technicalities and incompre-
hensible legalese. But equally important as a transparent review
of the facts was a psychological victory—that of convincing the
members of the jury that they should decide in his favor and
that of his client. He and the prosecutor were comparable to politicians from opposing parties fighting for constituents' votes.
Both rational and emotional arguments were equally valid.
Ballesteros had an attractive demeanor and he inspired people's
confidence. His ex-wife once told him he looked like the actor,
Daniel Day-Lewis. Of course, she had said that many years ago,
before their breakup.

Ballesteros had decided to begin his closing argument by
trying to parse some of the prosecutor's statements and reduce
them to absurdities in order to erode their credibility. He took a
sip of water directly from a plastic bottle and placed it back on
the table. After appropriately addressing the judge ('*if it pleases
the court*'), he began by presenting his conclusions in a well-
pitched, pleasant voice. "Ladies and gentlemen of the jury, before

I start presenting the evidence outlining the innocence of my client, I'd like you to think about a statement that the prosecutor made a few moments ago which I consider quite serious. She more or less stated that a person may be convicted solely based on circumstantial evidence in order that the crime rate not increase. It means that instead of the principle of the presumption of innocence currently established in our Constitution and our laws, we can move on to a kind of presumption of guilt. This, ladies and gentlemen, while impulsively stated by the prosecutor, is not correct. Our legal system is guided by the principle of '*in dubio pro reo*,' in other words, if there is reasonable doubt, you must decide in favor of the accused.

"Now that I have made this clear, let us review the facts of this case. It is true that Mr. Ribas was arrested at dawn at the Siesta housing complex. During the search warrant executed at his home, items were found that had been stolen from that same complex. And that is all. What does that evidence indicate? Only one thing: that Mr. Ribas committed the burglaries that he has confessed to having committed. But by no means can he be convicted for the death of Ms. López Demichellis. No item belonging to the victim was found during the search of Mr. Ribas' home. My client always carried out the burglaries well into the night and, according to the forensic report for Ms. López Demichellis, she was killed between three and four in the afternoon. In other words: in broad daylight. Furthermore, the houses that Mr. Ribas broke into were in another area, six kilometers away, where there were no alarm systems. Ms. López Demichellis' home did have an alarm, as was clearly indicated on the sign in front of her house. Why would my client take the risk of breaking into a home with a security alarm and in broad daylight? It makes no sense. Finally, and I consider this critical, forensic analysis found large quantities of chloroform in the victim's body. If she was already anesthetized, why strangle her? This is yet another contradiction that we can add to the others: first, the time of day in which Mr. Ribas is accused of breaking into the home; second, the home was protected by an alarm system and the other robberies committed by Mr. Ribas were carried out in homes that did not have this protection and were in another area; third, none of the victim's belongings were found in Mr. Ribas' home when the search warrant was carried out, while items from other robberies that the suspect confessed to were found. Finally, ask yourselves: if the victim was already anesthetized, why didn't Mr. Ribas just burglarize the house as he had done in other instances? What need was there to strangle the victim? Mr. Ribas has a criminal record, that is true, but for theft or robbery. There is no criminal history that links him to violent crimes. Overall, there are many components that more than establish reasonable doubt as to the guilt of the defendant.

"We have explained why my client confessed to having broken into that house. It is simply because he was promised drugs and my client was experiencing withdrawal symptoms. To make it stop he would have signed any confession they gave him at the time. If they had asked, he would also have confessed to being a member of Al-Qaeda and to have carried out the 2004 Madrid train bombings.

"In conclusion, I really must insist: if there is doubt, the law requires that you acquit. If you are completely convinced that Mr. Ribas perpetrated the homicide, then find in favor of guilt. But if you have any doubt, even the most minimal doubt, you must vote to acquit. And this is not my personal opinion, it is your obligation under the law."

7

When the jury foreman stood to read the findings of the facts in a loud and slightly nervous voice, Ballesteros knew what the verdict would be. Eduardo Ribas was found guilty of homicide with seven votes in favor and two opposed. In Spanish law, it was the minimum majority required, and it was enough to convict him. Now they would have to wait for the judge to prepare a decision and impose a sentence. It was possible that he could consider his client's drug addiction a mitigating factor. In any case, Ballesteros would appeal the verdict. He repeated over and over to himself that there was no substantial evidence that had determined his client's guilt.

After the jury was dismissed, Ballesteros started to organize the files that were on the table, place them into a cardboard folder and put them into his briefcase. The audience that had crowded the courtroom began to clear; there were barely a dozen people in the room. He cast a sidelong glance at the front row of the spectator seating and saw a beautiful woman wearing a black skirt and blazer over a white blouse. From some distance away, he could observe that her clothes were well made and impeccably tailored. There were no visible wrinkles, as if she had purchased them that same morning or had picked them up fresh from the dry cleaner. The woman's tanned complexion was as smooth and flawless as her outfit. She wore her curly black hair at a medium length that framed her face and highlighted her dark and intense eyes (though he couldn't make out the color at that distance). Full lips added a hint of sensuality to her appearance. She looked directly at Ballesteros, as if she wanted to speak with him. Ballesteros knew she was the victim's sister and he assumed that, as is often the case with family members of the victim, she would hate the defense attorney, who were frequently considered slightly less than the criminal's accomplice.

The woman and her parents, the only family who Ballesteros recognized, started walking toward the exit. A young man with a small voice recorder approached them. They exchanged a few words that Ballesteros could not hear, and the young man left. If there was a profession almost as hated as attorneys, Ballesteros thought, it was journalists. He imagined a hierarchy of hated professions. If it were up to him, Ballesteros was certain that the first tier would be populated by politicians. In second place were bankers and lawyers, though he couldn't determine the order. Third place could possibly be filled by public servants of any government office. The fourth and fifth spots could go to journalists and taxi drivers. Then there were those sectors that did not benefit from the esteem of public opinion, but performed essential functions: doctors, police officers, and professors. In short, perhaps the only ones that are indifferent to the spectrum of public opinion—and even enjoy their admiration— are artists. Paco had chosen wisely, he thought. For a moment, Ballesteros considered giving him a call to meet for a drink, but it was already 6:00 p.m. and he couldn't get a return flight to Ibiza until 9:00. Besides, although he was in the mood for a drink, he did not feel like talking. He'd rather be alone with his thoughts, and mentally review Eduardo Ribas' case to look for any possible errors and grounds for an appeal.

As he approached the exit, Ballesteros was shaken by a violent and frigid gust of wind coming from outside. It was raining intensely and the streets were flooded. Water was flowing through the roadway creating small rivulets that disappeared into the gutters. He hadn't brought an umbrella or appropriate shoes for treading in puddles. He waited a few minutes under the portico of the Provincial Court building, which shielded him from the rain, trying to decide what to do. He considered calling a taxi and going directly to the airport to kill a few hours while he waited for his flight, but changed his mind and decided to walk to a nearby bar that was sufficiently out of the way to ensure it wasn't frequented by people related to his profession. By the time he arrived, his clothes were drenched and his shoes and socks were soaked through. He walked over to the bar, ordered a whiskey, and sat at a table with his drink.

It was Thursday. On the following day, he would see his sixteen-year-old daughter who would be spending the weekend with him. Per the terms of his divorce, his visit schedule allowed him to spend alternating weekends with Julieta in addition to half of summer vacation, Christmas, and Easter week. For some time now, the relationship with his daughter hadn't been going in the direction Ballesteros would have liked. He attributed her ongoing confrontations and criticism of him to teenage rebellion. Nevertheless, he could not stop thinking that maybe he had done something wrong. Julieta possessed some wonderful qualities: she was an accomplished student and excelled in any activity that interested her; she had won a couple of photography contests and Paco had praised Julieta's drawings, even insisting she should attend painting classes. And yet the qualities that made Ballesteros most proud of his daughter were her ease and self-confidence. She was immune to the intimidating effect that the masses had on the individual. Since she was a young child, Julieta never felt self-conscious when speaking in front of an audience or practicing her clarinet solo in a café full of people. Ballesteros remembered an event that had occurred some time ago when his daughter was ten years old. He and Julieta had been standing in line at the Iberia Airlines counter to obtain their boarding passes for a weekend getaway to London. A well-dressed man with graying hair got in the line in front of them. Julieta pulled on the sleeve of Ballesteros' jacket and whispered, *'Dad, he's cutting in!'* Ballesteros didn't give much weight to his daughter's outrage and sluggishly replied, *'It doesn't matter. We have time to spare.'* She picked up her suitcase and with a determined expression stated, *'we have to defend our rights.'* She then stepped in front of the man that had slipped in front of them. Ballesteros followed and stood by her side. The gray-haired man said nothing.

Her confident boldness was a trait that Julieta had not

inherited from her mother or from him, who had both acknowledged being rather timid throughout their respective childhoods and well into their adulthood. Ballesteros appreciated and acknowledged the merits of his ex-wife, Yolanda, when it came to Julieta's education. Indeed, he would not have had the patience needed to review their daughter's schoolwork every day, as Yolanda had done for years. He was always engrossed in finding judicial solutions to intricate cases. During those years, he had dedicated more time to his goddammed job than to his daughter. Yolanda also had her own office and worked independently as a German interpreter, but she always found time to attend to their daughter's multiple demands, no matter how exhausted she was at the end of the day. Now Julieta could manage on her own and rejected his help, but it was clear that Yolanda had fostered not only Julieta's study habits, but also her self-confidence and assurance.

Although Ballesteros had not devoted much time to playing with his daughter or reviewing schoolwork with her, he felt he had made his own small contribution to her education by providing her with day to day praise and admonishment, advice (which Julieta ignored), and small sacrifices of which she was not aware. In his self-assessment, Ballesteros recognized that when he was his daughter's age, he had been a selfish and thoughtless adolescent who believed his parents' obligation was solely to satisfy his whims. Julieta was more mature and sensible than he had been when he was young. However, for some time now, his daughter was no longer a passive recipient of his parenting. She now responded with blunt criticism that Ballesteros experienced as painful jabs. He recognized that some of her rebukes were justified, such as when she criticized his unhealthy habits of smoking and drinking; however, sometimes it felt like she was simply looking for a fight. If he made fried potatoes with dinner, she wouldn't eat them; yet if he made a salad, she said she was tired of eating healthy foods. He could not seem to get it right. Ballesteros wondered if perhaps children of divorced parents felt they had to choose one side or the other and, in their case, Julieta had chosen her mother's side. He often felt he was experiencing a personality clash with his daughter. Perhaps he was being too authoritative, as his ex-wife had rebuked. He tried to do the best he could, the best he knew how, but he wasn't particularly happy with the results. Julieta was not communicative, and they didn't share a level of trust he would have liked. He was nostalgic for that trip to London because it was the last time he had felt unconditional love from his daughter, when she was ten years old. When had Julieta stopped loving him? It had been a slow process of which Ballesteros had been unaware. His daughter's sullenness when she arrived at his home and holed up in her room had increased over time and was itself becoming a more painful insult than the things she said out loud. He tried to console himself by thinking that adolescence was a necessary phase young people had to go through in order to cut the cord with their parents and achieve individual autonomy. They had to break away from their former compliance to find their own identity and independence. He tried to remember what he was like at fifteen and recalled an adolescent who was timid around strangers and unfriendly to his family, especially to his grandmother, who he would often respond to by shouting sharply. His behavior then, Ballesteros remembered with regret, was much worse than Julieta's behavior was now.

Ballesteros polished off his last sip of whiskey, now watered down from the melted ice, and held his empty glass up to the bartender to request another. The bartender came over with a tray holding a clean glass with ice and the bottle of Glenfiddich. He removed the used glass and poured him a new drink. As Ballesteros brought the fresh drink to his lips, he saw a reflection in the mirror at the end of the bar of a woman he recognized instantly. He had seen her in the courtroom earlier that afternoon, she was the victim's sister. After calmly placing her large umbrella in the stand near the entrance, she walked toward his table. Ballesteros did not believe in coincidences—well perhaps some but not others—and this one was the kind that made him suspicious. She was probably there to shame him for defending a criminal and to extol the virtues of her dead sister, whose life had been cut short for no reason. Or she might want to berate him for choosing to be a criminal attorney. However, it would be hard for Ballesteros to feel bad about being reprimanded by someone with beautiful stocking clad legs like the ones he could see reflected in the mirror as she approached. He decided to pretend he had not seen her. After all, he wasn't even sure she was coming to speak to him. She may have been looking for the bathroom, or perhaps it really was one of those coincidences.

"Good afternoon," she said stopping at his table. "May I speak with you?" Ballesteros faked mild surprise, arching his eyebrows in a gesture that seemed fake even to him.

"Yes, of course. Please sit." She sat in the chair in front of him, on the other side of the small, round table.

"I'm Raquel López. I've been attending the trial."

"Yes, I saw you in the courtroom. I'm sorry about your sister," Ballesteros replied trying to show his human side, though he thought his sympathy sounded artificial.

"The fact is, I'm not very satisfied with the results of the trial."

"What do you mean by that?" Ballesteros asked, this time with an authentically surprised look on his face.

"After seeing the trial, the evidence, and the allegations of both the prosecutor and your own, I'm not sure that the man who was convicted is actually my sister's murderer." Raquel López paused, waiting for Ballesteros' reaction as he looked at her thoughtfully. "There's also one more detail, something that I didn't notice at first but have been thinking about a lot since. I was the one who found my sister." Ballesteros realized that Raquel López talked about 'her sister' as if she were still alive. "I noticed something strange when I saw her lying on the bed and I finally realized what it was: her clothes. When I found her on the bed she was still wearing her nurse's uniform. My sister was very vain. She didn't like to go out wearing her work clothes. She always changed in the nurse's locker room both when she arrived and before she left. When she worked a morning shift, Ana preferred to take the bus. Even though there is a parking lot at the hospital, she didn't like rush hour traffic in Ibiza when everyone is going to work or driving their kids to school. She preferred to take the bus and read. And the truth is, I can't imagine her on the bus in her nurse's uniform."

"Maybe she was in a hurry."

"Yes, but it feels like there are just too many coincidences. Why would she be in more of a hurry that day than any other?"

"Hard to answer that. To be honest, I don't think my client is guilty either," Ballesteros responded. "Some circumstancial evidence suggests he is, but there is just as much that clears him. I am convinced that it wasn't him. I am telling you this honestly, not as a defense attorney. I'm saying it outside the courtroom, as if I were talking to a friend."

"Yes," she said, "but that begs the obvious question: if it wasn't your client, who killed her? Another thief? I don't know. It's all very confusing."

"The truth is the Civil Guard did not investigate other possibilities. They had already decided they had their guilty party and the investigation ended there. They only collected evidence that would convict him, and I don't think there was that much. Many details simply don't fit. And now we can add the clothes your sister was wearing to that list, which is also worth thinking about."

"Do you think it's true that he confessed because they offered him drugs?"

"Yes. I think it occurred just as Eduardo Ribas said it did."

"And don't you think the Civil Guard's conduct is almost criminal?"

"Well, it's complicated," he responded. "On the one hand, yes; on the other, no. The police and Civil Guard officers are used to dealing with miscreants who deny everything—if they have any common sense or experience. They have to be more astute than the criminals if they want to catch them, and sometimes they set traps that cross the legal line. They think they're doing the right thing, trying to get a confession, but then they could end up with situation like the Cuenca crime."

"Which crime?" She inquired.

"The Cuenca crime. Perhaps you're too young and haven't heard about that case," said Ballesteros, speaking to her in a more familiar tone now. "There was a movie about it and everything. It is considered one of the most egregious judicial mistakes that ever occurred in Spain. It happened in the early 20th century. A sheepherder disappeared right after he sold a flock of sheep. His family was sure that someone had robbed and killed him, and they blamed two other sheepherders who were the last to see him alive. The case closed because they couldn't prove that there was enough motivation for committing the crime. A few years go by and a new judge comes in who decides to reopen the case and find the guilty party at all costs. He orders the Civil Guard to arrest the two suspected sheepherders, and torture them until they get a confession. So, they arrest the men and subject them to all types of humiliation, torture, and deprivation until they end up confessing to having killed the man who disappeared. The case goes to trial and they are sent to prison. I don't know how long afterward, ten or twelve years perhaps, the local parish priest receives a request for the birth certificate of the man who disappeared: he was living in a nearby town and needed it to get married. Obviously, everyone realized that he was alive and that they had convicted two innocent people for a nonexistent murder. Anyway, if this guy had not gotten married or if he'd had a heart attack a couple months before, no one would have noticed the mistake.

"So, returning to the topic at hand, I believe that the judge that ordered the officers to torture the two sheepherders did so because he was convinced that they were guilty and that a confession had to be obtained at all costs, and that no one confesses to a crime they don't commit. And he underestimated the torture methods the Civil Guard was capable of inflicting. These days, those methods are more subtle. For instance, they offer drugs."

Ballesteros noticed that his story had roused this

woman's interest.

"I remember a more recent case, from maybe fourteen or fifteen years ago, when I was at university. I don't remember the details very well. I think it had to do with a girl who was murdered, and they convicted a woman that had been the girl's mother's lover," Raquel wondered if she had remembered this case because of the lesbian angle.

"Yes," the attorney nodded, "you're referring to the Rosa Bonet case. She was convicted by jury trial. All the media outlets suggested that her mother's lover was the guilty party, and the jury convicted her without any incriminating evidence. She spent more than a year in jail before they arrested Marc Garfield, a serial killer, and matched the DNA obtained at Rosa's crime scene to his. In that case, clearly the prosecutor carried a lot of the blame by leveling accusations without sufficient evidence, and then topped it off by convincing a jury which had already been tainted by trial by media."

"Honestly, it makes my hair stand on end to think that even today, in the 21st century, these things can happen," Raquel shuddered.

"The saddest part is that there have been cases where innocent people have been unjustly convicted and served out the entire sentence. Once someone has been convicted, the investigation is over. If the person is lucky, the truth gets discovered by accident, like in the cases we are discussing: a letter received after a few years, traces of DNA from a known criminal, or just pure coincidence." Ballesteros paused, looking at his glass. "Would you like a drink?"

"Coffee with milk, please. Let's see if I can warm up. This is some weather we're having!" Raquel exclaimed, rubbing her hands together and looking toward the windows near the entrance.

Hearing her mention the pounding rain, which had been irritating the attorney, didn't sound so bad coming from her lips. In fact, it sounded perfect. He lifted his hand to get the waiter's attention and ordered her coffee aloud.

"And what do your parents think?"

"I haven't shared my thoughts with them. I don't want to worry them. I think it's all the same to my parents if they convict this man or another. The only thing they are feeling is the death of my sister and there's no remedy for that. No judge can bring her back to life. I do want to be certain that my sister's murderer pays for what he has done. I want to see him in prison. No offense intended, but I believe the police have spent their time proving Mr. Ribas' guilt, while you have spent it trying to prove his innocence, and no one has bothered to find another possible suspect."

"It isn't my job to look for criminals," Ballesteros replied.

"And what if that's the best way to prove your client's innocence? And, at this point, what if it's the only way."

"Well, the Civil Guard has already closed the case. They're not going to do anything to find another possible guilty party. If we want to investigate, we will have to do it on our own. We should probably hire a private detective. And, although this may sound preposterous, I don't know of any in Ibiza. I mean, I don't know one that I think is a skilled professional," he clarified. "For a couple cases, I've had to use the services of private investigators, and the two I used both seemed amateurish."

Raquel López thought about it a moment before she answered: "I know one; an old friend from school. We studied psychology together at the University of Valencia."

"And how did he end up working as a private detective after studying psychology?"

"And why not? Not everything in life is as methodical as studying law and working as an attorney. Besides, Zarco was an expert at guessing the murderers in movies. You could be watching a suspense film with him for no longer than ten minutes, and Zarco had already solved it."

"I'm not sure that a knack for guessing movie murderers can be included on a resume. And obviously, I wouldn't want to go to the movies with him. Sounds annoying!"

"You could also look at it from another point of view, he's

an intelligent person. And I can guarantee that he's honest."

"These days, that's saying a lot. Anyway, we'll see. Life isn't like the movies. You don't always catch the bad guy. Do you have any children?" asked Ballesteros abruptly, although he knew he really wanted to ask if she was married or had a partner, if she was also returning to Ibiza on the 11:05 flight, and if she wanted to have dinner with him that evening.

"No," responded Raquel dryly, as if she wanted to protect her privacy. Ballesteros seemed an attractive man, but she needed more than attraction to get involved with a man that was a few years older than she. And she knew that mixing personal with professional matters was a combination as potentially explosive as nitroglycerine: any false move could blow you up.

"I have a sixteen-year-old daughter," said Ballesteros. "She's a teenager, and recently we haven't been getting along well."

"I have to go," responded Raquel, as she picked up her purse hanging on the arm rest, "My parents and I are taking the 6:40 flight and it's getting late. Tomorrow, I'll speak to Zarco and ask him to go see you, if that's alright, so you can provide the details about the case."

"That's fine." Ballesteros pulled a business card out of his wallet and gave it to the young woman. "He can come by my office after 9:00 a.m. Here is my address and phone number."

The attorney sat finishing his glass of whiskey and watched, through the mirror on the back wall, as Raquel picked up her umbrella and went out through the revolving door, without turning her head. The situation had made him feel a little uncomfortable. Why the hell had he started to talk about his daughter during his feeble attempt to move the conversation to a more personal level? Raquel had probably gotten the wrong impression. The truth was that Ballesteros, after his breakup with Yolanda and a few passionate and torrid relationships with women all of whom were ten years younger than he, was going through a phase in which sex was not one of his urgent priorities. He didn't lose his head or get swept away by pretty legs or breasts or sensuous lips, but Raquel had that indescribable something that made the attorney take notice. Of course, She was also probably ten or twelve years younger than him.

8

Álex Zarco was both surprised and delighted to get a call from Raquel López Demichellis. He remembered her as a paragon of beauty from their days together at the University of Valencia's psychology department. She was divine! Álex Zarco's amazement increased to infinity when she succinctly explained that she wanted to retain the services of his agency, Zarco & Cía., to investigate her sister's death, and arranged to meet him at Ballesteros' office the following morning at 10:00 o'clock. He insisted on meeting her for coffee at 9:30 at a nearby café before proceeding to the attorney's office.

Zarco had heard about the death of Ana López Demichellis from newspapers and television. Homicides in Ibiza were uncommon, and the media had dedicated major news segments to the crime, arrest, and subsequent trial; indeed, the sentence had been announced that same day. Zarco knew that the drug addict responsible for the girl's death had been sentenced to ten years in prison, and he was not clear about what it was Raquel wanted him to investigate.

Álex Zarco and Raquel López were the same age and had shared a classroom in school but had not established a friendship until they met again at the University of Valencia in their first class toward a degree in psychology, a major that Raquel planned to combine with law. The affinity that had sparked their friendship was their sexual tendencies: his homosexuality and her bisexuality. Neither of them conformed with generally accepted rules, which created the type of bond that unites individuals who separate themselves from what is considered "normal". Despite Spanish society having evolved toward greater tolerance by the end of the 20th century, the truth was that it hadn't changed enough so that gays and lesbians were on equal footing with heterosexuals. In large part, Raquel had made a significant contribution toward one of Álex Zarco's crucial life decisions: to open the closet door. Zarco had not yet stepped outside of that cramped container and had only come out to Raquel during an evening in which, contrary to his habit, he drank two beers and the alcohol had loosened his tongue. He gave a speech that seemed at once coherent and also completely absurd, revealing not only his sexual preferences but also his fear and shame. Raquel had responded to Zarco's honesty with her own secrets, which she had never done with her girl friends, and she had experienced a sense of relief. She enjoyed his uninhibited and childlike sense of humor and felt relaxed in his company. Zarco had allowed himself to be used by handsome students who approached him as a means to get close to Raquel. After graduation, Raquel moved to Madrid to study for the public finance management exam and, once she passed it, she settled in the capital city. During the first year, they called each other a couple times but later they lost touch. Álex had not heard from her until the phone call yesterday.

Álex Zarco was someone who might be called a *freak*, to use an Anglicism popular among Spanish speakers. Although he took immense joy in buying clothes as frequently as his budget would allow, during the fall and winter months—and well into the spring—he enfolded himself in a gray, old-fashioned trench coat which he'd inherited from his father who had died two years prior and wore a silk scarf around his neck like an ascot. If not an elegant detail, he thought, it was an acknowledgment of his personality. He did not skimp on the use of cologne. He liked the feeling of cleanliness provided by the scent and, every morning before he went outside, he sprayed himself with Eau Sauvage.

Zarco was not particularly attractive; he was somewhat overweight and prematurely balding. And at the age of thirty-three, Zarco was still a virgin. He had acknowledged his latent homosexuality to Raquel during an evening of secret sharing inspired by alcohol and the need to vent, but he referred to himself as a "magazine homosexual", which did not mean he would be on the cover of a gay magazine, but rather that he hadn't yet realized sexual relations with a flesh and blood human and had only relieved his libido by contemplating magazines with photos of shaven young men with enormous penises.

Álex Zarco had been practicing karate since he was twenty years old and, although he did not demonstrate the precision punches or agility or speed of his revered Bruce Lee, the result of training for six hours a week over twelve years at the Martial Arts Sports Club (MASC) had earned him a black belt in the Karate Do method. The MASC location was on a ground floor, had a blue tatami and a mirror on the back wall, and was popular with people that Zarco considered normal, which excluded gang members, goons, and club doormen, who were generally drawn to kickboxing. In order to obtain a black belt, it wasn't necessary to lift your foot to neck height; it just required concentration, coordination, and a balance that Zarco had achieved through years of perseverance. He had never used his karate techniques in a fight and did not even remember having been in any fight since his adolescence. In addition to being a personal defense system, karate provides character building and a quest for mental and physical balance, and its practice had given Álex Zarco confidence and self-assurance. He had, however, used it in his dreams. Since he was a child, Zarco had experienced nightmares in which he was pursued or attacked by an unknown assailant, but when he started practicing martial arts these distressing dreams disappeared. If some unknown attacker with evil intentions appeared in a nightmare, Zarco delivered a *tsuki* (direct thrust) to the face, or a *mawashi geri* (spin kick) to the ribs and left his assailant woozy.

The cliché that suggests the first objective of psychology students is to diagnose themselves rang true in Álex Zarco's case. By his third year, he had arrived at the conclusion that his timid character was partly due to the influence of his parents— who were barely connected to the outside world—as well as his low self-esteem. A few months later, he realized that his self-diagnosis was of no use at all since, as he had observed, human beings are prisoners of their own character and cannot achieve profound changes. No one can stop being fearful, timid, or irritable at will. We cannot even choose our own feelings. Free will was a chimera in a universe governed by infinite relationships of cause and effect. Raquel had encouraged him to obtain his doctorate or, at least, to author a paper about his theories. Zarco had stated: '*The only problem is that I only know one case: my own.*' And she had responded: '*How many cases do you think Freud or Jung learned about before they began? Their own. You only have to write about your own case and then substitute "I" with "the patient".*'

After obtaining his degree in psychology he did not pursue his doctorate, nor did he author a paper. In the spring of 2003, he suffered an acute nervous breakdown that led to hospitalization at a mental health facility for many months. Once discharged, he substituted the hospital cell with his room at his parents' home. His misanthropy increased and he hid like a hermit in his room. He only left the house on Mondays, Wednesdays, and Fridays to go to karate classes. His parents took care of his basic food and shelter needs, and when they could, they also provided occasional indulgences. He was an only child and, although they lived modestly, his parents would have made any sacrifice that would contribute to the happiness of their offspring. Álex Zarco spent his days and some nights holed up in his room reading detective and mystery novels. No other activity provided as much satisfaction as reading these books. He borrowed them from the Can Ventosa Library, located close to the gym where he practiced karate. He had read almost everything in this genre that had been published in Spanish: British authors, like Agatha Christie (perhaps his favorite), North American authors, Spaniards, Scandinavians (who had proliferated much in recent years), South Americans, Italians, Belgians, French, Swiss, Finnish, Greeks, and authors from other countries as well.

One afternoon, as he reread a novel starring Hercule Poirot, the longing to live an adventure among the upper class during the first half of 20th century England shook him to his core. Zarco unexpectedly had an idea, an inspiration, that he could re-make his own life into a novel in which he was the protagonist. And so he decided to dedicate his efforts, as well as part of his parents' savings, to becoming a private detective.

Without much effort, Zarco completed distance-learning courses and passed his exams to obtain a university degree in Private Investigation, which prepared him to work as a detective. He also obtained a weapons permit for private security. According to Spanish laws he could not carry a weapon unless he was working as a guard, and was supposed to store it for safekeeping at a facility authorized for that purpose. He opted to purchase a small Glock 17, 9 mm pistol, a model no longer manufactured, and a box of ammunition, on the black market. He stored the unloaded handgun on top of the closet in his bedroom. He did not take it outside of his home, but having it gave him a certain peace of mind in the event of a sudden emergency.

Once he had the diploma recognizing him as a private detective, he created a website advertising the different areas of investigative services offered by his detective agency, Zarco & Cía., and placed an advertisement in the local Ibizan newspaper, *Diario*. Álex was the only employee of the Zarco & Cía. Detective Agency, and he'd added the abbreviation of *Cía* after his last name to denote professionality and because, in addition to Cía being the Spanish abbreviation for 'company', he enjoyed using that particular Americanism which reminded him of the Central Intelligence Agency. With more preparation in theory than practice in investigation and surveillance methods, he began his career as a detective equipped with a reflex digital camera and a worn-out scooter that originally had been red but was now more of a discolored ochre thanks to the sun's harsh rays. On his first few assignments, he often lost the subject he was following and had to start over the next day. If tailing a subject became too complicated, he would take a few photos of the individual under surveillance in any innocuous situation and inform the jealous significant other (the majority of his clients came under this category) that his investigation had not uncovered any evidence of an affair—a statement that, while technically true, was not necessarily the reality in all cases.

His first client was an older woman, the owner of a small neighborhood supermarket, who suspected her husband was cheating on her. Zarco requested a duplicate of her husband's car key and asked what time her husband left the house to go to work. The following morning at 8:15, Zarco started tailing her husband's car through the streets of Ibiza and into a four-level parking garage close to his workplace, a prestigious administrative office. Zarco parked his scooter on the street and entered the parking garage through the pedestrian access door. He found the car on the second level, parked between a cement column and another vehicle. He opened the car door with the key his client had provided and placed a voice activated tape recorder (purchased with €120 his mother had loaned him) under the driver's seat. He hypothesized that people who wanted to hide a conversation would not make the call from their workplace, where they can be heard by a co-worker, or from their home where their partner or children could overhear. They also would not make the call on the street since they couldn't anticipate who they might run into. After giving it a lot of thought, Zarco concluded that the best place a person would be protected, safe, and secure from not being heard was inside their own car. Of course, Zarco could have given the tape recorder to his client with instructions on where to place it, but this might involve an error on her part and, while the ploy might still work, it would downplay the detective's efforts, so he situated the tape recorder himself. He left it fastened under the seat for a couple of days, and then returned to retrieve it the same way he had placed it: using the vehicle's duplicate key. He was lucky in his first attempt and discovered a conversation between the husband and his lover at the end of a workday: he told her that he had arranged to meet some friends for dinner, thereby covering his back with his wife and justifying his evening out. He would try to slip away around midnight and go to his lover's house. Zarco listened to the tape with euphoric triumph for both discovering the deceit and feeling happy for the woman who had hired him, who would finally learn the truth. The detective arranged to meet his client at her supermarket twenty minutes before it opened to the public. He pushed the play button on the tape recorder. He was satisfied with himself, his intelligence, and his cleverness. However, the crestfallen expression on the face of the supermarket owner while listening to her husband's syrupy voice as he spoke with his lover reminded Zarco that neither money nor knowledge can supply happiness. Especially the latter.

Slowly but surely, he was hired for more of these types of assignments: someone's jealous husband who wanted him to spy on his wife; or someone's boss who wanted to catch his employee *in flagrante* trying to take unjustifiable time off, or even parents who wanted to know where their young son was going at night and with whom, and if he was drinking or taking drugs. He had never investigated a murder or even an embezzlement case. Although his straightforward and routine cases could hardly be compared with the investigations carried out by any of the fictional heroes in his favorite novels, he liked his profession, and the task of solitary surveillance suited his withdrawn personality. To a certain extent, when he spied on his targets he felt in touch with the world at the same time that his covertness made him feel safe and sound.

Zarco had an aversion to people and regarded most of them as selfish, ignorant, and destructive. He only had to ride his motorcycle through the streets of Ibiza for half hour to confirm this low opinion, noting how cars would pull out in front of him ignoring all types of stop and yield signs, as if they didn't see him coming or didn't care that a motorcyclist had right-of-way. He felt particular aversion when the offender drove an SUV. The law of the strongest. And the heartless. He tried to mentally prepare himself so this kind of behavior did not perturb him, and turned to Buddhism to try and regain his composure and not allow aggression and negative energy that emanated from the actions of others to affect him. However, he was not always successful. Zarco also told himself that human beings were simply stupid, which was corroborated by their general disinterest in recycling. People were unaware that one of the major problems and dangers humanity was facing was damage to the environment. And to make matters worse, they justified their indifferent behavior by saying that it was ridiculous to separate plastic, glass, and paper, since municipal services were only going to throw it all into the same bin. Oh well. He hadn't broken the habit of finding descriptors for himself and now he self-defined as a "lone wolf", although this was not a home grown metaphor.

Step by step and without becoming discouraged, Zarco perfected his methods. With earnings from his work, he rented a three-room apartment that served as both a living space and office. He continued to acquite upgraded photographic equipment with powerful telephoto lenses, microphones that were able to pick up voices at hundreds of meters' distance, surveillance cameras the size of a button, spy software to install on computers—in short, a panoply of gadgets that, when placed accordingly, did all the work themselves.

When strictly following the laws and deontological ethics of the profession, spying on someone was only permitted on streets and public places. However, the nature of the cases he investigated forced him to skip both spatial and legal limits. Who was going to get a photograph or video of an adulterous wife or husband with their lover in a public park? The usual or logical custom would be to meet in the intimacy of a home or hotel room, far from prying eyes. When Zarco delivered reports and photos taken in a private residence (and thus a violation of privacy), he was careful to tell his clients that the pictures had been taken by an associate. In cases such as these, he also did not provide receipts for payment of services, in order to avoid leaving evidence that could connect him to this infringement on someone else's privacy, which could result in the loss of his license. In doing so, he not only violated various articles of the Spanish Constitution that guaranteed the right to privacy, to honor, to one's own image, secrecy of communications, and the inviolability of the dwelling, he was also defrauding the public treasury by not providing an invoice or charging VAT tax or declaring his total income.

Although he could be accused of illegal possession of weapons, crimes against personal privacy, tax infractions, and not always being sincere with his clients, the people who knew Zarco considered him an honest person.

Zarco arrived at the El Parque Inn café, situated in front of the plaza bearing the same name, fifteen minutes before his scheduled meeting with Raquel. Although the rain had stopped, the sky was covered in gray, almost black clouds, and the lights in the terrace and interior bar were on. He took off his trench coat, sat at a table, and asked the waiter for a Cola Cao hot chocolate and a croissant, which he ate with delight, dunking it first in the liquid chocolate. He wiped off his mouth and hands with several paper napkins and was turning his head just as Raquel crossed the doorway. He immediately recognized her eyes and striking lips. She appeared more beautiful than ten years ago, and certainly much more elegant. He noticed how some men at the bar looked at her more or less overtly as she approached. He stood up to greet her and they gave each other a kiss on each cheek. Raquel picked up the pleasant scent emanating from Zarco and remembered his fondness for the use of fragrances.

"It's been so long!" exclaimed Zarco.

"Absolutely! How great to see you!" She replied happily.

"What's going on in your life? Are you married? Do you have children?" Zarco launched into a barrage of questions.

"Neither of the two. I don't even have a boyfriend. And you? You can marry as well now."

"Well, I wouldn't be opposed to getting married, but I haven't found the right man. To be honest, I haven't even found the wrong man. You look amazing, darling!"

"Don't exaggerate. You haven't changed much either," she responded.

"Seriously?" asked Zarco, surprised. "Tell me the truth, don't I look a little unsightly? More fat and less hair," he declared, and then snorted: "too bad it isn't the other way around."

"Honestly, you look good. It's true that there's less hair, but nowadays you could shave it all off and be totally trendy."

"Look, I'm sorry about your sister," said Zarco, suddenly remembering the issue that had brought them together. "How are you feeling?"

"Fortunately or unfortunately, anything can be overcome. It was such a shock, finding her dead. I cannot describe how I felt. It was all so sudden. Human evil is terrifying." Raquel was rambling in disjointed sentences. "Evidently, some people are monsters. I don't remember a greater feeling of sadness and impotence in my entire life. Until then, the only close family deaths I'd experienced had been my grandfather and an uncle, but they died of illnesses, under normal circumstances and at an advanced age. It wasn't half as bad. Seven months have passed since Ana's death and I'm handling it better. I suppose we always survive in the end, we can't live in continuous sorrow."

"I understand what you mean. My father died two years ago and it was the hardest thing I have ever gone through. At first, I thought I would never get over it but, as you say, time heals everything—or almost everything." Zarco paused briefly before continuing, "Of course, the circumstances around your sister's death were unique. It's logical that you would suffer twice as much. What is it you said on the phone about investigating Ana's death? Wasn't the perpetrator already convicted? And, by the way, how did you know that I work as a private investigator?"

"So many questions! I knew you were a private investigator because my sister told me. I think she saw an advertisement in the newspaper and surmised it was you. Zarco is not a common name in Ibiza, and you'd always said you would love to be a private investigator. We thought it was a typical adolescent fantasy, but I see you've made it a reality."

Just then, Raquel remembered that her late sister had also informed her, without going into detail, that Zarco had been hospitalized at a mental health facility in Palma. He had always exhibited extravagant and antisocial behaviors that made him shy away from people. He had a high intellectual capacity and nonexistent social skills. When Zarco was a student, she'd had doubts that he would find a job because of his inability to relate to people or work on a team. She was happy that he had found an original way to earn a living, in keeping with his character and imagination. Private investigator! She looked attentively at her friend and found no trace of psychological decline in his gestures or his gaze, and thought it best to not ask him about his illness and his experience in the psychiatric hospital at their first meeting. There would be other opportunities later on.

"What are you thinking, Raquel?"

"I'm sorry, Álex, I was thinking about my sister."

"I imagine that talking about her brings back memories. Well then, tell me what you and the attorney want from me."

Raquel succinctly explained the intricacies of both the investigation and trial regarding the death of her sister: the suspicious confession of Eduardo Ribas, the lack of solid evidence, the incongruities revealed by the attorney, and the fact that her sister was wearing her nurse's uniform.

"I don't believe the man who was tried and convicted is the murderer," continued Raquel. "Too many things don't make sense. That's why we are going to meet with the attorney now. He'll give you the affidavit taken by the Civil Guard and explain what was said at the trial to fill you in. If, after your investigation, we come to the conclusion that Ribas was the killer, then that's it: he's already in jail. If not, the guilty party will have to be found."

"It is not going to be easy. This happened seven months ago and the physical evidence that there might have been at that time, fingerprints or other tangible proof, may be lost. How is it going for you at the Treasury Department? Last I heard, you had passed the entrance exams."

"Yes, that was many years ago. In fact, two years ago I made inspector through an internal promotion."

"Do you like your job?"

"In a general sense, yes I do. It has its moments. To a certain extent, one plays detective, tracking possible fraud. Right now, I have an interesting case. It's difficult, but interesting."

"I'm intrigued ..."

"Yes, but I can't tell you anymore. Discretion is an essential part of our job. In fact, I think I've already said too much."

"Raquel, honey, you haven't said anything at all. Don't get paranoid."

9

"Would you like some coffee?" asked Ballesteros. Raquel and Álex Zarco were seated in large, comfortable leather chairs on the opposite side of the large oak desk in the attorney's office. They shook their heads in the negative.

"We just had some," explained Zarco.

Ballesteros took out a bundle of photocopied pages from one of the drawers and offered it to Zarco. The papers had been hole-punched and bound with a gold-colored metal fastener.

"Here are the police's affidavit and proceedings from the trial. If you like, there are also recorded videos from the trial, but I reviewed the proceedings and the essential information is all there, Mr. Zarco."

"Don't speak to me so formally," protested Zarco.

"Sorry Álex, it's just a habit. Have you ever investigated a homicide before?"

"Yes, on a couple of occasions," lied the detective. "Of course, you know we can't meddle in an ongoing police investigation. In one instance I investigated an accidental death, though the family suspected it had been intentional. However, it was ultimately confirmed as an accident. Another time, I was asked to investigate the disappearance of a businessman and I discovered that he had been killed." Emboldened by how nicely the lie was unfolding, he decided to embellish and added, "The case was in the newspapers."

"Who was the businessman?"

"I can't say anything. Professional secret. I imagine that, as an attorney, you understand."

A shadow of a doubt regarding the detective's sincerity crossed Ballesteros' mind, but he decided to take him at his word.

"Have you thought about how you will begin the investigation?"

"First I have to thoroughly read the affidavit to see what the police officers did. Obviously, the investigation has to begin with the personal and professional background of ..." Zarco hesitated between using 'the victim' or 'the deceased' in front of Raquel, and finally opted for "... Raquel's sister. In most cases involving female deaths, the guilty party is a member of the victim's family or social environment."

"Yes, but in those cases they don't usually bother to conceal the crime by pretending it's a robbery," replied Ballesteros.

"True. As I said, before I begin I have to review the affidavit and trial proceedings to the last detail. Did your sister have a partner or an ex?" asked Zarco, directing the question to Raquel.

"No, she wasn't with anyone. She'd had a recent boyfriend, a doctor from Can Misses Hospital, but they broke up. I don't know much about my sister's life. We hardly saw each other, though we spoke on the phone at least once or twice a month."

"I'll go and see him," said Zarco. "While I'm there, I'll speak with hospital staff and attempt to reconstruct your sister's movements on that day and determine who the last person to see her was. The problem is that a lot of time has passed. When was the last time you saw your sister?"

"Well, the last time we saw each other was at Christmas. Christmas of 2011. Ana and my parents came to Madrid to spend the week and we celebrated Christmas Eve and New Years' Eve together."

"But wait, wasn't it you who found the body?!" asked Ballesteros surprised.

"One of life's random coincidences. I arrived in Ibiza that morning to visit my family and spend a few days with them, but not in time to see Ana alive. In fact, I arrived just in time to find my sister's body. Sometimes, fate plays nasty tricks on us."

10

On Friday afternoons, Ballesteros did not go to his office and worked from home instead. He lived in a duplex in the center of Ibiza. The lower level had a kitchen, living-dining area, laundry room, and a small bathroom. The upper floor contained three bedrooms, two bathrooms, and another room redesigned as an office where Ballesteros spent most of his time working. The large windows in the living room faced a central thorough-fare and buildings on the other side of the street; therefore, he generally kept the curtains drawn to retain his privacy. His ex-wife had kept the family home, a large chalet near Playa d'en Bossa. Ballesteros had decided to live in central Ibiza after his divorce with his daughter, Julieta, in mind, so she wouldn't have to depend on a car ride to meet up with her friends.

Julieta arrived on time that evening at 10:00 p.m., just as they'd agreed. She rang the intercom and Ballesteros buzzed her in through the automatic door. He waited for her at the open door of the apartment. Julieta greeted him with, "Hi dad." It was devoid of happiness. She gave Ballesteros two kisses on the cheek with an air of indifference that hurt him, although this was her usual pattern of behavior. She ran upstairs to her bedroom and from there yelled:

"What's for dinner?"

"Pizza."

"Good," she said unenthusiastically, despite the fact that it was one of her favorite foods.

At least, thought Ballesteros with relief, *she didn't say, 'not pizza again!' or 'always the same thing,' or something along those lines.*

"I'll shower and come down for dinner," yelled Julieta.

After she showered, she ran downstairs making a racket as she stomped on the wooden steps annoying her father, who said nothing in order to avoid a useless confrontation. He'd rather hold his recriminations for more important issues. They sat down to dinner in front of the television while watching an interesting documentary about World War II. Ballesteros drew upon any topic to start a conversation and asked his daughter how things were going with her classes and her friends, to which she provided minimal responses.

"Poor things!" Julieta exclaimed as she watched Warsaw transformed from a boisterous, thriving neighborhood to a ghetto which, after an attempted uprising, was reduced to a pile of rubble. Many Jews committed suicide and some women, after being captured by SS soldiers, detonated grenades they had hidden underneath their clothing. The survivors were sent to an extermination camp that the Germans euphemistically called work camps.

Ballesteros thought how times had changed, since now it was the Israelis who were mercilessly massacring Palestinians. He didn't comment about this aloud and let Julieta have her sadness about the Jewish people as she walked back up to her bedroom.

The land line rang with a start that made Ballesteros jump. He got up to reach for the wireless phone and saw on the screen that the call was from Yolanda, his ex-wife. She didn't call him very often and he assumed it was to remind Julieta of something.

"Hello," responded Ballesteros, as he put the receiver to his ear.

"Hi, Raúl. How are you?" Without waiting for his response, she continued, "Have you noticed anything strange about Julieta?"

"No, not really. Well, she's not very friendly with me and she doesn't talk much, but I suppose that's just part of adolescence. At least, that's what I want to believe."

"She seems very strange to me, especially on weekends. The other day, I noticed the smell of alcohol on her breath. Did she tell you she failed an exam? I also don't like those friends of hers—with their piercings and dyed hair. Besides, they're a year older than Julieta. They got left back a year, so they're basically the worst of the class. And have you seen the clothes your daughter wears? She looks like a vagrant."

"I think you're exaggerating a little. After all, they're just kids. I also let my hair grow out when I was sixteen and look at me now: in a suit and tie." Ballesteros was aware that using himself as an example would not inspire any sympathy from his ex-wife, but he'd simply blurted it out. They had reached a point in their relationship where no matter what he said, his ex would be irritated, just as she irritated him. He tried to redirect the conversation toward his daughter. "We've forgotten what youth and adolescence is like. A majority of young people her age drink a little on weekends. In fact, I'd say most young people do. And failing a subject isn't a big to-do. It surprises us because it's the first time she's failed anything, but I'm sure she'll bring home good grades at the end of the year. She doesn't have to get straight A's."

"Yes, but she didn't tell you about the failing grade."

"I don't think that's so strange. She didn't tell me about the failing grade in the same way she doesn't really tell me anything about her life."

"Raúl, like most men, it appears you have no idea what's going on!" barked Yolanda, with a contemptuous tone in her voice.

Ballesteros noticed it hadn't taken very long for Yolanda's latent feminism to emerge, right along with her talent for generalizing. Why didn't she just come out and say that he, Raúl Ballesteros, wasn't aware of anything? No, she wasn't just attacking him as an individual, she was attacking his gender. The fact that he was a man meant that he could not escape her criticism. He thought about responding in a diplomatic, politically correct fashion, but something inside him rebelled.

"And you, like most mothers, have an innate tendency toward melodrama!" he replied, raising his voice.

"Oh, that's a nice comeback, very colorful words, but it's still just macho bullshit. We're talking about your daughter!"

Ballesteros realized that she was launching into a tirade of hateful generalizations, and he had walked right into her trap. A game he would lose from the onset. He attempted to backtrack the conversation.

"Yolanda, I care about my daughter," he said patiently, "If I thought there was a problem, I would do something. But she seems perfectly fine to me. Yes, she got a failing grade, but I don't think it's anything major."

"Just do me one favor," Yolanda replied curtly. "If she goes out on Saturday, watch her when she gets home to see if she's acting odd … in case she drank or took something else."

"I'll do that, don't worry."

Ballesteros hung up the phone and speculated that his wife suffered from 'woman's illness,' an old-fashioned name for hysteria. To a certain extent, he was comforted by Yolanda's exaggerated concern for their daughter's wellbeing although her disproportionate worrying, on many occasions, caused her to make a mountain out of a molehill. Still, he decided to behave like a father and speak with Julieta.

He walked upstairs and stood in the open doorway of his daughter's bedroom. Julieta was lying on the bed, texting on her cell phone.

"Can we talk?"

Julieta looked at him in an unfriendly manner.

"What do you want to talk about?"

"Your mother told me that you failed a class."

"Yeah, I got a failing grade in history."

"What's that about? It's the first time you've failed."

"It's not a big deal! Only five people in the class passed the exam…"

"Was it very difficult?"

"Yes, very. Plus, nobody understands the teacher when she explains things. She's a miserable person!"

"I'm hoping you'll pass everything in June. You're not far from starting university and these days there's a lot of competition for particular careers …"

"I'm not going to study. I want to be a writer!"

"In order to be a writer, you also have to study. Do you think writers are ignorant?"

"What I need to do is travel a lot and live an exciting life."

"Yes of course, we can learn a lot from traveling. But some writers have never left their homes and still have written great works."

"Really? Name one!" challenged Julieta. Her father, as usual, spoke as if he were the guardian of truth, as though he knew everything about writers and literature, when he knew nothing about the subject. As far back as she could remember, Julieta had only seen her father read law books and newspapers. What the hell did he know about literature?

For his part, Ballesteros tried to think of an author who led a boring, unemotional life; one of those intellectual types who almost never left the library. He wasn't a great reader and knew few biographical facts about writers. He thought Juan Ramón Jiménez sounded a bit boring. Wasn't he the one who spent his life locked up in his own ivory tower?

"Well, for example, Juan Ramón Jiménez."

"Yeah, but I'm talking about current authors, not ones from the old days. I want to be a writer like Lucia Etxebarría." Ballesteros had never heard of her, but he couldn't give up that easily. Wasn't he a specialist in finding arguments to exonerate his clients? He could not allow a sixteen-year-old girl to beat him in an argument.

"The point is that in order to do anything you have to study and learn! Can you imagine a writer that makes grammatical errors or doesn't know where Peru is?"

"Dad, if you don't mind, I have to reply to a text," said Julieta, as she picked up her phone with both hands and started to type with her thumbs at breakneck speed.

Ballesteros had always told his daughter that the important thing was to be happy and that she should choose a profession that inspired her without worrying about how much money she could make. He had advised her to choose any career except the legal profession. However, being a writer seemed the same as not wanting to work at all. While it's true that some writers can make a living from their work, you could count those on one hand. He tried to calm down, reminding himself that his daughter still had another year before she finished high school, and she could change her mind. Writer! For Christ's sake!

The following evening, the sound of Julieta pounding down the stairs of the duplex shook Ballesteros out of an inattentive trance as he viewed a movie that had been on TV four or five times already.

"I'm meeting my friends. We'll have dinner at a pizzeria later," she told her father. She had put on some lipstick and light blue eye shadow on her lids. Ballesteros was not pleased in the least that his daughter was wearing makeup, but again, he bit his tongue to avoid another useless confrontation.

"You'll need money ..."

"Twenty euros is enough."

"I'll give you thirty, but you don't need to spend it all tonight," answered Ballesteros, as he pulled out his small leather wallet and took out a few bills. "You've got your phone?"

"Of course."

"Okay, well try not to let the battery run out and if you want me to pick you up somewhere just call. Otherwise, home by 1:00 a.m. Okay?"

"Mom lets me stay out till 2:30. And all my friends stay out till that time."

Ballesteros doubted his daughter was telling the truth. Still, after vacillating for a few seconds, he acquiesced.

"Okay, 2:30 then."

That evening, Ballesteros did not feel like working or drinking, and the weight of loneliness fell upon him suddenly. He felt depressed. He had been successful in his career and had gained the respect of his peers. He enjoyed the benefits of a comfortable financial situation, had an acceptable social life, and a beautiful and intelligent daughter. And yet: his job was exhausting; social events to which he was invited bored him; and he regarded those around him as vapid and superficial people who worried the whole damned day about money and appearances. Still, he didn't feel vastly different from them. Like it or not, he was part of that echelon of society made up of the nouveau riche and successful professionals. Of everyone around him, he could only call Paco his friend. And to make matters worse, his beautiful and intelligent daughter treated him with painful indifference. Life seemed like a real shitshow. Were things so bad that he was actually feeling sorry for himself? For the first time, Ballesteros felt he was getting old. He worried about the inexorable passage of time chipping away at his physical acuity and edging him toward the bitter end. He had needed reading glasses for nearly a year now, and with each passing day he became more aware that no one gets out of here alive, so to speak. These thoughts had not bothered him before, but now he had to make a conscious effort to avoid them. For an instant, Ballesteros considered calling Paco to meet for a drink and chat, but he immediately discarded the idea. Paco was probably with Tanya, his Moscovite muse. He and Paco would both turn forty-six years old this year, but Paco seemed ten years younger. Ballesteros surmised that the fact that Paco did not work and was dating a beautiful Russian who wasn't even thirty years old were two factors that contributed to his rejuvenation. There was no need for plastic surgery or skin repair creams: simply allowing a voluptuous young woman to take care of you and not having to lift a finger—because obviously painting is not work—is more than enough.

Right then, he decided to make the call that he'd actually wanted to make but had been putting off all afternoon. He had nothing to lose and could always use the investigation he was working on as an excuse. Besides, what the hell, Raquel had asked for his help and not the other way around. He picked up the phone and dialed the number. He heard Raquel's voice on the other end of the line.

"Hello ...?'

"It's Raúl."

"Right, your number is in my phone."

"I'd like to talk about a few things regarding the case."

"Okay. Tell me ..."

"I'd prefer to meet somewhere."

"Today won't work for me, but if it's important you can tell me on the phone," insisted Raquel.

"No, it's not really that important. It's just: do you think Zarco is competent?" he asked, trying to justify his call. "I don't know, I mean the way he looks, with that silk scarf and trench coat ... You know, he looks like a gay Colombo!"

"Colombo?" asked Raquel strangely, and Ballesteros realized that they belonged to two different generations. Raquel had not heard of Colombo or the Cuenca crime, much the same way that he hadn't heard of most singers and actors that captivated today's youth.

"Colombo was a detective in an old television series. I said that because he wore a trench coat similar to your friends'."

"On the other hand, what you said about being gay," Raquel paused a moment thinking about what she was going to say, "Haven't you heard that being gay is a man thing? In any case, Álex may be effeminate, but I think he's more asexual than homosexual." Raquel cleared her throat and, in a more serious tone asked, "You're not homophobic, are you? One of those people that thinks homosexuals are deviants or something like that, right?"

"No, of course not. It was not my intention to offend Zarco," Ballesteros tried to justify himself. "I'm only referring to his professional capacity. And if he has to follow someone, he will definitely not go unnoticed with that outlandish appearance."

"Maybe that's his strategy. If he were to take off his scarf and trench coat, do you think you would recognize him? Ultimately, we pay attention to what is superfluous in a person, and not to what is essential."

"Okay, maybe you're right. Let's see what happens."

There was a long pause, and Raquel broke the silence.

"If you like, we can meet another evening."

"Perfect. I'll call you when I'm not too busy with work."

"Or I'll call you."

Ballesteros poured himself a whiskey with ice and lit a cigarette. He opened the large window in the living room to clear the tobacco smoke and felt the sting of the cold evening air. At least it wasn't raining. He put the cigarette out in the ashtray and took the last sip of his whiskey.

Raquel had left the door open by saying *we can meet another evening*. On the other hand, she had also said she would call him, which could indirectly mean that she would prefer he not push too hard. Ballesteros undressed and got in the shower and felt the hot water as it cascaded down his body.

11

Álex Zarco walked through the main entrance of the Can Misses Hospital, walked toward a wall with a small red gadget on it, and pulled off a strip of paper with a number indicating his turn. The screen showed number 57 and he had number 78, so he would have to wait for 21 people to be seen before him. There were three young women behind a large counter and it didn't take long for his number to come up on the screen. Zarco approached the young redhead with a deadpan face that had called his number.

"Good day, my name is Álex Zarco and I'm a private detective. I'm investigating the death of a nurse that occurred seven months ago. The case is already closed, but I've been hired by the family. I don't know if you remember the matter or if you knew the young woman ..."

"Yes, of course I remember. I knew her by sight, but I can't help you now. Can't you see how many people are waiting their turn? You should speak with the Administrator."

"Do you take a lunch break?"

"Yes, around 11:00 o'clock."

"May I invite you to lunch?"

"I'm meeting a co-worker."

"If she doesn't mind, the three of us could have lunch together. Between the two of you, I'm sure you could provide valuable information."

The redhead hesitated a moment. Maybe talking to the detective would be interesting and fun.

"Okay. 11:00 o'clock at the Albatross Café. It's outside and to the left, across the street."

The Albatross Café was bustling. The two waiters helping customers from behind the counter were not enough to provide services. Zarco and the two young women picked up their respective lunches, coffees, and a Cola Cao hot chocolate at the counter, and found a table with three empty chairs around it. There were used cups, dishes, and glasses on the table. Zarco picked up the used dishware and took it to the counter. He paid the bill and asked the waiter for a receipt to include with his investigation expenses. The name of the redhead from reception was Luci, and she introduced him to her friend, Rosa, who also worked in the hospital office. The detective told them about the goal of the investigation.

"Did you know Ana López?"

"By sight, yes," said Luci, "but hundreds of people work at this hospital; there are more people here than in some towns. We knew each other by saying hello and good morning, but not much else."

"Besides, there's a sort of caste system here," interrupted Rosa, and explained, "the specialists interact with specialists, the family doctors with other family doctors, the anesthesiologists with each other, administrative personnel with their colleagues, and that's how everything works here."

"You forgot the cleaning staff," Luci pointed out ironically.

"Don't laugh, Luci. You know I'm not exaggerating."

"I know, girlfriend, don't get angry. It also seems logical to me that we are friendlier with the people we work closest with. And it's not as extreme as you make it sound: many doctors are friendly with cleaning staff or administrative personnel."

"Of course, if the nurse or assistant is attractive, she can be friendly with anyone, but you know there is a lot of classism among doctors."

"Do you remember seeing Ana López the day before her death?" asked Zarco, trying to redirect the conversation.

The two young women shook their heads in the negative.

"The only thing you can do is check the employee entry and exit log to find out what time she came in and what time she left," responded Rosa.

"And who can provide me with that log?"

"I suppose you would have to speak with the personnel chief or the Administrator."

"Do you know if she had any close friends or boyfriend

here at the hospital?"

"I often saw her with another nurse that works in the Emergency Department. Her name is Teresa, but I don't know her last name," said Luci.

"A few months ago, she was seeing a lot of a somewhat arrogant doctor, but I hadn't seen them together for a while ..." added Rosa.

"Can you give me more information about Teresa or that doctor?"

"Ugh!" sighed Rosa, "we just don't know eachother that well. There are so many people working here ..."

True, this place was indeed larger than a damned town, thought Zarco, and started to doubt he would obtain any clear information by asking doctors, nurses, and receptionists. Surely there was someone the deceased had a close relationship with at the hospital: colleagues, bosses, friends, someone she talked to on a daily basis.

"Did she work in the Emergency Department?" asked Zarco, though he already knew the answer was affirmative. "Who can I talk to there?"

"You should ask people from her shift," said Luci, "there are many of them, and they would trade shifts to take days off. On Ana's last day, I believe she worked the morning shift."

"Yes," confirmed Rosa, "the newspaper said she died in the afternoon. I figure she must have just arrived home and found the burglar. If you want to know who she worked with, you'd need to obtain the shift logs for that day. It's been a while and I don't know if they keep them that long. What kind of cases do you investigate?"

In a modest tone, Zarco told them about some of the kidnapping and murder cases he had solved, including the one about the missing entrepreneur written up in the newspaper. He did not provide many details and, obviously, did not reveal any names.

"Thanks for your help," said the detective. He took a few business cards out of his wallet. "I'll leave my card in case you re-member something, anything ... Or, of course, if you should one day need the services of a private investigator. One last question:

do you know if Ana López often left work wearing her uniform?"

The two young women looked at each other in mock disbelief.

"It would be strange!" exclaimed Luci. "There aren't many nurses that come in or leave in their uniform. They're quite vain."

"They sure are!" reiterated Rosa.

12

Zarco and Raquel López strolled along the ocean promenade with their hands in the pockets of their respective raincoats, their bodies shivering from the cold. Once in a while they'd pass a jogger.

"It's not going to be easy. Hundreds of people work at the hospital, it's larger than a town." Zarco repeated the same tune he'd heard that morning. "The only things the gals from reception could tell me, and they did seem a bit gossipy, were that your sister was dating a doctor and that she had a friend named Teresa who worked with her in the Emergency Department. But they couldn't give me much information. Would you happen to have the phone number of either her old boyfriend or Teresa? We could ask the hospital for a listing of doctors and nurses, but it would take time to obtain and review it."

"I know the boyfriend's name was Fran, and my sister had an address book where she kept phone numbers. She lost her cell phone once and consequently, all of her contacts. That's when she got into the habit of writing the phone number into her address book every time she added a contact to her phone."

"When you lose your cell phone these days, you almost become isolated from the rest of the world."

"I have the key to my sister's house. We could go and see if we find her address book."

"Yes. And while we're there we could have a look …" Zarco left out *at the scene of the crime.*

They got into the Opel Corsa that Raquel had rented for her stay in Ibiza and drove to her sister's house. The last stretch of road was unpaved, and she drove slowly to avoid the potholes caused by rain on the dirt road. She parked in a small vacant lot across from the metal fence that faced the courtyard of the house, then unlocked the padlock and pushed on one of the gate doors.

"I've only been here once since my sister died," said Raquel, as she put the key in the lock. "Well, I've actually been here twice: once on the day I found her, and another time when I came to clean and organize things a little. I also contacted a locksmith to put new locks on the main door and the terrace door. My parents haven't wanted to come, they can't face the memories. The house will look almost as it was when my sister was alive. I suppose we should donate her clothes to charity and sell the house."

"This must be hard for all of you."

The house was tidy. The lower level consisted of a small foyer, a simple living room, and a kitchen with a breakfast bar completely furnished with items from IKEA. On a modestly designed table, located next to a wall, Zarco saw an adjustable metallic lamp and a laptop computer.

"Was this your sister's computer?"

"Yes, of course," as she spoke, Raquel opened and closed drawers in the bookcase and inspected the shelves.

"And why didn't the burglar take it? It's an Apple, the best kind, and it looks new," commented Zarco, as if he were thinking out loud. He approached the window, raised the blind and drew back the sheer curtain a little. On the other side of the street, behind a row of symmetrically trimmed shrubs, there was a pool with crystal clear water, despite it being January. "Didn't the neighbors see or hear anything?"

"The two houses next door are usually vacant. The owners come to spend an occasional weekend, or during vacation season." Zarco went upstairs toward the bedroom where Ana López' corpse had been discovered. As with the rest of the house, it was clean and organized. He had a quick look in the bathroom: nothing looked out of place. It had been eight months since the date of the crime, and during that time the home had been cleaned and organized and the broken lock had been replaced. It would not be easy to find any clues about the murderer, he thought, as he slowly descended the stairs.

"I think I've found it!" yelled Raquel from the ground floor. "Yes, this is the address book. We need to see if all the phone numbers are written down."

She opened the red address book and looked under the letter F. She found a note with the name Fran, followed by a cell phone number. Then she looked up the letter T and found two entries for the name Teresa. One of them said *Teresa prof*, therefore, the number for her sister's friend must have been the one that simply indicated *Teresa*.

"These two phone numbers must be for Teresa and Fran," said Raquel as she copied them into the contacts of her phone. Zarco also copied them into his phone.

"I think it would be better if you accompanied me to visit them. I'm sure that if you are present, they will be less distrustful. I know from experience that people tend to be reticent when they speak to a private investigator. The truth is, we all have something to hide. Do you feel up to going with me?"

"Oh Álex! This is making me relive so many memories and feelings. But if you think it's best, I'll go with you to speak with them."

"I'd prefer we start by calling her friend. This way, when we speak with your sister's ex, we'll have a better preception of him. May I take the computer?"

"Why? Is yours broken?"

"Don't be cheeky, Raquel!" protested Zarco. "I know someone who can hack into it. Maybe we'll find some clues regarding what your sister was doing during her last days. It might also be helpful if you gave me her email address."

"You can have it. It's all about finding the bastard that killed her. But I don't like spying into anyone's privacy, let alone my sister's."

"Don't worry, our hacker is only interested in circumventing obstacles and getting into your sister's computer and emails. Once he is in, he won't care what's in there. It's a bit like undressing in front of a blind person."

"Right, but you and I have the gift of sight, and would be rummaging through Ana's privacy and her possible secrets."

13

Teresa lived on Calle de la Virgen, at the bottom of the rampart surrounding Dalt Vila, Ibiza's old town. It was an old-fashioned apartment that had been remodeled with plasterboard partitions and unmistakable IKEA furniture that resembled the items from Ana's house, where they had been just an hour earlier. The combination was modern and pleasant. It was beginning to get dark, and Teresa turned on a floor lamp located in a corner of the living room. Both women sat on the sofa and Zarco sat on an uncomfortable pouffe cushion in front of them.

"I think about your sister a lot," said Teresa. "What happened to her seems incredible. It's the kind of thing you hear about on the evening news on TV, but it always happens to other people. You never think something so horrible can happen to someone close to you."

"Yes, you were very good friends. I think about her a lot, too," responded Raquel.

"You said on the phone that you wanted to ask me some questions, though I don't know if I'll be able to help."

"We are trying to figure out what really happened to my sister."

"But the trial is over and they convicted that junkie," said Teresa, confused.

"Yes, but I'm not so sure it was him. Neither is his attorney. The police barely investigated."

"On the last morning that Ana was at the hospital, did the two of you work together?" interrupted Zarco.

"Yes, we worked the same shift."

"Do you remember the last time you saw her?"

"Not exactly, it was probably mid-morning," said Teresa. "I looked for her later but couldn't find her. There was a patient in ICU that Ana was supposed to be monitoring and he died. I tried to look for her to tell her so she could prepare the report, but I didn't find her. That must have been around two in the afternoon."

"Might she have already left?" asked Zarco.

"I don't think so. We are off at three. If she had to leave earlier, she would have let me or another co-worker know so we could cover for her."

"Did Ana's absence have something to do with the patient's death?" continued Zarco.

"No, certainly not. I remember perfectly. The patient was a man they had found on the street with three bullets in him. When they brought him in, he seemed almost dead. But the bullets hadn't touched any vital organs or main arteries and, after the surgery, it appeared he would recover. There may have been an unexpected reaction to the medications or respiratory depression due to the anesthesia. We see things like that every day at our job …"

"Was an autopsy performed?"

"I don't think so. It probably wasn't considered necessary, but I can't say for sure."

"Try to remember, please," insisted Zarco. "The last time you saw Ana that morning, what time was it?"

"Around 12:00 or 12:30 in the afternoon. I saw her walking with a doctor …"

"Do you know the name of the doctor?"

"No. It was the first time I'd seen him, that's why it got my attention. He walked strangely, as if he were limping, though I'm not sure. And he had a very serious face, although that's also normal in our profession; lots of responsibility and lots of stress."

"Limping and with a serious face. Could it have been Dr. House?" Zarco regretted his words as they were coming out of his mouth. "I'm sorry, it was a stupid joke. You were saying you didn't recognize him …"

"No. Many people work at the hospital. Sometimes new staff or doctors come in from other hospitals or from South America. It's impossible to know everyone."

"Have you heard from Fran, Ana's ex?" Zarco moved on.

"No. He is also a doctor in ICU but, since they broke up,

Ana tried as best she could to avoid running into him. I don't think Fran was working that morning."

"And what was the relationship between Ana and Fran?"

"Nonexistent. Since they broke up, I barely saw them exchange a couple words. Hello and goodbye and little else. They were polite but cold."

"Did he take the breakup well?"

"If it affected him, he didn't show it. Ana was the one who initiated the breakup because she didn't sense much interest on his part. Fran preferred to spend his weekend playing paddle tennis or watching a soccer game with his friends rather than spend it with Ana. She enjoyed hiking or taking short trips during her time off, and those things held little to no interest for him. They were very different people, and I suppose they both got tired of waiting for the other to change. After they broke up, Ana would often say she didn't understand how she'd put up with him for almost two years."

"Did Ana have another relationship after Fran?"

"I think she was seeing someone, but she didn't talk about it. I gleaned it from little details: she would leave the room when the phone rang; sometimes we'd made plans together and she would cancel at the last minute saying she was tired or some such excuse. I came to my own conclusions and assumed she was seeing someone from work, perhaps a married man, but that was mere speculation."

"Do you remember who the doctor in charge of ICU was on the day Ana disappeared?" Zarco continued the questioning.

"Yes, of course. The following day she didn't come to work and didn't even notify anyone that she wasn't coming in, and when Dr. Valdés came to ask me about it, he was mad as hell. It was the first time Ana missed work without calling in and, well, we found out later why she couldn't come in ..."

"Do you know if Ana had any enemies, or if there was someone she had a conflict with?"

"No, Ana was nice and easy to like. She got along well with patients, she didn't complain about work, and she was always there to lend a hand. Before, every ICU nurse was in charge of three patients; now, because of budget cuts, we're each in charge of four." Teresa paused thoughtfully, "Look, everywhere you go you can find jealous people. Some of them are bothered by a young, pretty and smiling woman; but if you're asking if she had an enemy capable of committing a crime against her, the answer is absolutely not."

"Not even Fran?" asked Zarco.

"No. I can't imagine him being at all aggressive. Besides, for Fran to feel hatred or jealousy toward Ana, there would have to be intense feelings and, like I said, I don't think there were any on the part of either of them."

"Teresa, I'm sorry I put you through this interrogation," apologized Zarco, "but I'd like to ask you for one more favor."

"If there's anything I can do to help …"

"Would you try to speak with your co-workers, the ones who worked the same shift when Ana disappeared, and see if you can find out who was the last to see her, what time, who she was with …"

"I'll try. Of course."

"Thank you, Teresa," added Raquel warmly. She moved closer and gave her a friendly goodbye kiss on each cheek.

"If you want to get together one day, call me," said Teresa. "I'll try to ask my co-workers and see if I can find anything out, though perhaps they'll think I'm a gossip."

14

Dr. Álvarez, 'Fran' to his friends, arranged to meet Raquel and Zarco at the tennis club café. The detective would have preferred to interview the decedent's ex at his home to gain some insight into his personality. Zarco thought it was possible to size up a person's character by observing the state of their living environment: by their furniture and appliances, whether it was organized or messy, clean or dirty, their refrigerator contents, and the books or DVDs on shelves –or lack thereof. However, Fran had scheduled their meeting at the tennis club, claiming that he had an afternoon paddle tennis match that would end at 8:00 o'clock. It also seemed understandable that he would prefer to maintain his privacy and meet with two strangers somewhere outside of his home.

Fran arrived at the café freshly showered, his hair still wet and combed back. Save for the waiter, they were the only people in the locale.

"Are you Raquel?" asked Fran smiling. "I wasn't aware that Ana had such a pretty sister."

"We came here to talk about something serious," interrupted Zarco.

"I was just being friendly ..."

That's something a sleazy Don Juan would say, thought Raquel. It wasn't a good first impression and she wondered what her sister had seen in this jerk with a toothpaste ad smile. He was good-looking, but not enough to put up with him for over a year. Nobody is that good-looking.

"Would you have a problem answering a few questions about Ana López?" asked Zarco. "Obviously, you're not obligated to respond."

"No problem at all," he replied with that same smile.

"When was the last time you saw Ana?" began Zarco.

"Well, we saw each other at the hospital one or two days

before she disappeared."

"You didn't see her the day she disappeared?"

"No. It's been some time since then but, given what happened, I would have remembered."

"Do you remember what you did that day?"

"That's difficult. Like I said, it's been a long time. I worked the night shift. We start at 11:00 p.m. and I don't remember anything special, just a normal day I suppose."

"And do you remember where you were between 3:00 and 4:00 o'clock in the afternoon?" pressed Zarco.

"Am I a suspect?" he asked, laughing openly.

"No. We're just trying to tie up all the loose ends and find out exactly what happened. Do you know if Ana had any enemies, owed money, or anything out of the ordinary?"

"I don't know about anything out of the ordinary in her life. She was the personification of normal, a nice girl, I can't imagine anyone who knew her would be capable of attacking her like that."

"Do you know who she was recently going out with?"

"The truth is no, I don't. I don't even know if she was going out with someone."

The conversation ended there, and Raquel and Zarco bade an icy goodbye to Fran. They headed to the parking lot and got into Raquel's car. The vehicle's windows were fogged up from the contrast between the cold temperature outside and the warm interior. They traveled across Avenida España and passed by the Vara del Rey walkway. The shops and local businesses had rolled down their metal shutters and there were barely any pedestrians on the streets.

"That guy is gay!" said Zarco.

"Álex, really?! What about the compliments and the looks he was giving me?"

"It was all a pose. He's not out of the closet yet and he's pretending to be very macho, but I can immediately tell when someone prefers cucumbers over lettuce."

"Okay, the cucumber thing is pretty graphic—but lettuce?"

"It's just an expression."

"Yeah, you all have lots of expressions. You also say if a guy is not gay, it's because he hasn't tried it yet. So, basically: he's gay if he tries it, and gay if he doesn't too," Raquel replied.

"Whether or not this guy is gay, what's clear is that he's not the least bit suspicious."

"Or he's an accomplished actor, or an innocent man," judged Raquel. "No one can pretend to be an asshole so convincingly. In the end, the most obvious answer is usually the correct one, so the guy they convicted will turn out to be the guilty one."

"Well, that's certainly a possibility. You can narrow down motives for killing someone to three: money, revenge, or crime of passion. Your sister's case doesn't seem to mesh with any of those, so it might be as the prosecutor suggested: involuntary manslaughter. The man went in there to steal, something went wrong, and he ended up killing your sister."

They parked the car on a street near the home of Raquel's parents.

"I'll walk you to the door," said Zarco.

"I don't know if we're wasting time and energy on this investigation."

"You're giving up so easily?" asked Zarco. "I think we've made some headway. First of all: we've ruled out her ex, who would normally be our number one suspect. Second, so far we've learned that the last person who saw your sister alive was Teresa, around 12:00 or 12:30 p.m., and that Ana was walking toward the elevator with a doctor that Teresa didn't recognize, therefore we'll have to find out who he is so we can question him."

"Do you think we're going to find him? An unknown doctor with a serious face?"

"Stranger things have happened," said Zarco optimistically. This investigation was giving him an adrenaline rush. "After 12:30 in the afternoon, Teresa couldn't find your sister even though she looked for her, so we might assume your sister had to go home for some reason but expected to return to work, which is why she didn't change clothes. She put a coat on over her uniform and that's it."

"Yeah, but if she returned home at 12:30—or let's even say

1:00 p.m.—that would have to be the time of death and not 3:00 o'clock. What happened during those two hours?"

"At the moment, it's hard to know. On the other hand, we also have your sister in charge of a patient who was shot three times and died in the hospital. That's two violent deaths in Ibiza in less than twenty-four hours … Hmm!" declared Zarco, without finishing the argument.

"Do you think they're connected?"

"Well, I don't know. But we have to investigate it. It's not normal for someone to be shot three times. It may be someone involved with drugs or prostitution, and those people don't fool around."

"Yes, but why kill the nurse who is taking care of him? I don't see the logic in that."

"And lastly," remarked Zarco, "we also have to figure out if Teresa's suspicions were true about whether your sister was secretly dating someone."

"We're not sure there was a mystery lover," replied Raquel.

"Right, but we have nothing to lose by trying to find out if he existed or not and, in case he did, ascertain his identity."

"And how are we going to do that?"

"It won't be complicated if we can get copies of phone bills from recent months. If Ana was seeing someone, she would have called him sometime."

"You're right, Álex," said Raquel with renewed energy. "Just as we agreed: maybe the man they convicted is guilty, but at least I want to dispel all doubt. I couldn't live with the uncertainty that perhaps we might have done more."

15

Ballesteros and Paco Marín were drinking beer at a crowded bar along the outskirts of the Vara del Rey area. There were two bottles of beer on the wooden table along with an order of *patatas bravas* tapas, compliments of the house.

"Have you ever heard of Lucia Etxebarría?" asked Ballesteros.

"The writer? Yes, of course."

"And what do you think?"

"I've read a couple of her books and I think they're very good. Some of the best out there right now."

"What does she write about?"

"Christ, Raúl! Is this an interrogation? Are you looking to gift a book to someone or something like that?"

"No, it just occurred to me to ask you. The other day, Julieta blurted out that she didn't want to continue her schooling because she wanted to be a writer. She wants to be like this Etxebarría person. Do you know if she went to college?"

"I don't know," Paco answered laughing. "I suppose she might have studied philology. Her writing is very good, very fluid, but I don't think you'd enjoy her novels."

"I'm almost certain of that. What does she write about?"

"From what I've read: love stories, psychological and sexual problems..."

"Another neurotic person! Shit! I don't even want to think about Julieta going in that direction."

"While it may be hard for you to accept," replied Paco, "Julieta is growing up. She'll be a woman before you know it. And, from what I know of her, she seems quite intelligent and responsible."

"Yes, she's been responsible up until now, but the other day she dropped this writer thing on me and, what can I say, it was not fucking funny at all!" When he was working, Ballesteros always used politically correct language, which was why he took guilty pleasure in spewing swear words and profanities in his private conversations.

Paco couldn't help but smile. Despite their longstanding friendship, he knew that Ballesteros' interests did not include the arts. He probably couldn't name a single work by Borges, and he certainly couldn't distinguish a Picasso painting from a Basquiat, even if he had heard of the American painter. He was, however, an avid film enthusiast and had an ample collection of both classic and current movies on DVD.

"Haven't you always said that the important thing is for her to be happy, and that money is secondary?" asked Paco in mocking reproach. "I sense an undercurrent of concern for your daughter's economic future."

"It's not just that. While I'm alive, Julieta will never want for anything. But I also don't want her to become a slacker."

"Holy shit, Raúl! Not all writers or artists are slackers! Some writers even work ten-hour days."

"Sure. And how many young people call themselves artists so they can jerk around all day?"

"Are you referring to me?" smiled Paco.

"Apart from the young person reference, the sentence could, in fact, apply to you."

"Raúl, we can't all be lawyers or surgeons. We not only can't but don't want to be. The amusing thing about this, and please don't take offense, is that you've always professed to having an open and tolerant attitude: my daughter can do whatever she wants. And now she tells you she wants to be a writer, and you don't approve. If she'd told you she wanted to be a police officer or firefighter, you probably wouldn't have liked that either."

"But look at the examples you're giving me! And with this economic slump the country is in … well, let's say it's not ideal to be deficient in education and skills!"

"It's better if you don't worry. Chances are with or without skills, she'll still end up unemployed."

Ballesteros was annoyed at Paco's long-established habit of joking around when he was trying to have a serious conversation. Sure, since *he* was set for life and could schedule his day around exercise, reading, and painting, it was natural to always be in a good mood and trivialize other people's problems. Paco didn't have children either and was unfamiliar with the invisible tether of parenthood. He decided to return the favor and annoy his friend.

"Paco, you shouldn't be in such a good mood. Haven't you heard that there's a bank deposit freeze looming over Spain? If I were you, I'd stash some money under a brick."

"Don't think I haven't thought about it. The worst thing would be if the euro disappeared, and I had to convert my money into pesetas or some other currency. I've also thought about transferring some to Switzerland. How much could I take out of the country without committing a crime?"

"I don't know right now. I'd have to research it. I'll call you tomorrow and let you know, but I don't think you can take out a very large quantity."

The waiter set two more bottles of beer down on the table. Both men picked up napkins, wiped off the bottle lip, and took a swallow. They both retained the habit of drinking straight out of the bottle. Ballesteros reached into the pocket of his coat, folded on the back of a chair, and pulled out a pack of cigarettes.

"Did you finally quit?" he asked, holding up the pack.

"No. I still smoke but only a little. This smoking thing sucks. Once you're hooked you can't stop," replied Paco.

"Want one?"

They walked out onto the street and stood, lit cigarettes in hand, next to a bar table with an ashtray at its center.

"One of the few positive things the PSOE political party managed to do was prohibit smoking in public spaces," said Ballesteros. "It's good for both non-smokers and smokers because it makes us smoke less. I remember it wasn't that long ago you could smoke in the courtroom. The billowy haze in that room was unbelievable."

"People also smoked on buses and airplanes, basically everywhere. And, changing the subject, you told me you'd found a private detective to investigate that nurse's murder ..."

"Yes. I already told you that case is full of holes. I don't believe Eduardo Ribas, the man who was convicted, is guilty of killing that girl. He was just in the wrong place at the wrong time and ran into a Civil Guard officer who was anxious to solve the case."

"Hey if he's not guilty, then the case has not been solved."

"As far as the police, judges, and press are concerned, it's solved."

"And have you made much headway in your investigations?"

"It's still too soon to tell. In any event, the investigator we've hired seems like a bit of a weirdo to me. The decedent's sister hired him. Anyway, we'll see what happens." Ballesteros crushed out his cigarette in the ashtray. "Now that I've tormented you with my problems about work and my adolescent daughter, it's your turn. How's it going with Tanya?"

"I would say that it's a summer romance that's lasting through the whole winter."

"In other words, there's an expiration date."

"Few things last a lifetime, Raúl. But for now, we're good."

"Have you talked about living together, marriage, children?"

"Actually, we have. She definitely wants to have children, though she's not in a hurry. And as for living together or getting married, we just spoke about it not that long ago. I feel really good with her, she makes me feel comfortable. But I often think about our age difference. There's a twenty-one year gap, no less! When you and I were younger and we saw a fifty-something guy with a beautiful girl from Russia or the Caribbean, what did we think? That she was with him for his money or to get her residency papers, or maybe both! Then it happens to you, and you think you're different, you're 'special'. And sometimes you screw it up. My money has given me a comfortable life, but it's also made me distrustful."

"Come on! You can move to a cheap apartment and tell her you're broke, that you barely have enough to live on, and see what happens."

"And if she stays with me? Then what do I tell her? That it was a test?"

"If she loves you when you're poor, then don't worry because she won't mind if you're really not."

"The truth is I go round and round the subject. I'm forty-five— almost forty-six—and she's only twenty-five years young. When she turns forty, I'll be sixty!"

"The important thing is how you feel," responded Ballesteros. "Don't try to predict the future. We could get hit by a car tomorrow and we won't make it to forty-six."

"Right. Do you know what she said the other day? She asked if I wanted to have a threesome."

"Holy shit! A threesome! With a guy or a girl?"

"With a girlfriend of hers. Can you imagine?"

"It's most men's sexual fantasy but, to be honest, this doesn't sound to me like a normal proposition. Society advances faster than my ability to adapt or to even understand. This generation is hedonistic: sex and binge drinking. I think I'm a little too old for that."

"And what about hippies? They're from the sixties: the decade you and I were born into. And they professed free love. The only difference is that back then they wore flowery shirts and long hair, and now they wear Zara or Pull & Bear clothes and they're waxed from top to bottom. They used to take LSD, and now it's ecstasy."

"The hippies wanted to change the world, and today's young people just want to avoid it and have a good time."

"Well, clearly, you talk like our parents used to. You've gone over to the other side," Paco taunted.

"I've been a father for a long time. But we were talking about you and Tanya, and we've gone off topic. Don't take this wrong, but I wouldn't trust a woman who suggested a threesome."

"Like I said, you have to understand that she's from a different generation. She sees sex as something completely natural. When we were kids, we were told that jerking off was a sin, and if you did it too much you could go blind. If you said that to a twelve-year-old kid today, he'd laugh in your face."

"Yes, that was definitely a repressive sexual education and we were just dim-witted teens, but I'm not so sure that an excess of freedom is all that good. Hasn't it ever occurred to you that if screwing is so natural for her, she might be getting a little somewhere else?"

"Well, actually yes. Some nights I've called Tanya. Not too late, of course—before midnight—and her phone is off, and I worry about whether she's at home or not. She doesn't have a landline, and she says she turns off her cell phone when she goes to sleep so it doesn't disturb her. She also travels a lot for work. Every ten or fifteen days she goes to Madrid or Barcelona, and sometimes it eats away at me. Should we go back inside?"

The two men went back to their seats at the wooden table and asked the waiter for two more beers.

"You could hire a private investigator."

"It seems a bit much to spy on your girlfriend."

"Look at it another way: you're not spying to find out if she has a lover, you're doing it to prove to yourself that you can trust her completely and to drive away the little green monster."

"I think I'll try your first idea: telling her that I'm broke and I have barely enough to live on."

"I was only kidding," clarified Ballesteros.

16

Ballesteros got up at 7:00 o'clock in the morning. After having vanquished his morning laziness, he put on his tracksuit and sneakers and went out for a jog. Ballesteros made himself get up early three days a week to go running. The first stretch of his journey was uncomfortable. He had to traverse several streets, stopping if the traffic light was red for pedestrians and then starting up again when it turned green. He started with a slow jog to warm up. Once he got to the ocean promenade, the path became obstacle-free. It was pleasant and he could increase his running cadence. He would invariably start to sweat within fifteen minutes and continued his run until he had completed the hour. Ballesteros often used that time to think about personal issues, which served to distract him from his physical exertion. The idea he had given Paco seemed too excessive to put into practice. Pretend to go bankrupt? For how long? It bordered on the ridiculous. He understood Paco's qualms about spying on Tanya; however, Ballesteros had never felt overly fond of the exuberant Russian girl. She was friendly and definitely had two very compelling reasons for attracting men, perhaps even three or four compelling reasons that were visibly evident. Ballesteros had noticed the insinuating looks Tanya gave him, using her eyes to remind him of just how sexy she was. That is not, thought Ballesteros, how one looks at her boyfriend's best friend, or for that matter, any other man. Paco definitely wore his age well (for being nearly fifty) and he maintained a bohemian lifestyle that attracted a certain type of woman. But his financial freedom was also attractive. He didn't brag about it, but it was obvious. It wouldn't be a bad idea to look into this young woman.

Ballesteros was sweating copiously by the time he made it back to the maze of city streets on his return to the penthouse. He noticed a slight twinge in his knees. It was yet another notch that marked the passage of time, he thought, likening it to the need to wear reading glasses. These two setbacks to his physical functioning had arrived suddenly, once he'd crossed the threshold of forty-five. He sprinted as he approached his home, and maintained a fast-paced stride until he was almost winded in the last few meters. Panting breathlessly, he stopped and stretched his calf muscles, placing the sole of his foot on a lamp-post and putting his leg in a sort of plank position. He thought about the shower that awaited him and he felt satisfied, as he always did when he finished running.

At about the same time that Ballesteros was running along the streets of Ibiza, Paco Marín was standing in front of his easel. He had gotten up that morning feeling tired, slightly hungover, and had not gone through his morning weight training session in the gym he'd installed in one of the bedrooms of his country home. He'd had coffee with milk and a piece of buttered toast with bitter orange marmalade for breakfast, and had gone straight to the studio to paint. He enjoyed that particular time of morning in which the machinery of civilization hadn't awakened, and calm silence prevailed.

Paco had prepared an assortment of colors on a large plastic plate that he used as a palette and started to dab the brush and spread the acrylic paints across the canvas with fast, spontaneous movements. He tried to fill the painting with vibrant colors and varying brush strokes: long, short, wide, narrow, thick, and diluted. At times, he also allowed the paint to drip or used a spatula. He wanted the painting to be an amalgamation of colors and a medley of shapes and textures. While he painted, his mind was devoid of daily problems. He forgot about the economic crisis that was ruining his country, the passage of time, his suspicions about Tanya, environmental destruction, selfishness, and evil, and human ignorance ...

He took a break, made himself another cup of coffee, and lit a cigarette. Then, with a cup in one hand and a cigarette in the other, he gazed at his work with satisfaction. He knew from experience that such satisfaction was deceiving and fleeting and that, frequently, the immense pleasure he obtained from viewing a recently completed painting would convert into frustration when he studied it again the following day.

As he took a drag from the cigarette, he imagined Tanya walking naked on the terrace of their hotel room at daybreak after that first night they'd spent together. He had been a little disturbed by her behavior, which he had considered shameless. *After all*, he thought, *Raúl and I are from the same generation, so perhaps we're not so different.*

He had met Tanya at the Ibizan airport one morning around the end of May. They had both arrived from Barcelona on an Iberia flight, and were standing together at the baggage carousel waiting for their respective suitcases. She was wearing jeans and a tight white shirt that highlighted her physical attributes. They were the only two passengers waiting for luggage, even though another fifty people had been on the same flight. Paco had looked at the monitor indicating that was the correct area to wait for their bags, but he thought it strange there were no other people waiting around the carousel where the luggage were supposed to appear except he and the attractive young woman standing next to him that he'd already noticed on the plane, so he asked her if she was also waiting for a suitcase from the Barcelona flight. She said yes with a smile, and they started to chat. He didn't remember what they talked about, but it had been a fluid and enjoyable conversation, as if they were old friends. He offered to give her a ride into the city in his car, which was in the airport parking lot, and she happily accepted.

That same evening, they'd met for dinner at a Japanese restaurant and later rented a room at the Gran Hotel where they made love. Paco generally didn't take women to his home on the first date and Tanya was no exception. He distinctly remembered Tanya's naked body outlined in the first light of dawn. She was walking barefoot on the terrace of the hotel room with her cell phone at her ear. Who had she called at that hour? It was the first time that thought had occurred to him, now seven months later. Paco was certain that she had initiated the call because otherwise he would have heard Tanya's phone ring. Why was he suddenly experiencing doubts and concocting questions? He was now pondering details that initially—when their relationship still seemed fleeting—did not seem important. As his interest in Tanya grew and their relationship became closer, he scrutinized some of her behaviors under the prism of a more demanding lens which was not above reproach.

Paco had decided to play out the plan that had been proposed, perhaps in jest, by his friend Raúl. It was by no means a perfect plan, and Paco knew it would not be viable to prolong the charade over an extended period of time. And yet it might provide a new perspective on his personal relationships and confirm to what point his comfortable financial situation shaped his friendships. Neither of his two sisters or any of his friends, not even Ballesteros or Tanya, knew the actual amount of his current fortune. He had not lied in telling them that he'd won the lottery, but he hadn't told them exactly how many millions of euros there were. But now he would be adding on a new lie: that of his bankruptcy. Of course, he wouldn't be the first lucky lottery winner to go flat broke after just a few years. It wouldn't sound preposterous to his family and friends that he'd made large property investments during Spain's infamous real estate bubble and that, after the housing sector crisis, these stagnant construction projects had lost most of their value. Since he was unable to keep up the payments, his luxurious home, his land, and the rest of his assets would soon be owned by the bank.

He smiled while imagining the reactions of those around him. His sisters would probably offer him some financial assistance while suggesting he look for work. Some of his superficial "friends" would definitely make themselves scarce. But how would Tanya respond? That was the big question. Of course, his scheme was juvenile and unseemly for a man that had entered his fourth decade some years ago. Paco recognized that his biological age did not correlate with his youthful spirit. Or, for all he knew, perhaps he was nearing that age when adults enter a second childhood and start behaving like kids. He decided to quash the clamoring voice in his head telling him this twisted farce was childish and that he was no longer a child. He remembered a saying his mother used to repeat: *a lie will always catch up with you.*

17

Álex Zarco sat in front of his computer screen in his apartment, taking little sips from a cup of Cola Cao hot chocolate as he typed on the keyboard with his free hand. The Demichellis case, the name he'd given this ongoing investigation, had plunged him into a state of hyperactivity as he tried to clarify all the facts. He had reviewed the police affidavit, the procedures from the preliminary hearing by Ibiza's Examining Court Number 2, and the trial proceedings, and he had not found any important information that Ballesteros or Raquel had not already shared with him. He wanted to leave nothing to chance, no matter how insignificant it appeared. His brain was working against the clock, trying to find the smallest detail that might have fallen through the cracks during the superficial police investigation. So far Ana's nurse friend, Teresa, had been the last person to see her alive. It was apparent that there were no witnesses to the homicide. In the scenario in which the killing played out, there was only the victim and the murderer (or murderers). Was it not elementary to investigate the victim's movements up to that point? The police team had not followed that line of investigation, probably because they were convinced they had already arrested the guilty party. Based on the premise that the murderer could be someone other than the man who had been convicted, there was only one other path: retrace Ana's steps until the moment of her disappearance. Zarco's biggest obstacle was the considerable amount of time that had elapsed. Why hadn't they called him sooner? Of course, at the beginning of the investigation, Raquel did not suspect that the unfolding of the trial would give rise to so many doubts regarding the culpability of the prisoner. In any case, there was no sense crying over spilt milk.

Teresa had reported seeing Ana in the company of an unknown doctor on or about 12:30 in the afternoon. Zarco would have to wait for the nurse to inquire with her co-workers and determine if any of them had seen Ana afterwards. If not, it would be as if she had vanished from the hospital at noon and shown up later at the scene of the crime.

He'd also have to investigate the deceased patient who had been under Ana's care. This didn't seem to be a line of inquiry that would go very far, but there were few available facts to work with. Still, it's quite unusual to find a guy in Ibiza with three bullets in his body. If the shooting had occurred the day before Ana's death, the initial court assigned to the case would have been Ibiza's Examining Court Number 1. Zarco was acutely aware of the instinctive scorn that court officials felt toward private investigators; therefore, it was going to be extremely difficult to gain access on his own to preliminary proceedings submitted regarding the shooting.

The investigator felt mild animosity for attorneys in general, who he considered a kettle of vultures ready to swoop down on carrion so they could enrich themselves on human misfortune and misery. Although he considered Ballesteros the prototype that embodied the vices and defects of said profession, he decided to call him and request his collaboration. Having to resort to asking the attorney for help was humiliating, but he knew that lawyers had easy access to court records even if they were not directly involved in the particular lawsuit since, in many cases, they enjoyed the trust of public servants who they dealt with on a daily basis. They might even argue that they were looking into whether they would need to appear at a civil proceeding and therefore have to review the file for applicable supporting documents.

Suddenly the phone rang, interrupting his thoughts. He picked it up and looked at the screen before pressing the key to take the call. He saw that it was Ballesteros and his face lit up with delight at the coincidence, since now he would be able to ask for the assistance he needed during their conversation, which would be less awkward than calling him to bluntly solicit the information.

"Hello?"

"Is this Álex Zarco?"

"Yes, it is."

"I'm calling you about a subject that has nothing at all to do with the investigation we're working on … I need you to recommend a trustworthy private investigator to follow someone."

18

"It wasn't hard at all," said Raquel as she held out several bills from the Vodafone telephone company detailing phone numbers and length of calls from Ana López' phone. "She had all her papers in one drawer and apparently, she saved all her bills: phone, water, electricity ... But it might be harder to figure out which of those numbers belongs to her mystery lover."

Zarco took the bill dated February 14 to March 13, 2012, from two months before Ana López' death and, after a quick perusal, he pointed to a number.

"Why do you think it's specifically that one? Other numbers are also repeated," argued Raquel.

"Yes, but I noticed that phone calls to this number tend to be made during the same time period, between 5:00 and 5:30 in the afternoon, and they're short calls. On the other hand, there are no calls to that number on weekends, which would fit the pattern for a married man. She calls him at a specific time, perhaps when he gets out of work or goes to pick up his kids at school, something like that."

"And the calls are short because they're only for setting a time to meet," noted Raquel.

"Exactly."

"And she didn't call at the arranged time on weekends because it's outside of his routine and he could be with his family," she added.

"Exactly!" agreed the detective again while giving his cell phone to his friend. "And there's only one way to be sure: call him."

"And what am I going to say?"

"The truth. That you're Ana López' sister and you'd like to speak with him privately. If I call him and tell him I'm a private detective he'll get defensive, regardless of whether he's implicated in your sister's death or not." Zarco insisted and gestured to the phone still resting in his hand, "Call him from mine."

Raquel quickly dialed the number. She heard the intermittent ringing of the phone. By the fourth ring, she doubted if someone would pick up when she suddenly heard a serious male voice on the line.

"Yes?"

"Good afternoon."

"Good afternoon," she heard the voice soften slightly, taking on that friendlier tone that Raquel often noticed when a man spoke to an unknown woman.

"Look … I don't know how to explain this," started Raquel hesitantly, "I am Ana López' sister and I'd like to talk to you. I know you two knew each other, "she asserted, while implying that she knew more. She perceived a tense silence on the other end of the line.

"What do you want?" responded the man in a forcefully calm voice.

"I just want to talk to you. It won't take much more than half an hour."

"I'm off work at 5:00 o'clock. We can meet at the café in front of the Can Misses Hospital at 5:10."

"Okay. See you there."

Raquel and Álex Zarco arrived promptly at the hospital café. They didn't know what the man they were scheduled to meet looked like—they didn't even know his name. Given where he worked, they had concluded that he was a doctor, although he could also be a nurse or work in the hospital as an administrator or even in maintenance. In the back of his mind, Zarco was sure he was a doctor due to the fact that Raquel's deceased sister was a nurse. The doctor-nurse relationship was a paradigm, much like that of the boss-secretary or pilot- stewardess. The detective believed that humans unconsciously followed particular behavior patterns that frequently ended up becoming clichés. They initially saw a stocky man with a prominent double chin sitting at one of the café tables. Raquel instantly ruled him out: she couldn't imagine her sister enjoying an evening of lovemaking with that person. She looked toward the door just as an attractive, tanned man who appeared in his mid-thirties came in. He had a thin, athletic body, and dark, penetrating eyes, and black hair cut short. She could imagine her sister with him. As he approached, Raquel stared at him intently while Zarco stayed in the background, ordering a couple of coffees from the waitress. The man walked toward her and she smiled, acknowledging that she was the one he was meeting. He held out his hand to greet her.

"Are you Ana's sister?"

"Yes. I'm Raquel. And you are?"

"Roberto Gomis. You look like your sister."

"Yes, there are some similarities." As she turned, she grabbed Zarco by the arm and introduced the two men: "Álex Zarco, Roberto Gomis."

"I don't understand," said Gomis, addressing Raquel and ignoring the extended hand that Zarco offered as a greeting. "I thought we were going to speak alone."

"Perhaps I wasn't clear," replied Raquel, "but I assure you we have our reasons. We are investigating my sister's death, and Álex is a private investigator I've hired. That's why he is here. We don't want to bother you or complicate anything."

"I don't actually see how I can help you," he replied annoyed.

"How long were you in a relationship with my sister?"

"Well, we had been seeing each other six or seven months before it … before her death."

"Did you go to the police after her death?"

"I didn't think it was necessary. I didn't know anything about the robbery at her home, and I couldn't offer any help."

"Didn't you think that perhaps the police could find clothing or something that belonged to you at Ana's house that could make you a suspect?"

"I had nothing to hide with regard to our relationship, and I felt it was nobody's business." He paused briefly to sip from a bottle of water the waitress had brought him, and continued: "I'm unsure if you know I'm married, and I have two daughters ages five and seven. I assumed that if the police came to see me I would tell them the truth, but I wasn't about to go to them."

"Of course," Zarco said sarcastically. Roberto fixed his eyes on Zarco and his face changed, taking on a seething expression. The blood gathered in his cheeks, reddening them suddenly. He appeared ready to pounce on the detective at any moment.

"You have no idea!" he spewed, raising his voice, "There was nothing I could do to help Ana. After she died, there was no point exposing our relationship. It was no one's business except hers and mine. It's not even your business."

"Please don't get angry," Raquel intervened, trying to reduce the tension in their conversation. "What we know for certain is that the officers in charge of the case did not investigate much."

"I don't understand what you two are looking for!" Roberto exclaimed. His voice had gone up a few decibels as he addressed Raquel. "The police arrested the man responsible for the robbery and killing of your sister. I know it's hard to accept a family member's death, but it's the only way to move forward. It's only human to make up demons and pursue them, and to utilize the craving for revenge to ease the pain, but you can't just assail someone with allegations."

"No one has accused you."

"Your investigator has offended me with his tone of voice." Roberto Gomis looked at his wristwatch. "Actually, I have to leave. I have other things to do. If you can think of something I can help with, let me know," he said with strained courtesy. "I've told you I have no relevant information."

"Did you care for my sister? Were you in love with her?"

As he reached for his coat, Roberto Gomis remembered the physical attraction he had felt for Ana. She had a shapely body, slim but with curves in the right places. Her body was the first thing that had attracted him to her but there had been more. A mutual fondness. They had met by chance a few times in the elevator and hospital hallways, and their conversation had flowed naturally, without the awkwardness sometimes felt during routine exchanges with strangers we aren't interested in talking to. There was a friendliness there and Roberto began to notice that she was attracted to him, which increased his desire for her. They ended up in bed on their first date. She knew that he was married and loved his wife and daughters, and that he had no intention of getting a divorce. He never lied to her or made false promises. Their relationship had been passionate and sexual and, to a certain extent, emotional. However, there had been no love on his part.

"That's not something that concerns either of you," Roberto Gomis responded curtly as he turned toward the exit.

Once Gomis had left the café, Zarco turned toward the waitress.

"Do you know that man that was standing here with us?"

"I know him by sight, he comes in often. He's with a group of doctors that comes in every day. Regular customers. Dr. Gomis is a plastic surgeon with a particularly good reputation, or so I've heard."

"Is cosmetic surgery performed here at Can Misses?" asked Zarco, surprised.

"I think they're cosmetic surgeries for health reasons. In the event of accidents or things like that," the waitress explained. "Not because someone wants a nicer nose or larger breasts."

"Ah!"

"You see, after working here for eleven years, I've even learned a little about medicine. And I won't even tell you about psychology! When a customer comes in, I already know if he's going to order a coffee, a Coke, or a double whiskey."

19

That morning, Ballesteros had gone to the main office of Ibiza's Court of Violence Against Women Number 1, to assist a defendant accused of domestic abuse battery who had expressly requested his services. The accused had refused services from the duty lawyer. Contrary to general opinion, a duty lawyer in Spain was not synonymous with legal aid. If the accused person's income was above twice the minimum wage, equaling 1,300 euros a month, he was required to pay the attorney fees. Only in the event that his income was below that amount, which was often the case with common criminals, was he awarded the benefit of legal aid.

Quick trials did not take place in the courtroom. Statements from the injured party, the accused, and possible witnesses were taken at the desk of a court reporter who transcribed their statements into the computer, under the judge's supervision. Afterwards, the case records were sent to the prosecutor who decided whether or not to draw up an indictment. If the accused acknowledged the events and agreed to the sentence requested by the representative of the Prosecution Ministry, the sentence was reduced by a third. If no agreement was reached, the case was referred to the corresponding criminal court for a new trial.

Ballesteros entered the Ibiza Court Building and went upstairs to the first floor where the offices of the Court of Violence Against Women were located, and asked for the clerk in charge of processing urgent proceedings. A plump young woman informed him that the records were managed by her co-worker, who had gone out for breakfast. Ballesteros stoically accepted the explanation. He knew from experience that it was useless to ask another clerk to allow him to see the file because they would find any excuse to refuse, and he would acquire a reputation for being a nuisance. He also knew from experience that breakfast could stretch out to forty-five minutes or even an hour. Public employees had bad reputations and received constant negative press, but if people really knew how their Department of Justice functioned, thought Ballesteros, citizens would refuse to pay their taxes and there would be protests and riots. Non-compliance with the seven-and-a-half-hour workday was widespread and condoned by the court administrators, who were in charge of monitoring and managing personnel and who generally looked the other way in order to avoid confrontations with their employees. It was true, of course, that in 2010, Prime Minister Zapatero's government had lowered their salaries, and the administration of the subsequent Prime Minister, Rajoy, had taken away their extra Christmas pay for the prior year. In nearly two and a half years, public employees had lost fifteen percent of their purchasing power, which didn't sit well with Ballesteros. He felt they should receive an appropriate salary but should also work the appropriate hours.

He remembered the information Zarco had requested and, to make use of his time while awaiting the return of the clerk in question, he walked to the offices of Ibiza's Examining Court Number 1, located two floors up. After a quick search, the clerk found the record number for previous court proceedings corresponding to those that had been formally filed regarding the fatal shooting that had occurred in May of 2012. The clerk pulled the file from the archives and gave it to Ballesteros. The attorney glanced through it quickly and made copies of the records. He read the findings at the end of the document, dated September of 2012. The proceedings had been provisionally archived, as the perpetrator was unknown. He thanked the clerk for the assistance provided, and returned to the Court of Violence Against Women.

Ballesteros disliked legal issues involving couples breaking up, whether it was a domestic violence complaint or a contentious divorce. In his extensive experience practicing law, he had never seen more intense hatred or bitter enemies than former spouses, especially when a third party was involved. Frequently, one of the parties experienced difficulty reintegrating into a social life that had slowly dwindled over the course of the marriage. When one half of the couple had rebuilt their life with another person while the other half plunged into loneliness, the result was excruciating to the extreme. That kind of pain spawns a desire to hurt the other and creates a snowball that rolls downhill and increases in size. Generally, the ex-wife uses the children as weapons, not respecting the visitation rights awarded to the father or allowing him to see the children according to the agreement, which results in non-compliance of parental responsibilities. The ex-husband then stops paying alimony, which constitutes a failure to pay child support. Of course, there were uncontested divorces and amicable separations, but those cases did not require attorneys except to fulfill legal requirements.

The clerk, who had returned from breakfast and was now back at her desk, gave Ballesteros the requested file. The attorney quickly glanced through the court records and was relieved to note that his client had not provided a statement while at the police station. He slowly read the injured party's complaint. The version of María José Zapata, the plaintiff, indicated that she and the accused (Derek Neumann, a German national) had been married in Ibiza in 2004, and had two children together, boys ages 6 and 4. In the past year, there had been arguments between both the husband and wife, and between the husband and his mother-in-law, regarding Derek's fondness for drinking. There had also been quarrels between María José and Derek's mother regarding the 'distinct German character of her mother-in-law', with no additional details, as if it were obvious that conflict and disagreement between these two nationalities were inevitable without specifying what these disagreements were, and always according to María José Zapata's version. The disputes of both the couple and their mothers had steadily escalated, reaching their breaking point when Derek received an offer from his company to work at a branch in Barcelona which included a substantial salary increase, a move opposed by María José and her mother. Over the recent Christmas holidays, there had been several intense arguments in which the word divorce had come up for the first time. In fact, María José had met with an attorney to obtain information regarding its requirements, procedures, and consequences.

Finally, yesterday, January 16, 2013, at around 10:30 p.m., Derek had staggered into his home where his wife greeted him with a belligerent attitude, reproaching him for being a bad husband and father, threatening him with divorce, and goading him to move out of the house. Derek was unfazed and, even sporting a crooked drunken smile, he went to the kitchen and uncorked a bottle of wine. This indifference escalated María José's anger, who's only outlet for venting was her sharp tongue. So she proceeded to upgrade the tone of her insults to obscenities and, realizing that claiming he was a bad father and husband didn't appear to bother Derek one iota and that the threat of divorce did not wipe that smile off his face, she moved on to attacking his manhood, alluding to both the size of his penis as well as his scant understanding of the female anatomy. María José knew too well that these words would offend a drunken German as well as a sober Spaniard, and vice versa. Derek, fully enraged, reacted by calling her a "filthy whore" and saying he was fed up with her and her goddamned mother. At that point, María José, overwhelmed by powerlessness, rage, and indignation, delivered a resounding smack to her husband's face. He responded with a similar blow that left his wife's face swollen and red. Once she overcame the shock and surprise, she grabbed her phone and ran into the bedroom of her still sleeping children, and she locked the door. Derek poured himself another glass of red wine and sat at the kitchen table.

Forty-five minutes later, the doorbell rang. Derek was in the bathroom brushing his teeth. It occurred to him that the only person who would show up at that hour was his witch of a mother-in-law, probably summoned by María José, so he continued with his oral hygiene. To his surprise, he heard a masculine voice speaking with his wife. He rinsed the toothpaste out of his mouth, walked out of the bathroom, and found himself facing two police officers who were staring at him steadily and seriously. One of them, without averting his eyes, informed him that he was going to be arrested for domestic abuse and that he had the right to remain silent, to not say anything that might be used against him, and the right to an attorney. While one of the officers read him his rights, the other made him turn with his hands behind his back and cuffed his wrists. Derek could not think clearly. "It was just a light slap," he said.

Ballesteros examined the injury report written at the Emergency Department and picked up on the concise phrases: "Contusion on left cheek. Reports aggression." The forensic report did not add much more of legal interest. It spelled out that the injury had required one basic ministration without the need for medical treatment or subsequent surgery, citing a healing period of two days with no restrictions. Put plainly: she had a mild contusion.

The version Derek recounted to Ballesteros in the holding cell differed in small, unsubstantial details from that of his wife, though they did coincide in essential and judicially relevant matters. Derek spoke perfect Spanish, manifested in his proficient use of profanity, and only a mild inflection when pronouncing his r's, g's and j's gave away his foreign accent.

"Before responding to the judge's questions, you need to understand a few things," said Ballesteros, trying to instruct his client. "First of all, you have to deny any word or action that might incriminate you. When you are asked if you insulted your wife, deny it. Or, at most, admit you called her selfish or greedy or something along those lines; something not strictly insulting. And more importantly: when you give a statement before the judge, you must deny having hit your wife. She has been seen by a doctor, and the medical examiner has provided an injury report. Therefore, you'll have to acknowledge there was a blow, but you must deny intentionality. Say that she smacked you, and when you tried to restrain her to avoid further attack, you struck her in the face *accidentally*," Ballesteros emphasized the last word.

"I don't understand anything. Can't I just say what happened? She insulted me and I insulted her. She smacked me and then I smacked her back. I know that's not right, but I don't think it's such a big deal."

"The fact is it *is* a big deal! In the best-case scenario and, if upon further review, your wife's injuries do not appear serious, the minimum sentence you could get for hitting her is six months to a year in jail. You wouldn't have to serve it because you have no criminal history and we would request a suspended sentence. But as of now, you do have a criminal history. And what's worse: your wife can request civil measures and a restraining order and, if the judge grants it, you may not be able to return home."

"And see my children?"

"Yes, you would be able to see them, but we're not going to get to that point. Just do as I say."

"I don't understand these Spanish laws! What about her? She hit and insulted me, too. What will happen to her?"

"Well, at best she could be charged with an offense and if she is found guilty, she'd have to pay a small fine of around 800 euros. But she is the victim here and you are the accused. You have to keep in mind that this is a law designed to protect women."

"And if I lie? Won't I be committing perjury?"

"No. As the accused and in accordance with the Spanish Constitution and procedural laws, you have the right to not tell the truth. Another point is that the judge and prosecutor create your version. Two things are important here. First and foremost, you must deny having insulted your wife or having hit her intentionally. Second, stay calm. Don't raise your voice or get irritated, regardless of how nasty your wife's attorney gets."

Derek Neumann looked at Ballesteros nervously. He did not appear to square with the advice he was receiving. Ballesteros was unfamiliar with German legislation regarding domestic violence, assuming that Germany had specific legislation to protect battered women instead of applying common laws.

In judicial law practice, the famous Spanish Organic Act from January, 2004, regarding Comprehensive Measures for Protection Against Gender-based Violence was considered disastrous, and additionally, useless. The legislature had designed a law to apply to domestic violence but had not anticipated that it could be implemented against any man who, in a moment of obfuscation, could insult or, per the wording of the law, "issue minor threats" to their partner or ex-partner. The law, and the courts of Violence Against Women, had not been useful in reducing the number of fatalities for one simple reason: women who met the profile of a battered woman did not go to court or to the police to file a report. Judges, prosecutors, and attorneys privately criticized the law, but did not dare to publicly object to it. Only a single Catalonian judge had openly expressed concerns to the media and had been scornfully criticized by feminist associations and political parties.

Ballesteros knew that it wasn't just the law but also media pressure directed at judges that worked against his client. A single thought hung like the sword of Damocles over the prosecutors and judges addressing violence against women when it came time to rule for prison or probation for the presumed abuser: *if I let him go free and he kills his wife, my name will be in all the headlines and news broadcasts tomorrow.* As a result, if there was any doubt at all, prosecutors and judges did not apply the presumption of innocence and instead remanded to custody.

Statistics evidenced that in 2007, there had been more than 41,000 criminal charges filed for domestic abuse. From among these, almost 4,000 had been withdrawn by the plaintiff. Only 5,000 of the court proceedings initiated had made it to sentencing and, of those, 20% were acquittals. There had been 4,000 convictions with sentences of varying lengths. What had happened with the 37,000 proceedings (which involved 37,000 men) that ended with a finding of dismissal or acquittal? Obviously abusers had to be detained and prosecuted, but the pendulum law was not a good model. Spanish lawmakers, despite their good intentions, had designed legislation allowing the use of a cannon to kill a mosquito, with no regard to collateral damage. And subsequent leaders had not dared touch that law due to fear of media and public pressure. It was certainly necessary to take measures to protect battered women, but the law demonstrated itself to be insufficient, and created unjust situations which did not appear to trouble anyone except the individual subjected to it.

Ballesteros refocused his thoughts on the man standing in front of him. Derek Neumann did not look well. His stringy hair was unkempt and his eyes were bloodshot, making him look a bit crazy. He emitted a mild, foul odor of sweat and alcohol. Ballesteros could not avoid the burgeoning of a tinge of chauvinism when he encountered a foreigner who'd settled in Ibiza and believed (perhaps rightly) that everything was better in his own country. The question that came to mind for these malcontent immigrants was: if you don't like Spain or Spaniards, why the hell do you choose to live here instead of Germany or France where everything works just swimmingly? But he knew he would not gain his client's trust by expressing his thoughts aloud, and he softened his tone.

"Look Derek, we Spaniards have our defects and we also have our virtues. We may be a frivolous country—all bullfights and flamenco—and perhaps our politicians are inept and corrupt, but this is where you live and you have to accept things as they are."

Ballesteros recalled the old joke that defined heaven as a country run by Germans, where the Swiss manage the money, the French cook, the Italians are fashion designers, and the Spaniards are the party planners. And then there was hell, a country run by Spaniards, where Italians manage the money, the British cook, the Germans are fashion designers, and the Swiss are the party planners. He filed that joke away in his head, and asked Derek Neumann again if he clearly understood the statement he needed to make. The German citizen softly nodded his head in affirmation.

María José Zapata, Derek's wife, was sitting in front of the court reporter's desk, between her attorney and Ballesteros, who sat in their own respective chairs while the court employee typed the plaintiff's information into the computer. The judge stood behind the court reporter and, while monitoring the computer screen, informed María José of her responsibility to be truthful and advised her of the penalties in the Penal Code regarding false testimony. The judge subsequently asked her if she would ratify the complaint she made at the police station, and María José responded in the affirmative. She acknowledged having slapped the accused in response to *his* (the manner in which she referred to her husband) insults. Then *he* had assaulted her. The judge asked if she felt threatened and if she was requesting a restraining order, to which she responded yes.

María José's attorney, who Ballesteros knew superficially and considered at the level of an ambulance chaser, did not pose any questions.

Ballesteros reminded María José that she had sworn to tell the truth, and then asked her if Mr. Neumann had assaulted her on any previous occasion. She responded that he had not, that it had been the first time, although she did state there had been some psychological abuse by way of insults and humiliation.

"I'm asking if you have filed a previous complaint," stated Ballesteros.

"No."

"And isn't it also true that you consulted with a lawyer to obtain information about divorce procedures?" asked Ballesteros.

"Your Honor," said María José's attorney, "this question is beside the point. We are here about domestic abuse that occurred yesterday. Whether my client sought information regarding divorce is irrelevant."

"Your Honor," interrupted Ballesteros, "my client is being charged with serious crimes, not only as they regard to sentencing but also the subsequent consequences that will arise in addition to the damage to his reputation, and I suspect these charges may be motivated by other purposes and not for presumed domestic abuse."

The judge conceded to Ballesteros, with the warning that he not stray from the facts. The attorney then re-worded his question.

"Please answer if it is true that you consulted with an attorney to obtain information regarding divorce proceedings."

"Yes, it is true. I consulted with Ms. Torres."

"And did your attorney inform you that by filing a domestic violence complaint you could obtain a restraining order against your husband and a divorce shortly thereafter?"

"Your Honor!" her attorney howled. "This is slander!"

"Look counselor," said the judge severely as he addressed Ballesteros, "focus on the charges against your client. Do not try to elaborate conspiracy theories."

"Excuse me, Your Honor, and attorney Torres as well if I

have offended her," said Ballesteros with false contrition, "I will ask one last question: do you believe Mr. Neumann struck you intentionally, with the purpose of causing you harm?"

"I'm positive!"

"And if, as you affirm, his intention was to harm you, why do you think he did not strike you a second time? Did you run away?"

"I did not run away, and I don't know why *he* didn't hit me a second time. I went to my children's bedroom, closed the door, and called the police. *He* stayed in the kitchen, drinking."

Ballesteros insisted on the testimony of the medical examiner, to whom he only posed one question: is it possible to determine if the mild contusion on the victim's cheek was caused by an intentional blow, or could it have been produced accidentally? The examiner replied that there was not sufficient information from examining the contusion to determine categorically one way or the other.

The last to testify was the defendant, Derek Neumann, who followed the advice of his attorney. He maintained his composure during his statement, and lied like a scoundrel while stating emphatically that he had involuntarily struck his wife while trying to keep her from attacking him.

The prosecutor did not find evidence to maintain the accusation and requested the dismissal of charges. The plaintiff's attorney maintained the charges of domestic violence and requested a sentence of one year in prison. Ballesteros requested a period of one day to present a written defense, and a date was scheduled for a ruling on the criminal case in two days. Derek Neumann was released on his own recognizance pending the oral hearing in Criminal Court Number 1, with a restraining order indicating he must remain 100 meters away from his wife, stay away from locations she frequented as well as the family home, and have no communications of any kind with the victim.

20

Zarco prepared himself a cup of Cola Cao hot chocolate, sat at his desk, and became completely engrossed in meticulously reading the copies of legal documents Ballesteros had given him, under the luminous light of his gooseneck lamp. He began to read slowly. He didn't want to miss even the slightest

detail. At sunrise on the 1st of May, 2012, near the industrial park on San Antonio highway, the body of Santiago Cañas had been found with three shots in his solar plexus, fired at point blank range. He was found unconscious and, miraculously, alive. His car, a BMW ATV, was found parked just a few meters from his wounded body. The interior of the vehicle was in order. Apparently, the assailant had not been searching for anything inside. Every indication suggested it had been an act of revenge. According to Santiago Cañas' family, friends, and neighbors, he had no known enemies and was not involved in any shady dealings. He was thirty-six years old, married, had a well-paying job in the hotel sector of Ibiza, and a home with the mortgage practically paid off. Subsequent investigations revealed that the morning before the shooting, he had withdrawn 50,000 euros from his account at La Caixa Bank. The scant clues suggested a vendetta, which contrasted with the personality profile provided by the people who knew him.

At the brink of death, Santiago Cañas had been transported by ambulance to Can Misses Hospital, where he underwent emergency surgery to extract the bullets lodged in his chest. The shots had cracked his sternum and one rib, but had not damaged any vital organs. The operation had been a success, and the surgeons expressed confidence in the patient's recovery. The following morning, Santiago Cañas' lifeless body was found lying on his bed in the critical care unit. The autopsy report indicated the cause of death was "cardiorespiratory arrest", which

Zarco translated as: he died because his heart stopped, and then he stopped breathing—which to him seemed like a truism. That same morning, the nurse in charge of his care had vanished and was later found dead in her home, the victim of a robbery. *Coincidence?* Zarco asked himself. He answered his own question by telling himself that there had to be a connection. Not only had there been two violent deaths in Ibiza over a period of less than twenty-four hours, which debunked all statistics regarding the crime rate on the island, there had also been a patient-nurse relationship between Ana López Demichellis and Santiago Cañas. It simply could not have been mere coincidence. For the first time, Zarco had the full realization that the two deaths were related, therefore excluding the drug-addicted thief that had been convicted—whose name he could not remember at that moment —as the author of the crime. The Civil Guard officers had not investigated the possible connection between the two crimes. In the report drawn up regarding Ana's death, there had been no reference to the shooting or subsequent death of Santiago Cañas. Of course, there were no clues tying them together but, while it seemed an unfounded hypothesis, Zarco was certain that a connection existed. The detective verified that both statements had been prepared by the Civil Guard Judicial Police team, the part of the law enforcement body tasked with investigating major crimes on the island which occurred outside of the city of Ibiza, whose jurisdiction was assumed by the National Police. In both cases, the lead investigator had been Sergeant Juan Ferrando.

The truth was, resolving a murder case was Zarco's professional desideratum. The private detective launched into his fantasy: he would solve both murders (which the Ibizan police had failed to do) and his name would be in the headlines. There would be interviews, he would gain prestige as a private detective, there would be a surge in demand for his services, he would hire a staff ... First, of course, he had to solve the case—or cases. Zarco applied the methods of renowned fictional detective, Hercule Poirot, who consistently used his gray matter correctly. He then added Cartesian skepticism, which started with methodic doubt. In other words: doubt all appearances and go directly to the facts which cannot be disbelieved. After that, use correctly applied intellect and arrive at irrefutable conclusions. The facts were there; they only needed to be taken to their logical outcome. The first thing was to determine if Ana López Demichellis and Santiago Cañas had any type of relationship prior to the day he had been admitted to the hospital.

He searched the file for the address and phone number of Santiago Cañas' widow and wrote it on a note he placed in his back pocket. He drained the last drop of Cola Cao, grabbed his trench coat from the hanger by the door, and off he went.

Zarco checked the time on his cell phone: 4:44 p.m. He had decided to simply show up at the widow's home instead of calling first. Of course, he knew his plan would be foiled if she was working and not at home, but he also knew that people were more apt to refuse to see someone who calls on the phone identifying himself as a private investigator, than if he shows up in person. He wrapped his scarf around his neck, put on his gloves and his indispensable helmet, and started up the scooter. The frigid air seeped in through his clothing even though he was warmly dressed. It was a bitterly cold winter and temperatures hovered at about zero degrees centigrade. Still, Zarco tolerated the cold better than the stifling August heat. In the winter, one could bundle up to fight off low temperatures. In summer, there was no escape. Even if he ventured outside in shorts and a tank top, the perspiration soon beaded his face and body, smothering it with an uncomfortable, sticky sensation. He arrived at Calle Baleares, parked the motorbike between a car and a dumpster, stored his helmet under the seat, and pressed the intercom belonging to the home of Isabel González, Santiago Cañas' widow. There was no response. He waited a little while and pressed it a second time. After a moment, he heard a distorted voice on the intercom, slightly sleepy and metallic.

"Yes ..." she said unenthusiastically.

"Good day. Are you Isabel González?"

"Yes. And I don't want to buy anything or hear any sales pitch."

"That's not why I'm here," explained Zarco, who understood the aversion to all kinds of propaganda. These days, no one escapes ongoing harassment from the various phone or insurance companies. "I want to talk about your husband's death ..."

"Who are you?"

"My name is Álex Zarco. I'm a private detective and I'm investigating a case that may be related to Santiago Cañas' death." He did not receive an answer, and added, "May I come up and ask you a few questions?"

In response, he heard the sound of the buzzer automatically opening the entrance door.

Zarco stepped off the elevator and found Isabel González waiting for him in the open doorway of her home. He greeted her by repeating his name and extending his hand. The hand she extended was flaccid. She was a slender woman with light eyes. She might be attractive when she dressed up; however, it was clear that on that particular morning she had made no effort at grooming. Her hair was messy, and the bags under her eyes suggested some self-neglect, which was confirmed by the alcohol on her breath as she approached him. She invited him inside and led him to a large living room while signaling for him to occupy either of the two sofas. She offered Zarco a drink, which he refused. She then served herself a glass of red wine and put a cigarette to her lips. The detective observed an ashtray overflowing with butts, but realized this was not the time for anti-smoking comments.

"You were saying?" stated Isabel, sitting on the sofa directly across from Zarco.

"Right, I wanted to ask a few questions about your husband's death."

"You mean about his murder," his wife pointed out.

"Yes, about his murder. I don't know if you were aware that the nurse who was in charge of his care was murdered on the same day your husband died. Her family has hired me to investigate her death, and I suspect her death may be related to what happened to your husband."

"Yes, I read about the nurse in the newspapers and thought the island of Ibiza must be losing the peace and tranquility that those of us who live here have enjoyed. And yet, according to you, these deaths are related? What's your theory? That the criminal who killed the nurse also killed my husband?"

"It's a bit more complicated than that. Our investigations are leading us to believe that the man who was convicted of killing the nurse may be innocent, at least of the homicide. Are you aware of whether your husband knew the nurse? I'm referring to whether he knew her prior to being admitted to Can Misses Hospital."

"No. As far as I know, he never met her. My husband was anesthetized during the brief time he survived in the hospital. And so he couldn't have had any communication with that nurse."

"Did the surgeon tell you what your husband's cause of death was?" asked Zarco.

Isabel González took a drag from her cigarette and slowly exhaled the smoke before responding.

"My husband was admitted to the hospital in very serious condition, as I assume you know, with three bullets in his chest. And yet it appeared the operation was successful. When it was done, the surgeon expressed optimism. He even said that the worst was over. And you know doctors are not prone to giving false hopes to family members. Yet the next morning Santiago was dead. The autopsy did not indicate a specific reason. The coroner said he died of respiratory depression, which may have been caused by the anesthesia, or that his heart did not endure the post-operative phase."

"I also read in the statement that your husband had withdrawn 50,000 euros from the bank that morning," said Zarco. "Do you know why he made that withdrawal?"

"I was just as surprised as anyone when I saw the bank withdrawal!" She extended the hand holding the cigarette between her thumb and index finger and poked around through the mountain of butts in the ashtray to put hers out at the bottom. "Of course, I didn't know he was taking that money out. He didn't tell me anything. And normally, he would have let me know because sooner or later I would have found out. The account at La Caixa Bank was in both our names and any day now I would have noticed a withdrawal of 50,000 euros."

"Did the police find any trace of the money?"

"They found nothing and didn't say anything about it. I

suggested that my husband could have been the victim of extortion. It seemed very suspicious that he withdrew that amount of money on the same day he was shot three times, but I think the officers preferred to go with the hypothesis that Santi was mixed up in drugs or gambling and suspected he needed the money to buy drugs or play in the casino." Zarco looked at her and said nothing. He had also backed the Civil Guard's hypothesis. If Santiago Cañas was being blackmailed, as his widow believed, killing him would have been senseless: the blackmailer would have lost his source of income. Isabel González grimaced with disappointment when she remembered the behavior of the officers, and she went on: "What's curious is that the officer in charge of the investigation was genuinely nice during my first meeting with him. Santi was still alive, and the officer seemed more interested in his recovery than anything else."

"I imagine you're referring to Sergeant Ferrando."

"Yes, I think that was his name, but I can't be sure."

"What kind of work did your husband do?" asked Zarco, although he already knew that he was a bigwig at a hotel chain. He was hopeful that Cañas' wife would provide details about her late husband's work.

"He was an executive for the Ibinat Hotel chain. He traveled to the Peninsula quite a bit for work to attend tourism trade shows or to meet with entrepreneurs or politicians. Ironically, he was terrified of flying. He always traveled to Denia or Barcelona by ferry, and then by car to his final destination: Seville, Madrid, or another city."

"I understand perfectly," responded Zarco, who was not at all comfortable with flying. "Fear of flying is not strange, what's strange is that those 500-ton flying behemoths full of people can stay in the air at all! Did your husband take his own car onto the ferry?"

"At first he would take his car, but for about a year now he preferred to rent one."

"Did you notice anything odd about your husband recently, before his death?"

"No. He had his ups and downs, like everyone, but nothing that would be considered out of the ordinary."

"Did he take any drugs—even sporadically?"

"No. I already told the police he didn't. He drank on weekends and on rare occasions he'd snort a line of coke at a party, but those instances were few and far between ... maybe on New Year's Eve or a special birthday, an event like that. And it was always someone else's, neither one of us ever bought coke."

Isabel González poured herself another glass of red wine and lit another cigarette.

"Since Santi died I don't take much care of myself," she said as she lifted both hands: the left holding the wine and the right holding the cigarette. "I drink and smoke a lot. In the end, we all pay for our sins and past mistakes, but frankly Santi never hurt anyone. Even after his death he was helping people."

"What do you mean?"

"What I just said. Even after his death he was helpful to someone. Santi was an organ donor. The shots did not injure his vital organs, so I suppose someone else is alive today thanks to his heart and lungs, or perhaps his eyes helped someone recover their sight. You see? I'm not like him. I'm not brave enough to donate my organs. I guess I'm superstitious or maybe just insensitive to others' misfortunes."

Zarco refrained from comment. He didn't need to know psychology to understand that this woman was in a deep depression which she was trying to suppress by self-medicating with alcohol. There was nothing he could say or do to help her. He got up, shook her hand, and left. As he walked to his car, he remembered her last sentence. She had said something like, we all pay for our sins and her deceased husband had no accounts to settle. At first, Zarco thought it was just a saying like any other or perhaps it was the result of her depressive state. But she may have been alluding to something real, to a specific occurrence, or to a sin which she had to pay for. The sentence crept into his brain and it hovered there for the rest of the day like a vulture on the prowl that can't decide whether to descend on its prey.

21

It was almost evening. The clock on the wall in Raúl Ballesteros' office indicated it was 6:40 p.m. when his cell phone rang. Raquel's name appeared on the iPhone screen. He wasn't expecting her to call; he'd imagined there would be a longer wait until their first date. Her call might be motivated by a detail related to the case they were investigating. Still, he was eager to hear her voice. He tapped the icon to answer the call and adjusted his voice to sound calm.

"Hello?"

"Hi, it's Raquel. Can you talk or are you busy?"

"I was preparing a defense brief for a trial I have in a couple of days," responded the attorney. He wanted to seem busy which, while true, gave a better impression than being idle, "but I have time to talk."

"Do you have any plans for this evening?"

"No, none," he said, thinking that even if he'd had a plan, he would have canceled it.

"Would you like to meet?"

"Yes, that would be fine. If you like, we could meet for dinner." Ballesteros mentally reviewed restaurants that might be open on a January weeknight in Ibiza. He considered Ama Lur, but reminded himself it was a rather fancy restaurant for a first date. Ideally, he was hoping for a simple locale with a good atmosphere and delectable food. He thought about the San Juan Bar, where they served homestyle food at ridiculously low prices, but remembered that the restaurant had shared tables. He did not want strangers to overhear them, especially on their first date where there would likely be awkward pauses, questions asked while getting acquainted, and the occasional boasting about one's own virtues. He realized he knew nothing about her culinary tastes.

"What type of food do you like?"

"Mostly everything, actually."

"Well, we could meet at Ses Canyes for a drink, and then go have dinner at the Indian restaurant on Avenida España."

"Perfect."

"Shall we meet at 9:00 p.m. at Ses Canyes, or is that too early for you?" asked Ballesteros.

She thought 9:00 p.m. would be fine. January days were short and the winter was cold, and early nightfall did not inspire her to go out much later than that. Nine o'clock seemed like the right time. Raquel hung up and wondered if she hadn't been too hasty in calling Ballesteros. Like any man, he could jump to the wrong conclusions. On the other hand, he was no longer a testosterone driven teenager who thought about sex every six seconds. And it was apparent that the investigation into her sister's death had created a bond between them that would justify any meeting. No, she wouldn't worry in advance. Better to wait and see how the evening played out.

Raquel had not gone on a date with a man since her last ill-fated relationship with Rafa, a good-looking narcissist (and a sexist) who she'd fallen in love with. She sometimes asked herself if what she'd felt for him could even be called love. She had read too much about love and the art of loving. In her mind, true love was selfless. It was about wanting good things for the other person, not possessing them. Raquel tried to remember the qualities that had attracted her to Rafa, but she couldn't. She suddenly pictured her most recent recollection of him: his arrogant demeanor, his know-it-all attitude (though he was actually quite ignorant), his desire to control her, their arguments, the harassment he had subjected her to after their breakup. He'd unleashed his hatred on her and had made sure she'd felt it. She remembered the messages he'd left on her cell phone, full of rancor and insults. Fortunately, all of that was over. The initial hatred he had seeded in her heart after their breakup had waned until it had become cold indifference. Since then, Raquel had dabbled in a few casual sexual encounters, always with women, and always superficial and short-term. She didn't want to get emotionally involved. She preferred fleeting relationships with women because she felt women had more pride than men. Perhaps their own female insecurities prevented them from diving in and declaring their love as some males did, who had to hear the word 'no' a hundred times before it seeped into their gray matter. In any case, she was drawn to feminine subtlety, whether born of insecurity or not, instead of the relentless masculine pestering that resulted from that gender's pigheadedness. Which dumbass had patented the idea that when women say 'no' they actually meant 'maybe'? When she said 'no', she simply meant 'no'. The jealousy she'd felt for Rafa in the beginning of their relationship now felt ridiculous to her, as did the emotional dependence she'd felt during his absence, or when he didn't answer her calls, or the antipathy she felt after their breakup every time she looked at her cell phone screen and saw a message from that pompous jerk who couldn't take no for an answer. She had gone from love to hate, and from hate to indifference in less than six months.

While Raquel had fought against prevalent educational models since her adolescence, some of them had permeated deeply. In western cultures, there was an established lifestyle pattern in which one of the necessary ingredients for achieving total happiness was to be part of a couple. And unconsciously following this model, she had always fantasized about finding her ideal partner. After her breakup with Rafa, she had discovered that being single provided her with freedom, tranquility, and a pleasant enjoyment which she was not inclined to relinquish, and which was exceedingly difficult to reconcile with life as a couple.

She had been attracted to Ballesteros' poise in the courtroom, as well as the combination of consideration and aplomb he had shown toward other participants of the judicial assemblage. He appeared an intelligent man; however, her experience cautioned her that the juxtaposition of the adjective *intelligent* with the noun *man* seemed a confounding conundrum.

She would wear something informal: jeans and a wool sweater.

22

Ballesteros arrived at Ses Canyes bar on time. The locale had a modern design, the walls were lined with cement and metal plates. He looked around and noticed that all the tables were occupied, and sat on a stool close to the bar. He ordered a bottle of beer and took a few short sips straight from the bottle. Five minutes later, Raquel walked through the door. They greeted each other with a customary light peck on each cheek. Ballesteros offered her his stool and grabbed another for himself. When Raquel took off her leather jacket, Ballesteros could not resist a fleeting glance at her prominent breasts outlined by her wool sweater. A moment later, he made eye contact with Raquel, who did not appear to have noticed the attorney's indiscretion. Up close, her eyes appeared more pale. Her look was soft and calm. Ballesteros noticed she was not wearing makeup or lipstick, or at least didn't seem to be. She ordered a small glass of beer and raised it as a toast before taking a sip.

"Have you discovered anything new?" asked Raquel.

"Well, all I know is what Zarco told me: that the last person to see your sister was a nurse friend of hers, and that it appears as if Ana was with a doctor at that time."

"Yes, I was with him when Teresa told us that."

"The truth is, I've changed my mind about Zarco," offered Ballesteros. "He is a bit extravagant, but perhaps I misjudged him."

"That tends to happen with Álex. When we were at university, he was the weird guy in the class. He always has been. The same when we were kids. His mother would dress him in polyester pants instead of jeans or corduroys, which is what most of us were wearing, and the other kids would snub him. I talked to him sometimes because I felt sorry for him, but soon I discovered he was very smart. I think sometimes we allow ourselves to judge people on first impressions, and first impressions can be misleading."

Ballesteros realized he knew nothing about Raquel's life, not her marital status or her profession, but it seemed absurdly rude to ask her bluntly if she was married or what her occupation was.

"If you didn't already know, what would you say I do for a living?" asked Ballesteros.

"Attorney."

"Well, that was easy! Is it written on my face? Alright, what if you had to guess something else?"

She put her hand on her chin and adopted a thinking expression.

"Hmmm ... well, I'd say you were a banker or a policeman."

"Shit! The crème de la crème, eh? Couldn't you have guessed airline pilot, professor, musician, scientist, or something like that? Do I really look like such an asshole?"

"Well, it's not that you look like an asshole. Quite the contrary: I think you look like a nice person, although somewhat serious. I guess it's because you're well-dressed and maybe a bit on the classic side. I certainly wouldn't say you're a drummer in a rock band."

"Alright then. I don't know if you managed to save that or completely ruin it," smiled the attorney as he gestured to the waiter to bring him another beer. He noticed Raquel's glass remained untouched and didn't order another for her. "I would guess you're a psychologist."

"I think I already told you I studied psychology, but I don't practice psychology. You're never going to guess."

"You're not also an attorney?"

"No, but you're not too far off: I'm a tax inspector. And yes, I majored in both law and psychology at the same time, so you can see that calling me an attorney wasn't an insult."

"Shit!"

"You use that word a lot."

"Well, only when I'm surprised. But in the past five minutes you've surprised me quite a few times. And what do you think of attorneys?"

"As a tax inspector or as a woman?" Without waiting for his reply, she continued: "As a tax inspector, I'll tell you that attorneys are more likely to commit fraud. Previously it was the hospitality industry, but since our modular tax system was developed, they don't need to cheat. And as a woman, except for my time as a student, I haven't met enough of you to form an opinion. Have you reserved a table?"

"Yes, at 9:30. In fifteen minutes."

Ballesteros hesitated for a moment. While Raquel had aroused his curiosity, he didn't want to jump into personal questions. These would come up in conversations on their own, he didn't need to force it. In his youth, Ballesteros had been shy around women. Paradoxically, in order to overcome his shyness, he would act boldly and foolishly when he was with a girl he liked in an attempt to disguise his withdrawn personality. As he got older, he learned that some women appreciated his shyness more than his bravado, and he was able to wait for the right moment before taking the first step.

"We've made some progress in the investigation," said Ballesteros, changing the subject. "Now we know who one of the last people to see your sister was."

"The truth is the Civil Guard officers investigated absolutely nothing," said Raquel irritably. "They didn't even speak to my sister's ex or make inquiries about her social life. I don't understand how the police work and I don't know if they adhere to any protocols in their investigations, but I certainly don't believe they were very diligent. They didn't move a finger to solve the case."

"They had already arrested the presumed perpetrator. Everything stopped there."

"I'm sure if the investigation had been about the sister of one of the officers, they would have worked harder," she replied.

"It's probably best if we forget the past. This case is now considered solved and closed to both the police and the judge. If we want them to reopen it, we have to obtain new evidence."

The walls in the Indian restaurant were covered with large colorful fabrics that were decorated with traditional images of elephants and Indian temples. A glimmering light illuminated the venue. Ballesteros hung his coat on a hook at the entrance and offered to hang Raquel's jacket alongside his. There were some tables at floor level with cushions around them to sit on. Both of them thought these would be exotically uncomfortable for dining and chose a table with the customary four-legged chairs. They reviewed the menu and ordered Indian cheese bread, Tandoori chicken, and basmati rice with vegetables, all to share. Ballesteros chose a bottle of Reserva red wine. The waiter poured a little of the wine into Ballesteros' glass. He looked at it against the light without overdoing the gesture, as if he made a habit of wine tasting. He took a light sip of the red liquid, savored it, and nodded his head in approval.

"Don't pour me too much," Raquel said to the waiter who had started filling her glass.

"Raquel, I believe wine is an essential part of relishing spicy Indian food," Ballesteros smiled.

"Yeah, but I don't like to drink a lot. I'd rather keep a clear head. I know in our country and many others, except Arab countries, alcohol is an integral part of social life, but I have personal reasons for not drinking."

"Personal reasons?"

She remained silent for a few seconds, wondering if she should respond honestly to his question.

"The truth is my ex drank in excess," she said. "At first, I also drank occasionally. Those were the days of wine and roses, like the movie. But then I started to realize that he couldn't stop and, moreover, he didn't want to stop. It was always the right time to have wine or a drink: as a cocktail, with lunch, before dinner, during dinner, after dinner. Until one morning I found him mixing himself a rum and Coke. That was when I decided to end the relationship. Don't think I'm a prude. I've had my share of merrymaking, but to me drinking is self-delusion and avoidance. People can't find reasons to be happy in their lives, so they throw back a couple of rum and cokes and they feel happy, even euphoric. I think it's an easy escape."

"If you look at it that way, I suppose you're right," agreed Ballesteros while putting his glass to his lips and deciding to use the occasion to inquire into Raquel's life. "Did you break up with your boyfriend a long time ago?"

"It's been a few months, but it's water under the bridge now. And honestly, I don't think talking about him is worthwhile. Tell me about you: are you working on any interesting cases? Respecting professional privacy, of course."

"Well, in fact, I have an alleged domestic violence case which I think is only *alleged* but given our new laws, all husbands and boyfriends that have allegations against them are guilty until they can prove the contrary."

Ballesteros perceived a change in Raquel's demeanor, as if she was now on guard against a threat.

"So you don't believe that women should be protected?" she asked ironically.

"Of course, women and all people who are victims of crimes should be protected, but I don't think the way to achieve that should be based on making all men suspects," responded Ballesteros vehemently. "Our current laws are supposed to apply to abusers, but in practice they are applied to any person whose partner files a complaint against them, and I think it's gotten out of hand."

"I think if that's how to save a life, it's well worth it."

"Right. And if we prohibited the use of cars then there wouldn't be traffic accidents," responded Ballesteros, slightly irritated and aware that the conversation was going down the wrong path while at the same time knowing that this topic exasperated him. On more than one occasion, he had become involved in these types of discussions in which he felt like a defender of reason who was up against an enormous media campaign. Although the outcome of the law was praiseworthy, the legal remedies were disproportionate and useless. And he was not going to bite his tongue. "The curious thing is the majority of fatality victims never filed a complaint. The inevitable profile of a battered woman is one who suffers abuse and is too afraid or doesn't know how to escape those circumstances. In other words, the women that really need protection don't file the complaint, and yet those that occasionally get pissed off at their partner file a complaint and have him arrested."

"We can't suddenly change society. It's a slow process, but

I believe we've made a first step. Besides, women have been discriminated against for centuries, so I don't think it's so terrible if men are on the receiving end of ten or twenty years of their own discrimination," said Raquel.

"I don't think that's the solution. It would be the same as saying that since black people in the United States have been discriminated against for centuries, it would now be fair to make laws discriminating against white people."

Raquel sighed. "I don't think you and I are going to agree on any subject."

"It surely seems that way," said Ballesteros, sensing and regretting that the evening was not going to end the way he had hoped. The conversation regarding his case, stemming from generalizations about domestic violence and flaws he perceived in laws regulating these types of crimes, had opened an insurmountable abyss between them. Raquel reminded him of Yolanda, his ex, who displayed her latent feminism and emotional armor against chauvinist aggressors she imagined all around her. He also recognized his own considerable defect of obsessively trying to win every argument by presenting his evidence with a fervor that bordered on intimidation. Why didn't he just limit himself to listening to others in general, and to Raquel that evening? To listen to what others thought and said without trying to impose his own opinions and judgments on them. He told himself that, precisely regarding the subject of domestic abuse and legal statutes, he—as well as a large majority of professionals that litigated every day in the reality of the courtroom —had an opinion which was substantiated on the pillars of an established institution. But the primary source of information for most other people were biased and alarming stories from news outlets and an incessant media barrage that, drip by drip, like drops of water slowly drilling through stone, shaped general opinion. According to media outlets in Spain, there were four problems that roused the country in the second decade of the 21st century: political corruption; the unemployment numbers; abuse; and of course, the line-up for Sunday's upcoming soccer match. Weren't AIDS, pollution, and climate change still problems? He was reminded of the Arabic proverb that roughly said:

don't say everything you know ... because he who says everything he knows ... often says what is not convenient. He would have preferred it if his dinner with Raquel had followed a more harmonious path; however, he had stuck his foot in it all the way and now there was no turning back. Raquel had definitely reminded him of Yolanda and, to be fair, he'd had pleasant, fun, and even magical moments with his ex. At least at first. "What do you think of the Indian bread?"

"It's delicious," answered Raquel, pulling off a piece with her hand and putting it in her mouth.

When they finished their dinner, Ballesteros insisted on walking her home. She refused the offer, telling him that he didn't have to worry about her because she was used to walking alone. But the attorney insisted, and she gave in. Deep down, Raquel appreciated these antiquated gallantries. They walked through the sparsely traveled streets. As they crossed Avenida Bartolomé Rosselló, an Arab man approached them with a bundle of newspapers under his arm and offered them one. Ballesteros automatically refused, scarcely giving the man a look.

"What was he thinking selling newspapers outside at midnight in the middle of winter?!" a perplexed Raquel asked.

"He must be desperate."

Ballesteros remained pensive as they approached her doorway. He held out his hand to say goodbye with a hint of a forced smile. She ignored the gesture and gave him a kiss on the cheek, catching the attorney off guard. Raquel smiled slightly when she saw the surprised expression on his face. He had, after all, been good company. Up to a point.

Ballesteros started to walk back home. That man selling newspapers along the empty streets at midnight had provoked a feeling of distress in him. That man may have come to Spain looking for a better future or, in other words, a poorly paying job that he may not even be able to find. That man might be facing dire economic straits while having to negotiate a western country's economic and cultural barriers. That man was trying to salvage his dignity by selling newspapers instead of just begging. Perhaps he had a wife and children. And yet Ballesteros had ignored him as one would sidestep a small and annoying obstacle. He had barely looked at the man's face. He quickened his step and turned onto another street looking for the Arab's location. He didn't see him on Avenida Bartolomé Rosselló and he continued scouring the streets at an accelerated pace. At last, he spotted a short, heavyset man at a distance walking in a slightly hunched over position. "Hey, hey!" he yelled, as he walked toward the man, who just stared at him expressionless. "Give me a couple of newspapers," Ballesteros asked as he opened out his wallet and took out a fifty-euro bill. A surprised look emerged on the Arab's face, and he apologized explaining that he didn't have any change. "It's for you," insisted Ballesteros. The man took the bill in disbelief and put it in his pant pocket while, in broken Spanish, he expressed his gratitude for the gesture and for the money with all his heart. He kissed the attorney's hand, saying: "May God grant you and your family the very best, all the best in the world."

23

On Thursday morning, the 17th of January, Álex Zarco received a visit from Xicu, the computer expert he had entrusted with examining Ana López' computer. Xicu was a hacker, a computer pirate, who frequently collaborated with the detective. Public institutions and private companies were reluctant to provide users' information to third parties, but Xicu knew how to evade their filters and cyber security measures, and he could sneak into local government files as well as business and private computers. The easiest method for gaining access to someone's computer was to send them a phishing email and, the moment they clicked on it, Xicu could get into their monitor, view all their information, and control their computer. Or he could also get in by sending a Facebook friend invitation and, when the recipient refuses the request, he could gain access to their computer. Getting into someone else's computer was child's play (and also a crime), and only slightly more difficult than accessing information from public files that didn't have complicated security measures.

Although this activity was openly illegal, Xicu had assisted Zarco on countless occasions. Both of them justified this flagrant infraction of the law by telling themselves they never used the information for purposes other than the interests of their clients, generally an unfaithful wife or husband.

Due to occupational hazards, in addition to a general mistrust in the confidentiality of communications, Xicu rarely used a cell phone or computer to contact Zarco, except in cases of extreme urgency. He simply showed up at the detective's apartment with no prior notice.

"Xicu, don't you sleep? It's 8:30 in the morning!" said Zarco.

"I figured you'd be awake. And you said you needed the

information right away." Xicu handed him the laptop that had belonged to Ana López Demichellis. "You can access the dead woman's computer and her email now. Here are the passwords for both," said Xicu, sounding pleased with himself as he handed over a piece of paper.

"I don't know how you do it ... figuring out computer passwords."

"The computer, like all things human, has its weak spots. That said, you do understand that I must safeguard my secrets."

"Yes, of course I understand," Zarco paused. "Listen, if I were to provide you with someone's first and last name, could you get me everything there is to know about that person online?"

"You'll have to give me a bit more information than that so I can narrow it down and find the person. A first and last name can bring up hundreds of people."

"His name is Roberto Gomis. He is a plastic surgeon at the Can Misses Hospital, and he lives on the island of Ibiza. That's all I know."

"That's enough. I'll get his ID info and then I'll be able to obtain a lot of information. What are you interested in? Properties? Bank accounts?"

"Anything you can find. Of course, it would be great to know his assets, account or credit card transactions, and vehicles. But I'm also interested in personal information. All I know is that he's married and has two daughters. I'd like to know about his family situation and his friends. And even his political leanings, if he has any. Basically: everything you can find."

"This is going to cost you more than hacking into the dead woman's computer. You know if I get caught one day they'll lock me up. And the truth is I can't think of any other way to make a living."

"You could open up your own shop and fix computers, that sort of thing."

"That would be like asking Picasso to paint your walls."

"You're right. And I would lose my best collaborator," fawned Zarco. "Don't worry about the money," he added, thinking he would be passing the bill on to Raquel and Ballesteros. "If

I can solve this case, there will be a before and an after for the Zarco and Cía Detective Agency. And you know you won't get caught."

"You can never be too sure, Álex. If I haven't been caught yet, it's because I always proceed with caution. Every day, there are more and more hackers who sell out, who cross over to the other side and become turncoats against us pirates."

"You mean the white hat hackers."

"Yes. They also call themselves samurais. They are jerks who sold their soul to the politically and economically corrupt system that manipulates us and, to add insult to injury, they think they're the heroes."

"Not everyone can be anti-establishment like you."

"Don't laugh, Álex. I'm pissed off as hell with these jerks and all this politicking. We're getting screwed on all sides: pension cuts, healthcare cuts, and cuts in the courts and in education. What does this mean for politicians? Simply put: savings. But for the people, it means a worse health care system, less services for the most disadvantaged, and an education system that's more inadequate than the one we already have. They've been talking for years about eliminating political appointees and elected councilmen, and yet they never do it. Apparently, politicians provide better benefits to society than doctors and teachers ..."

"I know, you're right, Xicu ..."

"And to make matters worse, the media makes those of us that are against the system appear ruthless." Xicu continued speaking with a passionate rhetoric that the detective was all too familiar with. "We want a real democracy. A democracy in which issues that are important to citizens are put to a referendum and politicians are required to implement their platforms and fulfill their campaign promises. They say if you don't vote you can't complain. But what's the point in voting for a politician who wins the election and then does whatever he wants? They talk out of both sides of their mouths. Well, I don't want to vote for the PP or the PSOE or any of our political parties that play by the ground rules they themselves set. I want to change those ground rules."

"Right. And that's why you dedicate yourself to hacking," said Zarco, in an attempt to change the conversation or at least hoping that his friend would end his anti-establishment rant. It was true that, without Xicu, a large part of his investigations would be doomed to fail, and giving him some attention every now and then was a small price to pay for his services.

"Yes, because of that, and because I like what I do. One day I'll hack into the computer of some world leader and shine some daylight on all the ins and outs of how the Americans, Germans, and multi-nationals are manipulating us. If a government spies on millions of its citizens, they justify it by alleging national security reasons or some such crap. But if I hack into someone else's computer, I could spend a few years in the pen. So you see, that's just the way things are."

Zarco was relieved when Xicu left his apartment. On the one hand, the anti-establishment blather that he'd already heard on other occasions was exhausting; and on the other, he was curious to examine whatever information might be found on Ana López' computer. He plugged the device in and turned it on. He saw a blank box with a small, blinking vertical line. When he entered the password that Xicu had provided, a series of icons were displayed. The detective scrutinized them closely, he wasn't sure what he was looking for. He wanted to gather as much information as he could about the victim, her friends and her contacts. He opened a file that contained images and looked through a series of Ana López' photos. Some appeared to have been taken abroad, during a trip. Others pictured her with friends. Some of them were of Ana with Fran, her last known boyfriend. Zarco did not find Dr. Gomis in any of them. Had they avoided all photos because they'd be evidence of adultery, or had they been subsequently erased? For now, this was an unanswered question like so many others.

He made his way into Ana's email using the other password provided by Xicu, but also found no relevant information. She didn't have hundreds of messages saved; it appeared she liked to erase emails that she'd already read. One of them was undoubtedly from Dr. Roberto Gomis, dated January 14, 2012, a few months before her death. Zarco opened it and read an extensive missive in which Gomis discussed his feelings for Ana in a romantic tone, without resorting to sentimental drivel. Zarco had to admit that he liked the letter and that Gomis knew how to charm a woman. He read a couple other emails, especially those that had been sent by men, searching for a resentful lover that hadn't tolerated the breakup. If these men existed, they hadn't sent any emails or Ana had erased them. Xicu could recover deleted emails, but Zarco weighed the possibility that perhaps they wouldn't provide any valuable information. After two and a half hours in front of the computer, he gave up. If anyone had motive to kill the girl, it had not been disclosed in her computer network.

Zarco went outside and got into his old car, a Volkswagen Polo, which he'd inherited from his father. The car would soon be 20 years old. He got onto the highway and headed toward the road to Santa Eulalia. Although the gear shift and steering wheel had the stiffness of an old car and the windows went up and down with the crank of a handle, the motor still worked with the precision of a Swiss watch: it started up the first time, used little gas, and easily passed the vehicle inspection test. On two separate occasions, he'd left the headlights on which had drained the battery. The problem had been solved by calling his insurances' road assistance; they'd sent a tow truck to recharge the battery. Since then, every time he parked the Volkswagen, he would return to it a few minutes later to toggle the light lever and ensure he had not left the lights on. Some nights, when he was just about to fall asleep, he was seized by doubt. He would get out of bed and go out to the street, covering his pajamas with his trench coat, to verify that the vehicle lights were off. At least, Zarco thought in those moments of optimism, he hadn't drained the battery a third time.

As he drove, he paid attention to the license plates of cars that passed him on the road. He had a superstitious belief that if he saw a license plate with more than one number 4, he would be lucky for the rest of the day. He didn't remember why he'd started believing that he would be afforded luck if he came across the number 4, or why he had chosen that number. His lucky number was simply 4. He passed a small van whose license number included 1444—he didn't notice the letters— and his mood improved. Today might be a wonderful day!

Twenty minutes later, he arrived at the entrance of the Civil Guard police station in Santa Eulalia. He got out of his car, smoothed out the lapels on his trench coat, and walked up the four steps that led him to a small office. He opened the door and found a distracted young man dressed in the traditional green Civil Guard uniform. He appeared surprised to see Zarco. After a few questions regarding the reason for the private detective's visit, the officer agreed to inform Sergeant Ferrando of Zarco's arrival. He left his cubicle and returned after just a few minutes to apprise Zarco that the sergeant would see him. He motioned with his hand for Zarco to follow and led him to a small and unorganized office belonging to the sergeant. Ferrando was on his feet. He greeted Zarco with *Good day*, and, with polite formality, invited him to take a seat in front of him, on the other side of the small desk. Zarco recognized the photo of the sergeant which had been published the day before in the Ibizan newspaper, *Diario*. Ferrando had been decorated for rescuing a civilian. A young man had broken his leg while climbing near the Atlantis cove. The rescue helicopter had only been able to get close enough to throw him a rope and a harness, but the young man was paralyzed with fear. According to the newspaper article, the sergeant had scaled down a vertical wall to reach the injured man and fitted him with the harness. It had been a heroic performance.

"I'm Sergeant Ferrando." He introduced himself bluntly and, modulating his voice to sound friendly, he asked, "Are you a private detective?"

"In fact, I am. My name is Álex Zarco."

"I generally don't meet with private detectives, but the officer told me you had a lead about the murder at the industrial park, and it wouldn't hurt to hear ideas from someone outside the corps. Are you Ibizan?"

"Yes, I was born on the island, although my parents are from a town in Seville. You are not from here either," Zarco affirmed, instead of asking the question.

"No, I'm from Cullera, in the province of Valencia. I requested a transfer to Ibiza eight months ago. Life is good here. Besides, you can be in Denia in just a few hours by ferry, and you can get to Barcelona or Madrid or anywhere else on the Peninsula within an hour by plane."

"That's true. However, some people who come from the Peninsula get overwhelmed. The idea of having to take a plane or a boat to get off the island makes them feel like prisoners. So, you practically had just arrived here and began investigating the murders."

"Yes, that's right. I was stationed in Denia, but I needed a change and thought I'd come to the island. Shortly after I got here, the wave of robberies started, and then came the shooting." Sergeant Ferrando sat up slightly in his chair leaning his body into the desk. "The guard informed me that you work for that attorney, Ballesteros, and that you have information regarding the murder at the industrial park."

"Well, that's partly true. At the moment, the only lead I have is about the other murder, the one regarding the nurse."

"What the hell?! That case is closed!" said the sergeant, raising his voice. "Didn't anyone tell you that there was a trial not long ago in which a man was convicted for having perpetrated that homicide? I suppose you also know that you cannot interfere with a police investigation."

"Yes, I know. Although, the police investigation is actually closed. I just wanted to explain my theory. Does it not seem strange that there were two murders in Ibiza almost within twenty-four hours of each other? And furthermore, that the murdered nurse was in charge of providing care for the man who was shot? In other words: both people who were killed had contact, even if it was brief."

"Detective, I believe if you go down that road, this meeting will be a waste of time for both of us. I'll remind you that the perpetrator of the crime against the nurse has been convicted because he confessed, among other reasons, although he later denied it during the trial," said the sergeant, looking directly at Zarco and hardening the expression on his face. Zarco recalled that, at the trial, Eduardo Ribas had stated that he had confessed in exchange for drugs and had indicated that Ferrando had been the perpetrator of that bribe. Zarco had screwed things up: defending Eduardo Ribas' innocence had implied an indictment of the methods used by the sergeant. He'd stormed in like a bull in a china shop and didn't know how to pull it back.

"Perhaps you're right," conceded Zarco. "Can you tell me anything about the other murder, the shooting at the industrial park?"

"The truth is we didn't find much," responded the sergeant, regaining his calm. "We tried to follow the usual leads, that is, see if he had any contact with drug mafias or shady businesses, but he appeared clean. We also investigated the situation with his family and friends but discovered nothing. And that's where it stopped. We came to a dead end. Unless we get a tip or make an unexpected discovery, it will be an unsolved case. Yes, perhaps it is rare that two crimes occurred within a couple of days, but sometimes coincidences happen."

"His wife told me that the morning her husband was killed, he had withdrawn 50,000 euros from their account. Did you find out anything about the money?"

"Not a trace. We don't know if it was to purchase something or to pay off a debt or blackmail. I don't know. Like I told you the dead guy appeared clean: no drugs, gambling, or other known vices." The sergeant paused and opened his hands in a conciliatory gesture. "By the way, what's that information, the lead that you said you had regarding the nurse's murder?"

Zarco thought the question was strange. Hadn't the officer just told him, in an overbearing tone, that the case was closed? He tried to hide the surprise on his face and spoke with fake modesty: "It's not a big deal, really. I think I found the last person that spoke with Ana López, a friend of hers that was also a nurse. Apparently, the morning Ana disappeared, she saw Ana leave with a doctor she didn't recognize. After that, no one—that I know of—saw her alive again. It might have been a lead, but since the case is closed like you said, there's nothing to scratch there."

"True, Zarco. Don't waste your time. Tell the attorney that there's nothing wrong with losing a case. Not all clients are going to be innocent or be acquitted. And leave the murderers to the professionals," he said with an arrogant tone that bothered Zarco.

24

The detective unenthusiastically walked down the steps leading to the vacant lot that had been allocated as a parking area. The conversation with the Civil Guard sergeant had bothered him. Zarco tried to mentally prepare himself on a daily basis to avoid becoming affected by the negative attitudes of other people. He could not allow his mood to be undermined by the arrogant behavior of a police officer, or any other individual that goes through life intimidating others with their insolence. Zarco tried to attain a level of Buddhist enlightenment in which the negativity of external actors could not affect him. However, although he repeated this litany to himself consistently, his blood still boiled whenever he ran into a bully. Sadly, he encountered knuckle draggers like these on a daily basis. And if he didn't meet them on the street, they showed up on his TV screen. He had a long way to go to attain sagacity and immunity.

He was opening the car door, lost in his own thoughts, when he heard a voice behind him calling out his name.

"Álex!"

He turned and saw a uniformed Civil Guard officer walking toward him. It was corporal Reira. Lucas Reira had been Zarco's neighbor for many years and, as children, they'd play together on the street. Lucas' family later moved to Sant Jordi and, although the youngsters had lost touch, the embers of their old friendship and mutual affection remained. Lucas always had a smile on his face, and friends knew him by the nickname *Riera* or *Riese*, a Spanish word for laughter. He approached Zarco and gripped his hand strongly while patting him on the shoulder.

"What are you doing here?" asked Lucas. "You didn't get a ticket or something, did you?"

"No. Nothing like that. I came to speak with the sergeant."

"And how did that go? He's not a bad guy, but he has a foul temper."

"I think he was courteous; almost friendly I would say. At least up until the end of the conversation when I noticed a tone of superiority and contempt toward other people, in this particular case, toward me."

"Well, if that's how it went, you don't know how lucky you are. I don't know if he'll stay on the island long, but the truth is he kicks our asses. He acts like we are in the army during wartime." Zarco observed that Lucas' smile had not faded, even when he was complaining. "We've tried to drop some hints that, here in Ibiza, things work differently, more relaxed. Even the Civil Guard is more relaxed here! But no: he's old school. That said, he's definitely got some balls! I don't know if you saw the article in the paper from a few days ago. The guy slid down a wall to save a tourist. If the sergeant hadn't shown up, that foreigner would have died there. And he made a judge take a breathalyzer test!" he said with admiration.

"I read about saving the kid, but breathalyzing a judge? Where did that happen? Here? In Ibiza?" asked Zarco incredulously.

"No, when he was in Denia. I heard that, to a certain extent, he had to come to Ibiza because of that incident."

"The truth is I'm surprised that an officer would make a judge blow into the bag." Zarco was starting to feel some admiration for Ferrando. It's one thing to be inflexible toward an ordinary citizen, but something totally different to have that attitude with a judge.

"Yes, that's why I said the guy's got balls. It didn't happen just because—it's actually a long story: the sergeant's girlfriend had an accident just before he came to Ibiza. She was crossing the street at a crosswalk when a car turned the corner at a fast speed and ran her over, and then he just took off. The hypothesis that went around was that the driver had been drinking and fled the scene of the accident so he wouldn't have to take a breathalyzer test. You know that if you're not driving drunk, a traffic accident or running someone down would be, at worst, reckless endangerment. It turns out Sergeant Ferrando is a judicial police officer and works on complicated investigations. But not long after his girlfriend had the accident, he started spending time with patrol cops at sobriety checkpoints. I suppose he was trying to find the guy who ran her over. His girlfriend only remembered that the car that hit her was a white ATV. Do you know what kind of car the judge drove?"

"A white ATV?"

"With deductive reasoning skills like those, you'll go far," joked Lucas. "The point is they stopped the car. The driver calmly stepped out of the car and, with a slightly annoyed voice, identified himself as a judge from one of Denia's courts. Up to that point, everything went well. Until Ferrando said, in a very formal voice: *Your Honor, this is a routine sobriety check. Would you be so kind as to blow into the breathalyzer?* And that's when everything hit the fan. The judge responded violently saying that he would not, asked him if he knew who he was talking to ... basically, things were said. The sergeant told the judge that if he refused to take the breathalyzer, he could be accused of failing to obey a lawful order from a police officer. Things went from bad to worse. The judge said he didn't have to obey a police officer and that it was in fact the other way around: the officer was there to obey him. Then the police impounded the vehicle. The judge called a taxi, and Ferrando wrote a report which included the judge's refusal to take the breathalyzer test and, in the section where they explain the driver's outward appearance, the sergeant took the judge down hard: distracted walking, slurring his words, aggressive attitude. The following morning, Ferrando was not rewarded for his actions. The commander called him in and told him he'd gotten a call from the judge complaining about the treatment he'd received. Apparently, the judge told the commander he would be filing a complaint against Ferrando accusing him of some crime or another against his reputation and abuse of authority. The fact is that, since he didn't actually take the sobriety test, it was Ferrando's word against the judge's and, well ... you know how that went."

"But there were other patrolmen present."

"Sure, but forcing them to make a statement against a judge would be putting them in a predicament. Ferrando himself had to face the consequences for something he alone had done."

"And what happened?"

135

"Well, you can imagine. The police report disappeared—or was filed away—and both the judge and the sergeant forgot the whole thing. Or they pretended to forget. Obviously, Ferrando does not get along well with the judicial branch. Have you ever seen a judge convicted of driving under the influence of alcohol? And do you think there has never been a member of the judicial branch that has driven while intoxicated? So that's where things are. Certainly, if a judge commits a serious crime, we'll go after him, of course, but for that kind of bullshit, we generally turn a blind eye."

"That goes without saying. What I don't understand is how Ferrando could lose his head like that. I mean, we're all equal under the law, and he was doing his duty, but even with very little experience you know when to look the other way."

"The thing is his girlfriend has been in a wheelchair since the accident," Lucas said, trying to explain. "And her condition appears to be irreversible."

"What a story! Did the judge have anything to do with Ferrando's girlfriend's accident? I'm asking because of the similarity of the car."

"No. It was just a coincidence. There are lots of white ATVs. Still, the sergeant investigated him. But the judge had a good alibi: he was in Madrid at a seminar on the day of the accident. And what about you? What's up with the sergeant? If I can ask ..."

"Of course, absolutely. I came to talk to him about a couple of issues I was investigating from last year. Do you know anything about the murder of that nurse or of the guy they found full of bullets at the industrial park eight months ago?"

"Well, we caught the guy who killed the nurse, and as for the other one, we weren't able to find the murderer or the motive. Personally, I think it was the wife. When someone is killed without an apparent motive, the murderer is always someone close to the victim. Statistics don't lie. For sure the wife contracted a killer to put a few shots in her husband. She inherits whatever the dead guy's got and she's free to take off with her lover."

"And the fifty grand that the dead guy withdrew from his

account that same morning? How do you explain that?"

"To pay off the killer! Some women are twisted. She knew that if she goes to the bank and takes out 50K euros on the same or next day that her husband is killed, all the suspicion falls on her, so she bamboozles her husband with some story, and he's the one who takes out the money."

"That seems a bit backward, but I suppose stranger things have happened. And, changing the subject, do you think your sergeant is capable of bribing someone to confess to a crime?"

"What do you mean?

"Is he capable of offering a junkie drugs to confess to a crime?"

"Álex, that's thin ice. Every day we have to deal with the worst of our society and, although some have their doubts, we really are the good guys. I won't deny that sometimes we pressure a suspect to spill it, but I can assure you we don't cross the line." Lucas Riera spoke in a hurried voice.

"No offense, Lucas," said Zarco, thinking that the corporal had gone off on a tangent and hadn't answered his question. But Zarco was also aware that it wasn't wise to insist.

"Álex, I'm not offended, but I've really had it with this image people have of us. What do you all think? That we have a secret torture chamber where we make people confess? What you don't know is that the sergeant, while he may seem like an asshole, is also a consummate professional. He's the best there is. When he investigated the robberies at Cap Martinet, he even inhaled the chloroform himself to determine its effects."

"Well, he could have determined that by giving chloroform to a cat or a dog. That's the scientific way to experiment."

"He wanted to confirm for himself how long it would take the victims to recover and, therefore, the time the thief would have to burglarize the house. Like I said, he's a professional. Just like José Mourhino: you can like him or not, but his professionalism can't be denied."

"Like who?"

"I'd forgotten you don't like soccer. Mourhino is Real Madrid's coach."

"Oh, right, I heard something about him. And as if I

hadn't heard about Real Madrid's team! Or Barça! Everyday they talk about them on the news for over 20 minutes. Alright thanks, Lucas, I've got to run. It was great seeing you. Give my regards to your parents."

"I will. And give my regards to your mother."

Zarco got into his car and rolled down the window. He heard Sergeant Ferrando's voice: "What were you talking about with that faggot detective?" He didn't hear Corporal Riera's response. He started up the car and left the parking area. *That's what today's heroes are like*, thought Zarco, *they save climbers, make judges take breathalyzer tests and yet, deep down, they're a bunch of homophobic douchebags.*

25

Ballesteros ate his usual breakfast of orange juice, coffee with milk, and a croissant, at a café in the neighborhood where his office was located. Afterwards, he started walking toward his law firm with an incipient headache. He'd recently experienced difficulty falling asleep. He often awoke at four or five in the morning and was unable to get back to sleep. He would toss and turn in his bed in a sort of limbo, without the necessary energy to get up but not tired enough to sleep.

The oral hearing against Derek Neumann for alleged domestic violence was scheduled for that same morning. It was a simple case that did not require much advanced preparation. If the client followed Ballesteros' instructions and stated he had not touched his wife, he would end up a free man. There wasn't any evidence, just two contradictory versions of the event. His wife's injuries did not carry enough weight and it had in no way been proven that the defendant had intentionally caused them. The prosecutor, unless he had changed his mind in the days that had elapsed, would not be presenting charges. Ballesteros and his client would only have to deal with the accusations made by the attorney the represented the plaintiff. Ballesteros went into his office, took out a box of effervescent aspirin, dissolved one in a glass of water and observed the fizzing of the carbonated bubbles in the liquid. It had been a long time since he'd contemplated moral dilemmas when instructing a client to lie in court. It was all established in the rights of the accused ("the right to not plead guilty and to not testify against oneself" as stated in the Spanish Constitution), and the job of a good attorney rested on using all the resources at his disposal to get an acquittal, or at least the most favorable sentence for the defendant.

Additionally in this particular case, an acknowledgment of the facts by Mr. Neumann would carry a guilty verdict and a disproportionate sentence. Derek Neumann was not an abuser, or at least no more than his wife. Both parties had clashed during a moment of heated anger. The difference rested in the fact that Derek would get nine months in prison, in addition to both safety and civil measures that would regulate his future relationship with his sons.

Ballesteros' secretary lightly tapped on the door with her knuckle and without waiting for a response, as was her custom, she entered his office carrying a large manilla envelope that she placed on the table.

"A woman brought it this morning."

Ballesteros looked at it with curiosity. It had no identifying letterhead or return address. The cover showed the attorney's name written in thick black marker. He opened it, tearing the flap, and recognized that it came from the private investigator he had hired at Zarco's recommendation to surveil Paco's girlfriend. The report was approximately twenty pages in length, joined with a spiral wire binding and a plastic, transparent cover. He didn't expect to find anything unusual and casually glanced over the pages until a paragraph caught his attention and he began reading the content carefully. His expression changed from initial surprise to shock, and by the time he'd finished reading the report, placing it back in the envelope, his face reflected dismay. He hadn't imagined he would find information that could be so troubling and disconcerting to his state of mind.

26

Zarco had set up an acrylic whiteboard on one of the walls in his office where he had written names, dates, and diagrams in distinct color markers. On one side, in red, he had the trajectory of events leading up to the death of Ana López Demichellis. In blue, he had outlined a summary of the death of Santiago Cañas. Both the red and blue lines converged at a single point in time and space: the morning of May 2nd, 2012, at the Can Misses Hospital in Ibiza. On that particular morning, the man that had been shot died; and Ana López, the nurse in charge of his care, had disappeared. Both incidents occurred at the same hospital and on the same date. It could not be a coincidence. He had underlined a sentence on the whiteboard next to the name of Cañas' widow: *she's hiding something.* What could she be hiding? He didn't believe the version suggested by his friend, Officer Reira, was correct: that she was the guilty party. No. It's true that within a close family circle one could find perpetrators of a multitude of homicides, but he just didn't see Cañas' widow contracting a killer to shoot her husband. He had witnessed the pain and desperation in the woman's eyes and face. She was hiding something, but it wasn't a murder. Another name showed up on the board: Dr. Roberto Gomis. Thus far, he was the only one directly connected to both the hospital and to Ana López. But nothing linked him to Santiago Cañas. Gomis hadn't performed Cañas' surgery and it didn't appear that they even knew each other. It was the broken link in the chain that could have incriminated the doctor. Zarco could find no motive that would lead Dr. Gomis to shoot Cañas. Did he discover that Cañas and Ana López were lovers and killed them in a fit of jealousy? That was pure speculation. There also wasn't the slightest evidence that the nurse had known the dying patient before he was admitted to the hospital.

The incessant ringing of the doorbell interrupted the detective's mental digressions. He made his way to the front door with growing annoyance. Whomever was pressing that bell was in a big hurry. He didn't think any salesperson would announce themselves in such an outrageously loud manner since it would be counterproductive to a receptive attitude from the inhabitants of the home. Zarco's expression softened as he opened the door and saw Raquel López standing in front of him. Without saying hello or waiting for him to say anything, she frantically rushed into the apartment.

"I can see you're in a hurry!" exclaimed Zarco. "Is something wrong?"

"Well, yes! I just received a called from Teresa, my sister's nurse friend who we were talking to the other day ..."

"Yes," interrupted Zarco, "I remember her perfectly."

"She called me on the phone about half an hour ago. She was extremely nervous. She told me she'd recognized the doctor that was accompanying my sister the day she disappeared from the hospital."

"And who was it?"

"She didn't have time to explain. We got cut off. I tried to call her back three or four times afterwards, but she didn't pick up. I thought I'd go to her house and see her, but I came to get you first. I thought you could go with me."

"I don't know if that's a satisfactory excuse for pounding my doorbell."

"I'm sorry, Álex. I was nervous. I started to imagine strange and awful things. And after my sister's death, I suppose I'm sensitive to everything that is somehow associated with her."

"Don't worry, Raquel, I was kidding. Every time my mother is late returning from shopping or from church, I think she might have had an accident. I'll put my boots on and we'll go see Teresa."

While Zarco was putting on his worn-out leather boots and tying up the laces, Raquel peaked through the door of the detective's office and stared, dumbfounded, at the back wall where she could see the whiteboard with blue and red scribbles, and names, numbers, and arrows pointing from one side to another. There were dozens of newspaper clippings around the board.

"Let's go," said Zarco, putting on his trench coat and wrapping a thick scarf around his neck.

They walked out to the street and, although the temperature was low, they decided to take the scooter. It would get them there faster. Zarco preferred the motorbike as his mode of transport around the city. Zigzagging around cars eliminated getting stuck in a traffic jam, he could usually park right in front of his destination, and it hardly used any gas. Traffic was slow throughout the city streets and Zarco weaved around vehicles, guiding the motorcycle with expertise. His clothes did not repel the frigid humidity in the air: it snuck in through the small openings of his sleeves and filtered through his wool sweater. The plastic visors on the helmets were not hermetically sealed and the cold got in through the cracks, whipping at the young duo's faces. When they got to the end of Avenida España, he stopped at a red light. They inattentively stared at a digital clock that rose up like a giant T at the upper end of the Vara del Rey walkway. It was 7:45 p.m. The light turned green at the same time that the clock switched to a temperature reading of 5 degrees centigrade. He headed for the Port, crossed the boom gate, and parked in the outskirts of the old quarter. Zarco and Raquel got off the motorbike and stashed the helmets in the under-seat storage compartment. Raquel lightly rubbed her arms and thighs to offset the cold. The pedestrian streets of the old quarter were deserted, in contrast with the usual summer hubbub when the island filled up with diverse crowds of people from various parts of the world.

Zarco enjoyed the winter calm. During the summer months, hoards of tourists laid waste to Ibiza in search of the three S's (sea, sun, and sex), to which the detective added the three D's (discos, drinks, and drugs). Obviously, the island's economy was almost exclusively based on tourism, and it had to be considered a necessary evil. But fortunately, high season was limited to the months of July and August. Although bars and stores remained open throughout September and tourists could still be seen, their numbers were beginning to decline. By October, the foreign invaders had disappeared and most establishments closed their doors. This was especially noticeable near the Port and the old quarter, where the private investigator was now walking with his friend.

From the street, they could see the light was on in Teresa's apartment. It was a small complex with two floors, and two apartments on each floor. The door to the building was open. They walked upstairs to the second floor and rang the bell. There was no answer. They heard no movement inside. After a short wait, Zarco rang the doorbell again a bit more forcefully. Raquel gestured that he shouldn't overdo it. "Maybe she's in the bathroom," she whispered. After a while, Zarco tried it again, leaving his index finger on the bell for a long while.

"It's impossible that she hasn't heard us," said Zarco. "I wonder if her boyfriend is with her and they're in the middle of it."

"Don't be silly. She called me no more than half hour ago."

"Maybe you should call her cell."

Raquel reached into her purse, took out her phone, and dialed Teresa's number. A few seconds later, they heard it ringing inside the apartment. Zarco and Raquel looked at each other.

"Her phone is ringing," she said. "What should we do?"

"She may have suddenly gone out and left her phone at home."

"Álex, I'm starting to get worried. I've been trying to reach Teresa since our call got cut off and I haven't been able to. The lights are on in the apartment and her phone is inside. I think she may have had some kind of accident; a fall or something. I don't know."

"If you want, we can go inside," offered Zarco.

"Really?"

"Unless she locked the deadbolt, it's not very hard to open a door like this one. Of course, we would be entering someone else's home without their permission, which could be considered unlawful entry."

"If you can open the door, open it! I'll take responsibility. We can explain it to Teresa and she will understand."

Zarco took a credit card out of his wallet and slipped it through the crack between the door and the frame, moving the plastic card up and down and tilting it while searching for the latch. He felt it bump against the metal piece and pushed the card in, trying to shove it in like a wedge and wiggle it, to separate the latch from the strike plate. After a few failed tries, he felt the card enter easily, pushing the spring in toward the wooden frame. The door opened. Raquel stared at him in amazement.

"I didn't realize it was so easy to open a door," she gasped. "I thought opening a door with a credit card was an urban legend. From now on, I will always lock the deadbolt when I leave my house."

"Good idea," answered Zarco as he lowered the tone of his voice and softly pushed at the door which opened noiselessly.

Zarco entered first. He walked through a small hallway where there was a coat rack on the wall with a couple coats hanging from its hooks. The living room door was open and the light was on. He took a few stealthy steps and entered the bedroom. He saw Teresa's body lying face up on the carpet with her eyes open and a large blood stain soaking through her pajama and spreading over her torso.

"Don't come in here, Raquel," he said stretching out his arm so she wouldn't walk into the room.

"What's going on?"

"She's dead! She's been stabbed repeatedly!"

"Oh my God! But I just spoke with her moments ago! Álex, call for emergency services!"

"Wait a second, Raquel: we'll call the police but first we have to figure out what we're going to say. What should we tell them? That we broke in and found her dead body? You know we private investigators are not extremely popular with the cops."

"Álex, don't complicate things. I'll take full responsibility.

And given what happened, I think we were justified in opening the door. We aren't going to make things worse by saying that the door was already opened or some such lie."

"You're right. Besides, we could obscure the facts. Call 911. The National Police will come. We'll see how this turns out."

The patrol car arrived 15 minutes later, after Zarco'd had some time to look around the room. He knew that as soon as the police arrived, there would be no more opportunity to snoop around. He had put on the same gloves he used to ride his motorbike. Although they were thick and not meant for easy handling, he would avoid leaving fingerprints at the scene of the crime. Zarco found a bloody knife next to Teresa's body which the killer had likely dropped on purpose in order to avoid staining his clothes or carrying it out to the street. Zarco assumed no fingerprints would be found on the murder weapon. Next to the knife, he saw the young woman's cell phone covered with blood splatter. The television was on, and he could see muted images on the screen. The remote was lying on a coffee table in the center of the room. A small side table with a lamp was adjacent to the corner of the sofa, which had a shelf underneath with various newspapers in an organized pile. Zarco looked through them: they were copies of the Ibizan newspaper, *Diario*, from days prior. The detective entered the kitchen and opened the cupboard under the countertop. He looked in the waste basket: leftover wrappers and vegetables, nothing out of the ordinary. With the exception of the murder weapon, the killer had not left a single trace.

When the police arrived, Zarco and Raquel were waiting discreetly in the entrance hall. The police officers, both of whom were young and tall with wide backs and short hair, took down their information and asked them matter-of-factly whether they knew the victim and how they'd found the body. Both officers' eyes briefly looked away from Raquel's face and furtively directed their gaze at other parts of her attractive anatomy. Keenly aware of the officers' glances out of the corners of their eyes, she explained what had occurred, leaving out Zarco's brief search.

An hour later, the examining judge, court secretary, and

forensic pathologist arrived. This time, it was the female judge that checked out the young officers and looked Raquel and Zarco up and down as well. The judge was an attractive woman, barely over thirty. Her gestures denoted an arrogant authority with the undisguised attitude of someone who was accustomed to being obeyed. With a tone that would not suffer a reply, she crisply told Zarco and Raquel to go home and to go to the court office the following morning to provide proper witness statements.

Raquel and Zarco left the apartment and walked toward the motorcycle. The detective asked Raquel if she was feeling alright. She responded in the affirmative and asked:

"Did you see how that judge was looking at us?"

"Yes. She looked at me as if I were a weirdo, and she looked at you as if she were gauging whether or not you were more attractive than she was which, in all respects, you are."

"She was a rather unpleasant lady."

"The coppers were also looking at you—I don't know if you noticed," Zarco added.

"Yes, but their look was more innocent, for lack of a better word. It was easy to figure out what they were thinking. However, I had no idea what was going through that woman's head."

"Mirror, mirror, on the wall, who is the fairest of them all?" joked Zarco, and with a change in tone, he added, "I'll take you home. I don't want you to leave alone after what we've just seen."

They got on the bike and started on their way. They stopped at a red light on the street near the Port. Through his rearview mirror, Zarco saw a white car stop behind them. Was he getting paranoid, or had he just seen that vehicle parked near his motorcycle at the Port? The light turned green and Zarco signaled left with his indicator. He saw the white car do the same. He decided to perform a definitive test and, driving slowly, he turned right, then right again, and then right again: a drive around the block.

"What are you doing, Álex?" yelled Raquel, lifting the visor on her helmet so he could hear her.

"Raquel, stay calm, I think we're being followed by the car behind us. I just made an absurd maneuver, going around the block, and it's still behind us. Don't look and just hold on tight."

He accelerated the bike and drove toward Avenida Bartolomé Rosselló, the busiest street at that hour, where he would be able to dodge his pursuer. When they got to the end of the side-street that opened onto the avenue, Zarco was discouraged to find very little traffic. A car driving on the avenue approached the side-street where they had stopped and cut them off, blocking their exit. Zarco decided to take a gamble and twisted the throttle on the bike. The motorcycle whipped across both lanes of the avenue. The car driving in the main lane stopped abruptly and angrily blasted his horn. With his brain swimming in adrenaline, Zarco put his arm up with an open palm in an apologetic gesture, and took a look backward. The car that was following them had stopped for another vehicle who had the right-of-way. Zarco made a few turns without thinking about where they were, and then abruptly wheeled around and parked the bike behind a large garbage container. They waited for a few seconds. The car did not appear.

"I think we lost him," said Zarco.

"Are you absolutely sure he was following us?"

"I'm positive, Raquel. I went completely around the block and the car followed us."

"Did you see the license plate?"

"No. It was impossible. I saw the car in the rearview and could see its headlights, but little else. I couldn't even see if there were one or two passengers inside the car. The only thing I know I saw was a large white car, like a minivan."

"Álex, I'm frightened," cried Raquel. "I'm afraid to get back on the bike."

"I understand. We could call a taxi."

"No, I have another idea," she said, taking out her cell phone and dialing Ballesteros.

27

Ballesteros was not having what one might call a good day. His morning had transpired according to plan, and the trial against Derek Neumann had turned out as expected. The plaintiff, his wife, had not provided any new evidence, and thus the public prosecutor had requested an acquittal for the defendant. The plaintiff's defense attorney concurred with that request; however, the plaintiff herself asked for a sentence of nine months in jail and made an additional demand for a restraining order. Ballesteros' experience told him that if the prosecutor had not requested a jail sentence, it would be hard for the judge to impose one. Everything indicated that the balance of justice would lean in favor of his client. Still, he had been unable to breathe easily since he had read the report from the detective agency hired to follow Tanya.

The trial was over by 1:30 p.m. Ballesteros went home and began preparing spaghetti with garlic and chili pepper. He put an abundant amount of water to boil in a pot, uncorked a bottle of red wine, and poured himself a generous glass. When the water reached a boiling point, he threw in a handful of salt and plunged the spaghetti into the pot. He had always enjoyed cooking and thought he had a talent for it. Memories from his student days came to mind, when he shared an apartment with Paco and Joan in Barcelona. The dish he was now preparing had been their usual fare. It was easy to make, cheap, and delicious. He peeled and chopped three garlic cloves into thin slices which he fried in a pan with chili pepper. He strained the spaghetti and poured it onto a plate, topped it with the garlic and chili pepper stir-fry and finished it off with grated parmesan cheese. It was ready. He caught a few strands of spaghetti on his fork and twirled it around before putting it in his mouth. It was truly a simple and delicious meal. Yolanda, his ex, had told him many times that he could have been successful if he'd chosen to open a restaurant.

Ballesteros had slept badly the night before and he felt tired. Breaking with his usual routine, he decided to lie down on the couch and take a nap while he listened to the news in the background. Although the wine had made him drowsy, he could not fall asleep. He felt uneasy due to the contents of the report, and because he was unsure if he'd done the right thing by hiring someone to investigate Tanya. *I did it because I didn't expect to find anything,* he justified to himself. *It's like feeling mild aches and pains and going to the doctor, thinking he will say the discomfort is innocuous and you're perfectly healthy. But the trouble is when you go to the doctor with mild aches and pains and you're diagnosed with cancer.* Wasn't his mistrust and subsequent hiring of the private detective completely justified given the content of the report? Wasn't Paco already planning to stage an absurd sham by pretending to be bankrupt?

By mid-afternoon, he took a shower to wake himself up. He got dressed, called his secretary to let her know he would not be returning to the office and headed for Paco's newly rented apartment, located in a building on Calle General Gotarredona, close to Ballesteros' house. It was a small apartment, and had a breakfast bar separating the living room from the two square meter kitchen. There was a door next to the sofa that opened into the bedroom, where there was another door to access the bathroom. The livable surface area was no larger than thirty square meters. Apart from that, the building was only about ten years old, and the apartment appeared clean and comfortable although Ballesteros supposed that being otherwise used to a luxurious country home, his friend's stay in that building would be a short one. Paco was sitting in front of a medium-sized canvas resting on an easel, located in a corner of the living room. There was an uncovered cardboard box at his feet jammed full of acrylic paint tubes and several water-filled glass containers next to it that held submerged brushes of assorted sizes, with their bristles in the water and their handles sticking out.

When he opened the door, Paco was surprised to find Ballesteros standing in the doorway, since he knew that his friend did not generally break with his strict afternoon routine of focusing exclusively on his work. Paco assumed his friend was simply curious to see the new apartment.

"Raúl! What a surprise!" he exclaimed looking pleased.

"This isn't a bad little place, except for the dimensions. You won't even last a week here."

"You may be right," admitted Paco. "Want a beer?"

"Sure. What are you paying for this place?"

"Four hundred euros, "answered Paco while he opened the refrigerator and took out two beers. He opened the bottles and offered one to his friend. "Not bad for Ibiza."

"I certainly didn't believe there was anything rentable left here for under six hundred. Not even a miniature apartment. Don't you miss your house?"

"Well, yes. Apart from the small space, there is no central heating and it's noticeable. And then there's housekeeping, which I also don't have, and I'd already forgotten what sweeping and cleaning the floor was like. I guess that's what makes the small size a plus: there's less to clean."

"And what does Tanya think?"

"The truth is she hasn't complained. I even feel like a bit of a jackass because of this farce I've created. It's not apropos for a mature man."

"Don't get your hopes up, you're not a mature man. Except for your age, of course," quipped Ballesteros.

"That's an important piece of information! Anyway, like I was saying, I'm delighted with Tanya. I told her I was penniless and that I had to let go of the country home and other creature comforts and, do you know what she said? She said not to worry about it, that we'd be okay. Basically, she didn't run away. I think she's even paying more attention to me. That's why I feel a fool, embarrassed by my own behavior."

Ballesteros looked toward the brown envelope he had laid

on a small table. There was no doubt that his friend was in love and the contents of that envelope could shatter his illusions and possibly their friendship. He asked himself what he would prefer if he were in Paco's shoes, and the resounding response was to know the truth. He spoke in a hesitant voice:

"Paco, I hired a private detective to follow Tanya and she discovered things you aren't going to like."

"A detective?" asked Paco with incredulity, while trying to assimilate the information. "You've stepped over the line, Raúl! You have sunk really low, and you've dragged me down with you. What did you discover? That she has a lover and a child she hasn't told me about?"

"Much worse. I think she's an opportunist. The day after you told her you'd had to sell your house, she went to the property registry office and confirmed it was still in your name. She knows you're not broke. And that's not all. Do you remember her trip to Madrid last weekend? Well, she met up with a guy and he wasn't her lover: he was her client. Tanya works as an escort. Apparently, the guy that hired her was significantly older. They had dinner at a prominent restaurant. When they left, he accompanied her to her hotel, and they said their goodbyes. Angela, the detective, made inquiries at the agency where Tanya works, and was informed that they also offer all types of sexual services."

"Christ, Raúl! You always think you know more than other people, and that it gives you permission to judge them. You know nothing about Tanya! She lived a miserable childhood and, since she was fifteen years old, men have been trying to take advantage of her. So, yes, it's possible she's had to work as an escort to get ahead. Yet you think you're better than her because you have a luxury office and social status, but in your own way, you prostitute yourself as well. What's worse for society: sleeping with some pathetic guy or doing everything possible to leave a criminal out on the streets?"

"Shit, Paco! It's not the same thing to draft a defense statement than it is to give someone a blowjob!" countered Ballesteros.

"You put your intelligence and hard work at the service of the worst scum in this country. You defend all sorts of criminals knowing that they're guilty lowlifes that have ruined the lives of other people."

"Look, you may be right, I don't always feel particularly proud of my work, but for fuck's sake! Tanya is a whore!"

"And you're no saint. The truth is, I don't even know what our friendship is based on, "said Paco, making an effort to remain calm. "I believe you and I have nothing in common anymore save a friendship from our youth we've been trying to hold on to. You are a close-minded man, Raúl. You aren't interested in art or anything else that isn't your work. Sometimes reading something that isn't the Penal Code can expand our minds and help us to understand others. It makes us more human."

Ballesteros thought that no matter how many literary works or novels he read, he still would not understand his friend. Their points of view differed on so many topics, but that hadn't stopped their friendship from enduring throughout the years. In politics, he sympathized with the right, while Paco leaned left. In religion, he was a faithful Catholic—though he didn't attend mass—while Paco teetered from agnosticism to atheism. He felt himself a Spaniard; Paco, a citizen of the world. He wasn't interested in art, which was his friend's passion, nor was he interested in philosophy or literature, activities he considered a waste of time. He had honestly tried to help Paco with the best of intentions, and had been motivated only by his affection for his friend and his fear that Tanya might be a con artist. And it was starting to look like she was. A mature man with money and a stunning, foreign young woman was a bad combination. Ballesteros didn't consider himself chauvinistic or xenophobic, nor did he have other types of prejudices. Things were just what they were. And to make matters worse, she was a whore. It was utterly absurd. He could try to admonish Paco, who had himself also been unsure about Tanya's love for him; otherwise, he wouldn't be feigning financial ruin. But his friend had turned a deaf ear, and dragging out the conversation was not conducive to a good outcome. Paco had gone to the doctor to confirm that he was in great health, and he didn't want to hear otherwise.

Ballesteros got up, picked up his coat, and started walking toward the door.

"Paco, I don't know what you're thinking, but I just wanted you to see things as they are. I tried to help you, but you're a grown man and you're responsible for your own decisions."

"Take this with you," said Paco, handing him the brown envelope. Ballesteros took it silently and headed out the door.

28

Paco walked into the bedroom, took a large suitcase from the upper shelf of the built-in closet, placed it on the bed and opened it. He slowly started taking his pants off the hangers and laying them at the bottom of the suitcase. He had decided to go back to his house. To his life. He felt nervous. He and Raúl had argued in the past, but none had been as violent or about such a serious subject as this. It hurt that his friend had spied on Tanya: as if he'd watched her from inside her bedroom, as if he'd defiled a sanctuary. It was true that while they had a couple of beers they'd talked about the possibility of contracting a detective agency, but a friend couldn't just decide on his own to spy on another man's girlfriend. Raúl had told him that Tanya worked for an escort agency, which possibly included sexual services. Paco felt resentful that Tanya had not been honest with him. Of course, he hadn't been completely honest with her either. Does total honesty even exist? We all hide away our secrets, fears, mistakes. Nobody bares their soul without reservation. Not even to our closest friend or our partner, or even to our confessor or psychiatrist. The only thing that mattered was that he loved Tanya and he was convinced that she felt the same about him. True, there was a 20-year age gap between them. Who knows if Tanya was looking to him to be the father figure she'd never had. He could go crazy trying to find psychological reasons for every emotion.

As he was not tied down to a fixed work schedule and had more than enough money in the bank, it would be feasible for them to pack their bags that same evening and travel to South America, or get lost in some island in the Pacific. They could settle down in any unknown location and start over. He needed to talk to her, though he didn't know what he would say. He could justify his false bankruptcy by saying it was a joke meant for his family and friends. He wouldn't tell her that Raúl had hired a private investigator to follow her. Paco suddenly realized that he was about to start this new phase of supposed maturity with new lies. We complicate our own existence, he thought. Perhaps honesty is overrated.

Admittedly, he knew very little about Tanya's past. She was born in Moscow in 1986, when Russia was still part of the Union of Soviet Socialist Republics—the USSR—before it was dissolved in the early 90s. Tanya's childhood and adolescence had occurred during an erratic decade in which Russia repudiated its socialist past and carried out the largest privatization in history. A new wealthy social class was born, while poverty was also extended to many citizens who had to do without the free services that had previously been provided by the State. The Soviet State had been a tyrannical father, treating its children with stringent discipline but still maintaining minimum conditions of work, food, healthcare, and education. When that disappeared, capitalism replaced socialism and much of the population did not know how to adapt to the new labor market conditions. The government-owned company where Tanya's parents had worked for decades was privatized, and they were let go along with another two thousand workers. They had not amassed a single ruble as their income had not allowed them to save, and they could not have imagined that the all-powerful Soviet State that took care of them and provided them with work would one day abandon them. On the other hand, inflation was out of control and prices skyrocketed from one day to the next. In the 90s, the suicide rate in Russia increased, putting it in second place worldwide behind Greenland. Tanya's family, like thousands of other Russian families, found themselves headed for poverty. Her father finally found work as an assistant garbage man, in charge of placing containers onto the truck's hook lifts and loading trash into the hopper in the back of the truck.

Tanya did not have a happy childhood. Although her parents never physically mistreated her, save the occasional slap, she seldom received affection. In the mornings, she attended secondary school and in the afternoons she helped at home with cleaning, shopping, and other tasks assigned by her mother. When Tanya turned 15 years old, she got a job at McDonald's and stopped going to school, although she continued studying Spanish through distance-learning courses. Her dream was to go to Spain: the country with a warm climate and cheerful people.

Her father died one night while stepping off the wrong side of the garbage truck. A car traveling at high speed knocked him down and killed him. Her mother was compensated, and received a pension that allowed her to live out a modest life.

This was the compendium of Tanya's childhood and family that Paco knew about. When she turned 20 years old, she was able to realize her dream of coming to Spain. She lived in Madrid, where she worked as a Russian translator for a year and a half, before settling down in Ibiza.

Paco heard the familiar sound of a key unlocking the door. Tanya appeared in the doorway with that smile that could light up any room.

"What are you doing?" she asked, pointing to the suitcase laying open on the bed. "Are you moving to another house again?"

Paco moved closer and kissed her on the lips.

"Can I ask you a question?" he said.

"Of course."

"You have to answer honestly."

"Well, that would depend on the question. But I'll try." Tanya felt slightly uneasy. Paco seemed to be talking around the question. Why didn't he get straight to the point?

"What do you think about our relationship? I mean, do you think we have a future together? You're a beautiful woman and you are almost twenty years younger than me."

For just a second Tanya felt relieved, as if a threat had been hanging over her and, suddenly, she'd awakened from sleep only to realize it had just been a nightmare. She looked directly into Paco's eyes without altering her expression to exaggerate her feelings so that he could see she was being sincere, as if sincerity could be perceived at a glance.

"Paco, your question is a little strange. I think we're good together. It's been almost a year now and, the truth is, I haven't planned out the future. Sometimes I think I'd like to get married and have a child, but I'm also fine like this. We're not in a hurry. True, there is an age difference between us, but I can't really see myself with a man under 30-with all of that boasting and blathering. Do you know what I like about you? It's that, even though it was clear that you lived well and you surely had money, which was obvious by just walking into your country house or even your loft, you never bragged about anything or talked about money. I can't stomach people who spend their day talking about how much they earn, and their business, and their investments and, to make matters worse, they think they can impress you with the number of zeros in their bank account. You don't care about any of that. You have a comfortable life. You told me you won the lottery, but you haven't been swept away by materialism. You have a simple car, and you dress unpretentiously. I think that, to a certain extent, what seduced me about you was your naturalness. You never tried to impress me. And I think that's what other people, what your friends, like about you: that you are just yourself. And don't think what I'm saying is nonsense because people usually spend a lot of time trying to make an impression. We want to be accepted by others and we often do it the wrong way."

Paco was moved by Tanya's words. He really loved her. Perhaps now it was time to bare his soul, to be himself. He hadn't told her about his fears, his insecurities, his jealousies. He had also been deceitful, by trying to appear stronger than he was.

"Would you marry me?"

Tanya hesitated for an instant, trying to guess if he was joking with her. She looked at Paco and knew he was being serious.

"You seem in a strange mood, Paco. Do you think we know each other well enough to get married?"

"I know you better than you imagine. And you are right: I am acting a bit strange. I had an argument with Raúl this afternoon."

29

Ballesteros walked across the luxurious lobby of his building decorated with white marble walls and flooring and pressed the button for the elevator. His argument with Paco had left him feeling glum. His friend was in love, and love doesn't listen to reason. Until then, Ballesteros had never contemplated the significance of the phrase: love is blind. It's blind and deaf. The ringer on his phone interrupted his thoughts. He took it out of his coat pocket and saw Raquel's name on the screen.

"Hello," he said in a neutral tone.

"Raúl, I'm with Zarco in the lobby of a building on Calle Juan de Austria. Could you come and get us?" Raquel spoke in short, abrupt sentences. "It's important. There's been a new murder. A friend of my sister's. And we think we're being followed."

"A murder? You're being followed?" asked Ballesteros, trying to digest the information. "I don't understand. Have you called the police?"

"No. What were we supposed to tell them?" cried out Raquel. "We think a white car is following us. Can you come? Please. I'm frightened."

"I'm on my way. I'll get my car and be there in five minutes. Do you know the number of the building?"

"No. We're in a lobby located halfway down the street, near some garbage containers."

"I'll be right there. When I get close to the containers, I'll give a few short honks on the horn."

Calle Juan de Austria was close to Ballesteros' home. He took the elevator down to the underground parking, got into his car and was on the specified street just a few minutes later. He was driving slowly, and saw another car fly by on a perpendicu-

lar avenue. Ballesteros could not distinguish the color of the vehicle from a distance, but he was sure it wasn't a white passenger
car. He reduced his speed to a near stop as he approached the
garbage and recycle bins. He saw a lobby across the street, but
the interior lights were off, and he couldn't see people inside. He
stopped the car and tapped the steering wheel to give two short
honks. Álex Zarco's burly figure emerged from the lobby, looked
toward both sides of the street, and gestured with his hand
toward the glass entrance door. Raquel came out and strode
quickly to the parked vehicle. She and Zarco occupied the back
seat.

"Let's go!" urged Raquel nervously.

"Stay calm," replied Ballesteros. "We're leaving now. I
didn't see any suspicious vehicle on the way. The garage in my
building is close by. If you like, we can go to my house, and you
can tell me what happened. Would that be alright?"

"Yes," replied Zarco. "We'll be safe there."

Ballesteros toasted some bread, grated some tomato into
a bowl and placed a dish on the table with thinly sliced ser-
rano ham and an assortment of cheeses. On a separate plate, he
served salmon and smoked herring.

"Would you like some red wine?" he asked. Zarco opted
for a non-alcoholic beer and Raquel chose a Diet Coke, which, to
the attorney, seemed like a gastronomic aberration. Pairing Iber-
ian ham or *Cabrales* cheese with a Coke is like drinking a glass of
milk while eating a *paella*.

Between bites, Zarco and Raquel described the events of
that disturbing and tragic evening: how Raquel had been contacted by Teresa and later could not be reached despite calling
her back insistently; how she went to get Álex and how they
entered her apartment and found her dead body; and how they
realized a car was following them when they left the apartment
where the murder had been committed.

"Are you sure you were being followed? Couldn't it have
been a mere coincidence?"

"It was not a coincidence," stated Zarco. "I purposely went completely around the block, and that car stayed right behind us. I don't know the reason or what they were looking for, but they were definitely following us."

"The logical explanation is that it had to do with Teresa's murder," opined Raquel. "They may have seen us leave the apartment and then followed to find out more about us."

"Maybe they went around the block because they were looking for parking," suggested Ballesteros without much conviction, trying to come up with an alternate explanation.

"What is clear," interjected Zarco, speaking with certitude, "is that Teresa's murder is related to your sisters' and, I believe, with Santiago Cañas' death as well. Teresa called you, "he continued, speaking directly to Raquel, "because she remembered something. As far as we know, she was the last person to see your sister alive. Perhaps she saw the man who had accompanied your sister in the hospital on the day she disappeared. But I don't understand how the killer would know that. If he considered Teresa a liability, he could have killed her long ago. It doesn't make sense to wait seven months."

"Maybe he didn't know she'd seen him with my sister, and then Teresa said or did something that made him suspicious." Raquel paused and added: "I'm frightened."

"Look, it's not everyday a person finds a corpse and is subsequently pursued through the streets of Ibiza," said Zarco, trying to downplay the situation.

"Do you want to sleep here tonight?" offered Ballesteros. "I only have two bedrooms, but the sofa is comfortable, and we can manage."

Raquel accepted the invitation. She was scared. She had been afraid many times in her life. She'd been a fearful child that had needed the hall light on until she was sixteen years old so she could sleep. Later, she'd been frightened to walk along some deserted streets late at night, and there had been several other situations as well. But those fears were the products of her imagination, or survival instincts that make us cautious. This time, there was a real killer on the loose who had murdered someone that same afternoon.

Ballesteros went into his daughter's bedroom and searched for a winter pajama to offer Raquel.

"This belongs to my daughter," he said, handing the clothing to Raquel, "She is almost your height. I think there are some new toothbrushes in the bathroom drawer. If you'd like to stay," he continued, turning to Zarco, "I can also loan you pajamas. You can sleep in my bedroom, and I'll take the couch."

"You've got everything covered, "said Raquel, accepting the pajama. She felt extremely relaxed after the cluster of emotions that had accumulated throughout the day. "The pajamas are nice and look warm."

"I won't be staying," stated the detective, "I'd rather sleep in my own bed. Thanks anyway for the offer."

Zarco called a taxi to pick him up in front of the lobby and take him home. When he got out of the cab, he looked toward both sides of the street and didn't see anyone. He didn't know to what extent his pursuer knew him and Raquel, and perhaps believed they knew more than they did, Zarco speculated, as he put his key into the locked lobby door and opened it. He entered quickly, pushed the door closed and secured the latch behind him without waiting for the auto-lock to kick in. He raced up the stairs with long strides and entered his apartment, turning the key twice to lock the front door, and then entered his bedroom. Zarco placed a chair next to his closet, climbed on it, and swept the top of the closet with his hand until it ran into a couple of cardboard boxes. He took them down and sat on the edge of the bed to open the first box, which contained an antique Glock in excellent condition. It was practically new. He removed the magazine from the stock, it could hold seventeen cartridges. He opened the other box, took out a handful of bullets, and placed them in the magazine, filling it halfway. With the weapon in hand, Zarco checked the rest of the house to assure himself that no one had entered and was laying in wait. He carefully opened the kitchen door and nudged it until it touched the wall, confirming that no one was hiding behind it, and then turned on the light. He checked his office and the bathroom. He returned to his bedroom and checked under the bed; all he found there were his old house slippers. He stored the gun in the drawer of his night-stand. Now he felt safer. If someone connected to Teresa's killing —and presumably to the murders of Ana López and Santiago Cañas as well—had followed them that night, it was because they were getting close, although Zarco had not yet found any light to show him the path forward. For the moment, he could find only one point in common among the three victims: Can Misses Hospital. The two murdered girls worked there as nurses and the man who had been shot had died in their intensive care unit.

30

It was nearly dawn when Zarco walked into the hospital lobby, which was illuminated by an intense white light emanating from fluorescent tubes. He had bags under his eyes and felt tired. And just like every time he entered a health facility, the close proximity to sickness and death put him in a bad mood. It reminded him of his own mortality and that, sooner or later, he would wind up in a bed in that institution or one just like it. He tried to shake off those thoughts as he walked toward the reception desk. None of the girls he had spoken with on his first visit were there. He couldn't remember their names but was sure he'd written them down. He took a small notebook out of the inside pocket of his trench coat and looked at his notes from a few days back. On the page corresponding to January 12th, he found the names of Lucia Torres and Rosa Guasch, Can Misses Hospital clerks. He walked to the front desk and approached an older woman.

"Do you know Rosa and Luci?" the detective asked in an attempt to demonstrate a camaraderie with the two young women, as if they were good friends.

"Yes, I know them," responded the woman. "What do you want?"

Zarco had the feeling that the woman was getting defensive, as if she suspected that he was trying to extract a favor because of his friendship with the girls. He intuited that the woman was making it clear that she wasn't buying it.

"Well, I'd like to speak with them. I'm a private detective and I'm investigating the murder of Ana López. I don't know if you remember it. And possibly Teresa Marí's as well, the one that occurred yesterday."

"Oh my God!" she exclaimed. "I read it in the newspaper!

That's all we've been talking about here. Two dead nurses! Do you think there's a nurse killer out there?"

"No, don't worry about that. I can't divulge any details, but our investigations indicate that it's not a serial killer. I very much doubt another nurse will be killed," confirmed Zarco with more conviction than he actually felt.

"Thank goodness! I mean, poor things—those two girls. But at least it's a relief that this won't happen to other young women in this hospital. Are you sure?"

"Completely. Do you know a doctor named Roberto Gomis?" inquired the detective.

"Yes, of course. He's a surgeon."

"Do you know where I can find him?"

"His office is on the second floor."

"Thanks. Can you tell me who I can obtain information from regarding Teresa Marí?"

"Well, you could ask the Administrator or the Chief of Staff, though I don't know if he can see you. His office is on the lower level, down that hall," she said, directing him toward a long hallway with countless doors on each side.

Zarco didn't get any clear leads. Both the hospital Administrator and the Chief of Staff told him they were too busy and had no relevant information. The Chief of Staff referred him to the union representative who apparently knew all the ins and outs of the hospital and would have more time to talk to him. But when Zarco walked to the union representative's office, he saw a handwritten note taped to the door: *I am out of the office for work reasons. For any questions, please call 698508525.*

Zarco went up to the second floor and, as he turned a corner, he ran into Dr. Roberto Gomis filling a plastic cup at a water dispenser. The doctor's face expressed displeasure when he looked directly at Zarco.

"What do you want?" he spit out.

"Could I speak with you for a moment? I assume you've heard that another nurse from this hospital was murdered yesterday."

"Yes. Bad news travels fast. But I don't understand why you're coming to see me. Do you think I killed her?"

"I wanted to see if you could provide me with some information."

"This is really beyond the pale! The other day, I agreed to meet with you and Ana's sister as a simple courtesy. But for you to show up here all of a sudden and ask me about a poor girl that has just been killed is absurd, not to mention harassment! You're not a police officer or anything of the kind. You can't just show up here and ask me questions. You're fleecing Ana's sister and taking advantage of the emotional state she's in while she tries to do something, even posthumously, for her deceased sister. And since there's nothing left for her to do, her mind has created the existence of an unknown murderer that must be found out."

Zarco felt awkward, aware that he could not compel the overbearing doctor to have a conversation with him. He decided to throw down the gauntlet. It seemed to work in movies, and they were often based on reality.

"You appear to have something to hide," he insinuated.

"Look, stop busting my balls or I'll file a harassment complaint against you," the doctor stated as he turned around and walked away.

Zarco reckoned that people just didn't take private detectives seriously. They considered them busybodies. He would have loved to turn into Philip Marlowe at that moment and deliver a clever and scathing reply, full of implied threats. He couldn't think of any however, and opted to leave the hospital. His hopes of obtaining some useful information had already been low and, given the results, his visit had been a complete waste of time and self-esteem. He had reached an impasse. That damned hospital was the junction point for the three victims. The only suspect, Dr. Roberto Gomis, might have had reason to kill Ana, but Zarco couldn't see the doctor's connection to the other two murders. A 'normal' person could commit murder in a moment of obfuscation, hate, or fear, but perpetrating three murders was more complex. It was out of the ordinary and suggested the possible presence of organized crime or, at least, a professional killer.

He sensed he was getting closer to crucial information, if only he could organize the scattershot facts that had piled up in his brain. The path that might have allowed him to establish a connecting thread between them seemed to have vanished with the death of Teresa. The fact that he and Raquel had been followed the previous evening meant the murderer did not feel safe. What was his purpose in following them? Was it to find out something about them, or was there another reason? He couldn't know. That's why he had prepared himself for the worst option, he thought, while confirming that his Glock was resting in the pocket of his trench coat. He suddenly remembered a sentence that had been going round in his head since he'd heard it a few days before. It had been uttered from the mouth of Santiago Cañas' widow and, while he hadn't given it much thought, it had taken root in his brain and he now knew he needed clarification. What had she said exactly? That we must all pay for our sins or our mistakes but that her deceased husband hadn't committed any? It was something along those lines. But if her husband hadn't made a mistake, there was only one other explanation: it was she who had to atone for a sin.

31

Ballesteros got up, went into the bathroom directly connected to his bedroom, cast a quick look at his face in the mirror, and got into the shower. He turned on the water and let it run a little to warm it up. He'd slept well and felt rested. He'd awakened at 4:10 a.m. according to the digital clock on his nightstand, but contrary to his habit of staying awake, Ballesteros had gone back into a deep sleep a few minutes later.

While he showered he thought briefly about Raquel, asleep in the bedroom next to his. He was pleased that she had spent the previous night there when she'd felt she was in trouble. He was unsure if the car chase described by Raquel and Zarco had really occurred or had been born of a paranoid crisis caused by the discovery of the dead body of someone they knew. The previous evening, Ballesteros and Raquel had sustained a short and friendly chat before going to bed. The tensions that had emerged during their first dinner together seemed to have dissipated. Still, as Ballesteros did not know how the events of that afternoon had affected her, he had made no attempts to move closer to her or make any insinuation before she went to bed. Each to his own.

He remembered his argument with Paco and regretfully acknowledged that his friend was partly right, you can't go around spying on someone at the drop of a hat. Ballesteros told himself that he hadn't done it out of morbid curiosity, but to protect Paco. If Tanya's dirty laundry hadn't come to the surface, he wouldn't have said anything. He'd have shredded the report and forgotten about the whole thing. But after discovering that Tanya was engaged in prostitution–or one of its variants—he'd felt a moral obligation to tell his friend. At least, that was how he had reasoned it out. He had been hoisted by his own petard, as the saying goes, and it had opened a deep schism in their friendship. Until the afternoon of their quarrel, he had not seen what was completely obvious: Paco was like a teenager in love. All Ballesteros could do now was allow some time to pass and wait for the flood waters to subside.

He stepped out of the shower, dried himself, and put on a dark suit and clean shirt; he seldom wore a tie. Raquel hadn't yet shown any signs of life. Her bedroom door was closed and Ballesteros assumed she was still asleep. She was in no danger there, and he did not think she would feel frightened when she awoke. He took out a notepad and pen, and wrote: *Good morning, Raquel. I had to go to work. Feel free to make yourself some breakfast with anything in the refrigerator or cupboards. I made some coffee. You can warm it up in the microwave. If you need anything, call me. Warmly, Raúl.* He picked up his coat and headed for the office.

Ballesteros had no client visits scheduled for that morning, nor was he scheduled for a duty shift, so he dedicated his time to reviewing some unfinished business. Antonio Torres, the attorney with whom he often worked, called Ballesteros mid-morning to inform him that he'd just been notified of the sentencing regarding Derek Newmann's domestic abuse case. He advanced the verdict by phone, and let Ballesteros know he was on his way to the office to provide him with a copy of the ruling. The judge had declared an acquittal for the accused. The resolution was not yet final and it was possible that the wife's attorney could file an appeal; nevertheless, with a favorable verdict from the court and without an indictment from the prosecutor, it was improbable that the Court of Appeals would overturn the verdict. It was also unlikely that the defense attorney for the presumed victim would be so overconfident as to file the appeal. Ballesteros called his client and communicated the favorable result, while at the same time advising him to take a civil route when filing for divorce and, if at all possible, to do so by mutual consent.

"What does mutual consent mean?" asked Derek Neumann.

"Well, to put it plainly, you and your wife should agree on who stays in the family home and who leaves; which of you will claim responsibility for care and custody of the children—normally it would be her; how much alimony and child support you will have to pay for your children and which days they will spend with you under your care," explained Ballesteros in the simplest way he knew how.

"And if I don't want to pay her anything?"

The attorney noted that his client's speech was slurred, and he attributed it to a morning intake of alcohol. Not the best remedy to calm the nerves. However, Ballesteros said nothing. He was only his client's attorney, not his doctor or his spiritual adviser.

"Look, Derek, the financial support is not for her, it's for your children, and I want to be clear that a mutual consent divorce would be your best option. The end result will be nearly the same and you will save yourself a year of lawsuits and legal fees. The most sensible thing you can do is forget about the past and, in the future, try to resolve your issues by talking them through. It would be the best approach for both of you and for your children."

"How can I forget that I spent a night in jail and that she took me to court for domestic violence?! The verdict says I am innocent, but I'm sure if an acquaintance speaks with my wife, they will come away suspecting me of being a wife abuser. That can't be fixed with a verdict. Can't I accuse her of filing a false accusation? In Germany ..."

Ballesteros was tempted to hang up the phone. He knew this couple's war had just begun and he disliked marital conflicts. It wasn't enough that his client had been declared innocent: he wanted vengeance. He wanted to ruin her life.

"Derek, just be glad that it worked out," interrupted the attorney. "Things could have been much worse. Try to relax and don't exacerbate the situation. I know the Spanish criminal justice system is not the best in the world and it's quite possibly better in Germany. Almost everything is better in Germany. But we are in Spain."

"Yes. I'm thinking of returning to my own country. And as for the divorce, will you be my attorney?"

"No. I don't work in civil matters, but I'll recommend a trustworthy attorney. I have to hang up now. We'll talk again soon."

Ballesteros was tired of Derek Neumann. He was tired of his clients in general. And of his profession. Although movies about the justice system often depict the attorney as a rock star that gets his client acquitted after delivering an irrefutable closing argument, in an actual Spanish courtroom the attorney is the low man on the totem pole. During legal statements made at police stations, the attorney is at the mercy of police guidelines. In court, the attorney is subjected to written and non-written rules imposed by judges, court clerks, and public officials, to say nothing of the absurd pretenses of many clients, who believe that because they are paying the bill he must adhere to their instructions, as if he were an interior decorator working on a remodel. The hotshot maverick attorney that takes on the judiciary system, brandishing arguments about the Constitution and the law does not actually exist. His primary work is done in the office or from his home, reviewing legal precedence and the minutiae of the case, and examining the faults and flaws of an investigation to determine if some piece of evidence against his client might be unlawful and, consequently, dismissed. Only in oral proceedings did an attorney take on a significant role. It was true that he earned more in one routine workday than a police officer, a civil servant, and a judge combined, which in part compensated for the stress he was under. But it also gave rise to envy and a desire for retribution from many of the other actors in the halls of justice.

On the other hand, he loved jurisprudence. Despite the inherent defects in laws, like most things man-made, he believed that humanity had advanced toward greater justice and equity: slavery had been abolished; women enjoyed the same rights as men (at least under the law); wars had been reduced (at least in western countries); and there was greater tolerance toward immigrants, homosexuals, and other minorities. There was even a black president in the United States, something that would have been absolutely unheard of five decades before when whites had exclusivity to bars and buses to avoid intermingling with blacks. And the law had played a decisive role in all of these considerable advancements. Yes, he loved the law. What he couldn't tolerate were the people he had to deal with: volatile clients, apathetic public servants, and arrogant judges. He needed a vacation. He checked his calendar and counted almost seven months until August.

32

Zarco dipped a cookie into his mug of Cola Cao hot chocolate and was in the process of putting it into his mouth when he was startled by the sound of the intercom. He took a quick glance at the kitchen clock to check the time and verified that it was 12:20 a.m. There was only one person that would show up at his home at that hour without calling: Xicu. That also meant he had some valuable information. Zarco unhooked the intercom handset and mechanically asked who it was, though he already knew what the answer would be.

"Open the door." It was his friend's voice.

"Do you know what time it is?"

"Geniuses never sleep!" said Xicu.

"Geniuses are pests," answered Zarco while simultaneously pressing the button that opened the door to the building. He knew that behind the façade of genius his friend feigned were a multitude of hidden psychological complexes, and that Xicu's inability to find a normal job had led him to focus completely on the world of information technology. To a certain extent, Zarco saw himself reflected in Xicu: both were recluses, misanthropes, and dedicated to professions (if the way they made a living could be qualified as such) which were outside the usual margins. He went to his bedroom, picked up the Glock, and placed it in a kitchen drawer.

Xicu climbed the stairs in giant strides and in under a minute he'd made it to the second floor, where the detective's home and office were located. He darted into the apartment, headed toward the kitchen, and found Zarco taking a sip from his mug.

"Would you like some hot chocolate?" asked the detective. "I have one every night before I go to sleep."

"No, thanks. I only came to bring you the information you wanted. I'll go and sleep later. I haven't had a wink of sleep in forty-eight hours, which means this is going to cost you 900 big, fat euros."

"For a day and a half of work?"

"Some people earn that in an hour."

"And some don't earn it in a month."

"Álex, don't haggle me. You said it was urgent and I've brought you what you wanted in record time: the doctor and his wife's emails, credit cards, bank accounts, and passwords. You could even obtain the 900 euros to pay me from him. And you know this is a special price for a friend."

"I know, Xicu, I was joking. I don't have any cash on hand, I'll give it to you tomorrow." The detective thought about his bank account where he had little more than 1,000 euros. The following day, he would tell Xicu that he'd pay him for the work in two installments, or he would have to ask Raquel for an advance on his fees. Neither option was pleasant, but it was better than being in the red. Although he'd recently completed a few jobs that had provided appropriate compensation, he'd purchased a sophisticated computer and some gadgets for his investigations that had left his account balance with just enough to cover his monthly expenses. It was still mid-month, and the automatic mortgage payment wouldn't be deducted until early February. He needed to make a deposit within the next 15 days.

"No problem, "said Xicu, handing him a page full of notes. "Here are the email addresses for the doctor and his wife and their passwords. And also their bank accounts. You can access those with their ID numbers and the passwords I wrote down for you. You'll enter as if you were the actual user, and you can also view activity on their credit cards. Try not to perform too many searches because the last one is recorded, and they may realize someone has gained access. If you have to look at their accounts, only enter one time and, if possible, do it in the wee hours of the morning to be certain that neither he nor she are online. Do the same with their email: try to get all the information you need in one single login. I haven't gotten into their Facebook, Twitter, or other social media accounts. They're public forums and I assumed you were looking for information that is not available to everyone. If you have any questions, give me a call."

"What I just understood was that I can access their bank accounts. Can I make a transfer?"

"Normally, in order to make a transfer, the bank will use additional security measures such as sending a passcode to the cell number they have on file. In any case, if you do it they'll catch you. If you transferred money to your account, for example, it would be quite easy to trace. They'd arrest you in a couple of hours. It would only be viable if you were to transfer an exceptionally large amount of money into your foreign account, and then jump on a plane immediately afterwards. Still, I imagine the banks have alert mechanisms in place that track large financial transactions. Basically, it would be best if you didn't try to take the doctor's money. They'll catch you, and then they'll catch me."

"Don't worry, Xicu, I have no intention of transferring money to my account. I was simply curious to know what my limitations are when encroaching on the lives of others. We currently have access to almost everything through these devices," commented Zarco as he pointed to the screen on his personal computer.

He bid farewell to Xicu and looked impatiently toward the kitchen clock. The time was 12:40 in the morning. He prepared an instant coffee for himself with a substantial amount of sugar so he could perk up, and he sat down in front of the TV. His body was not used to caffeine, and he knew that a single cup of coffee would keep him up all night. He had to wait until 2:30 or 3:00 a.m. to access the email and bank accounts of Roberto Gomis and his wife, María Ribas.

Additionally, in order to stay within safety margins, he could login to each email and account only once, per Xicu's instructions. He calculated he could meander through the couple's electronic data for three and a half hours: from 2:30 to 6:00

a.m. He didn't think anyone would get up that early unless they suffered from insomnia.

By 2:00 a.m., he was bored from waiting and watching television shows and felt impatient to go through Roberto Gomis' confidential information. Zarco decided he would no longer delay signing in to the doctor's computer. He recognized that not keeping to the schedule he had set was not up to professional standards. However, as he often told himself, we're only human. As he keyed in the password to slip into Roberto Gomis' bank account, he wondered if it would actually work. Deep down he still could not believe the miracles Xicu could perform, despite having witnessed many of them during the years they had been collaborating together. He clicked the *Enter* key and watched in amazement as he accessed the plastic surgeons' bank accounts. At first glance, he didn't see anything unusual. The balance showed little more than 30,000 euros in his checking account, and a balance of 52,366.54 euros on his mortgage. He viewed details for purchases and payments on the credit card, and also found nothing out of the ordinary: a flight to Madrid, two nights in a hotel, several charges at gas stations, and some shopping. Zarco was disappointed. What did he think he would find? A credit card payment labeled 'contract killer'? At any rate, thought the detective, there was no need to review current activity, just charges made around the time of the first two murders in early May of last year. There was a remote possibility that he could roughly trace Gomis' steps. Any payment made at an establishment close to the place where Santiago Cañas was shot or near the house where Ana López was killed at a coincidental time might place Gomis at the scene of the crime. After several attempts, he was able to find his way into Gomis' May 2012 bank statement. Again, he found nothing. Only normal expenses for the mortgage, some receipts, and little else. He attempted to trace credit card expenses for that same month but was unable to find a way to do it.

Zarco opened the Yahoo page and entered the email address. He typed in the username: robertogomis33, and keyed in the password that Xicu had provided. The detective was beginning to feel discouraged. Perhaps the information he'd find there would be just as worthless as what he'd obtained from Ana López' computer. He was going to have to justify a 900 euros expense and a breach of information privacy to Raquel and Ballesteros with no useful information to show for it. The inbox showed four unread messages: two of them seemed like advertisements from pharmaceutical companies and the other two, from Josu Zulaika and Joan Vives, appeared to be friends. Either way, if there had been any strange communications in recent months, Gomis could have easily deleted the messages. A small tab in the margin indicated that no one from their contact list was online at that moment. Still, Zarco was nervous. All he needed was for one of Gomis' friends to be online at that hour, notice that his email was active, and decide he wanted to open a chat. If that occurred, Zarco would have to log out quickly. He opened some recent messages that had been sent to other people and found nothing of value. Dr. Gomis appeared to frequently visit a site for contact with women, but nothing connected him to crimes or illegal activity. He continued to scroll back pages until he found emails sent in April of 2012. He found none sent to Ana López. In early May, he found one email with the subject: a success. He opened it and started to read. It appeared to have been sent to a personal friend. Gomis stated that his wife's kidney transplant had been a success, and that he had to wait for the post-op to ensure that the organ was not rejected, but that hopefully his wife would then be free from her daily servitude to the dialysis machine. The email was dated May 5th. Zarco looked up at the whiteboard where he had documented relevant facts of his investigation in colored sharpies and saw that everything began on May 2nd, the date that Santiago Cañas and Ana López were killed. He remembered the sorrowful expression on Cañas' widow's face as she informed him that her husband had been an organ donor. He took a screen print from the computer and then printed the email sent by the doctor. Meanwhile, Teresa had been the last person to see Ana López alive, and she had reported that Ana had been accompanied by a doctor. The pieces were starting to fit.

33

Ballesteros and Raquel López stared fixedly at Zarco, who was smiling with an air of triumph he was trying to disguise. Despite not having slept, the detective appeared full of vitality. Raquel and Zarco were sitting in leather armchairs while Ballesteros sat on the other side of the elegant oak desk in the attorney's office.

"I've discovered the connection," said Zarco calmly.

"Alright, Álex, that's what you told me on the phone. Can you provide more details and tell us what you've learned?"

Ballesteros remained silent waiting for the detective's explanation.

"I'll try," responded Zarco looking alternately at Raquel and the attorney. "As you know, from the onset I've suggested the hypothesis that the first two murders had to be related. I believe the nurse was killed later because she saw or discovered something. Basically, the violent deaths of two people within just a few hours could not have been a coincidence, not to mention that those same two people had been in contact with each other, even if it was brief. What was the nexus? It was the location where these two people overlapped. Can Misses Hospital. However, Cañas and your sister, "he said, looking at Raquel, "did not know each other. We were missing a motive, and I believe I've found it. Don't ask me how, but I've gained access to Dr. Roberto Gomis' computer. We know he had a romantic relationship with Ana. It appears that Dr. Gomis also knew Cañas: Gomis' wife received a donor kidney the day after Cañas died. Cañas was an organ donor. Therefore, Gomis is the connection between Cañas and Ana."

"That doesn't prove anything," interrupted Ballesteros. "Perhaps Gomis may have taken advantage of his position as a surgeon to move his wife up on the transplant list, but from there to killing a man is quite a stretch."

"I may not have evidence for what I'm suggesting and the little I have may not be admissible in court, but now we know where we should focus our investigation."

"Álex, don't be offended, but I don't see the logic here either," voiced Raquel. "What are you trying to say? That Dr. Gomis shot that poor man three times so his wife could have his kidney? That seems a bit much. And I still don't understand why he would also kill my sister."

"Because your sister found out," insisted Zarco, who was beginning to feel the exhaustion of having spent all night in front of a computer screen. "I can't explain myself clearly right now. I haven't slept all night. But there has to be a nexus. The third death—the nurse—can't be a coincidence. She was your sister's friend and she also worked at the hospital. Teresa told us she saw your sister in the company of a doctor the day she was killed. Who's to say it wasn't Gomis?"

"Teresa said that she saw my sister with a doctor that had an unfriendly face, who she didn't know. Gomis doesn't fit that description. On the one hand, he doesn't have an unfriendly face, although he is, in fact, rather unfriendly. And on the other hand, he's been working at Can Misses for a long time and his specialty is plastic surgery. Teresa worked in the ICU, and she surely knew him."

"And how do you explain the 50,000 euros that Cañas withdrew from the bank that morning? What was the reason for that?" asked Ballesteros.

Zarco stared broodingly at the floor. He had no response. He was aware that he had rushed into an elaboration of his theories before tying up all the loose ends. The discovery of an incidental connection between the doctor and Cañas had been enough to launch him into a series of hypotheses that he could not confirm. He'd allowed himself to be led by euphoria and by his animosity toward the surgeon, and he hadn't thoroughly analyzed the details of the situation. The only valid hypothesis would be one that clarifies the minutiae; just a general idea was not enough. A low mood swing was now taking hold of him. What if it had all been nothing more than a series of coincidences? And what if everything had occurred just as the Civil Guard officer had said: Cañas was killed by a professional gunman and Ana López was killed by a thief who broke into her house?

"Perhaps the 50,000 euros have nothing to do with the crime. It may have been pure coincidence that on that same day he withdrew a lot of money from the bank," protested Zarco, lacking conviction.

"That doesn't make any sense," said Ballesteros. "In any event, the 50,000 should have shown up somewhere and, to date, whatever Cañas did with that money or his reason for withdrawing it from the bank remains unknown. Furthermore, if the doctor intended to use Cañas' organs, it wouldn't make any sense to shoot him three times in the chest. According to what we were told, it was a miracle the bullets didn't hit his vital organs." And in a more paternal tone, he added, "You should sleep a little. You'll be able to see things more clearly afterwards."

"Álex, I'll accompany you home," offered Raquel gently, resting her hand on the detective's knee.

"I think I've made a fool of myself with my investigation," replied Zarco, crestfallen, and also thinking that he couldn't bill Raquel and the attorney for those 900 euros that Xicu had asked for. And on the first of the month, he would have to pay his bills: telephone, mortgage, social security, etc. He was exhausted and disheartened, and he was also annoyed by Ballesteros' sympathetic tone, speaking to him like the adult that patiently reprimands a child.

"You have not made a fool of yourself, Álex," said Raquel. "What you've uncovered isn't wrong. I can't imagine it was an easy task to obtain all of that information, but your hypothesis that a doctor would kill three people to obtain a kidney is not plausible."

"You're right. I got ahead of myself. Still, I'm sure the

doctor is hiding something and that he played a role, directly or indirectly, in Ana's death," said Zarco dejectedly. "I'm going to go sleep for a few hours. You don't need to go with me, Raquel, but thanks for the offer."

34

At noon, Ballesteros received a call from his ex-wife. It was odd that she'd call him in the morning and he sensed she didn't have good news. Yolanda got straight to the point: his daughter had been arrested together with three boys and another girl.

"Wasn't she in school?" asked Ballesteros.

"She should have been, but no, she wasn't. If she had been at school she wouldn't have been arrested."

"And why was she arrested? Did she steal something?"

"No. They were smoking joints."

"That's not a crime."

"Spoken like a true attorney!" she said. Ballesteros made an effort to remain quiet. He was not free from marital conflicts either, despite being divorced. She continued, "It isn't a crime, but instead of being in class she was at the park smoking a joint."

"So then, why are you talking about an arrest?"

"What do I know about these things?! The local police found them with drugs and told them they would all be fined."

"Yes, that's true. A fine—and that's it."

"What do you mean: that's it?"

"Sorry, but when you said 'arrest' I thought it was something worse..."

"That's not enough for you?" Yolanda barked.

"Well, no. Obviously, we need to have a serious conversation with Julieta. She has to think about what she wants to do with her life. But she's a goddammed teenager."

"For years now, we've been blaming everything on her adolescence. I suppose our daughter also bears some of the blame. And I think we do, too." Yolanda accentuated the pronoun 'we' to ensure that Ballesteros understood that the plural of 'we' could be substituted for the singular 'you'.

"You also bear some of the blame. You're the cool dad, the understanding dad."

Ballesteros felt about to explode. He still remembered his irritation after the conversation with Derek Neumann, an angry husband he found impossible to reason with, and now he was experiencing the same absurdity with his hysterical ex.

"The important thing now is not to find fault but find solutions," he said, struggling to control himself.

"There you go again with your words of wisdom! Talk to your daughter!"

Ballesteros listened to the *click* on the other end indicating that Yolanda had hung up the phone without saying goodbye or giving him time to say anything. Yolanda could drown in a glass of water. She got carried away with hysteria and exaggerated things to the extreme. Despite having a better understanding of the situation, Ballesteros couldn't avoid being infected by her anxiety—as if it were the flu. Therefore, as an antidote against the hysteria virus, the attorney chose to minimize the problem. Hadn't he smoked a joint or two when he was young? Isn't alcohol more detrimental to your health than hashish? A person who smokes joints tends to be more relaxed and peaceful, while drinkers lean toward euphoric and aggressive behavior. One only had to observe the hoards of drunken English tourists that arrive in the popular Ibizan town of San Antonio during summer months and destroy hotel rooms or pull side-view mirrors off parked cars. Ballesteros was in favor of legalizing drugs. Although his position regarding this topic, published in an interview in the Ibizan newspaper, *Diario*, had generated discussions with his colleagues and criticism from the families of those directly affected, his standpoint remained the same. History confirmed that Prohibition, such as the paradigm example from the United States, had not stopped people from their consumption. But it did generate the enrichment of organized crime by smuggling illegal substances. What basis do lawmakers have for permitting gambling and alcohol, which ruins lives and families, and not allowing the consumption of hashish or marijuana? Couldn't state governments see that by legalizing drugs, they could put an end to the mafias and criminal organizations that were profiting from the sale of illegal substances? Were they not aware that drug trafficking was the second most lucrative business in the world, after arms dealing, and that its legalization might end economic crises in western countries and allow greater development in third world countries?

Obviously, he was going to have to speak to his daughter, but he wouldn't do it as an authoritative father, he would be understanding. He would tell her that he didn't see any harm in smoking joints during recreational activities, such as on weekends. After all, his daughter was going to continue smoking hash or drinking beer whether he allowed it or not. But it was entirely different to cut classes at school in order to smoke joints. He would also caution his daughter about health risks resulting from tobacco as well as joints and alcohol, though he already knew what his daughter's response would be: *if it's so bad for your health, why do you drink and smoke?* And he would have no response except to acknowledge that we all have our own contradictions. Yes, roughly speaking, he would say something along those lines. Attorney and father of an adolescent. He wouldn't wish that on anyone, except perhaps his ex. He checked his vacation calendar again: seven months left and it seemed like an eternity.

35

Zarco had spent the past two days in the grip of a deep depression. He was at the bottom of a dark hole, one that he'd been in many times before. While it was a familiar place and he knew he'd eventually climb out, at that moment he couldn't find a glimmer of hope. He felt unstable, on the edge of a precipice. He'd spent hours lying in bed trying to find sleep to no avail. He'd tried to reread an Agatha Christie novel but couldn't focus on the words and, after spending five minutes on the same page, he put the book back down on the nightstand. Admittedly, he'd been depressed many times before for no apparent reason. Humans, it turns out, have a consequential chemical composition: one sharp drop in our lithium levels and we get depressed. But in addition to being demoralized, he felt humiliated. This criminal investigation had put him in very close proximity with the outside world, and he had not been prepared for it. But now he understood. Up until that time, his work as a private investigator had not required much social contact except with the client that hired him. He had been limited to following and spying on his targets with sophisticated photographic equipment and recording devices. He'd installed surveillance devices into their homes or hacked into their computers with Xicu's help. In those situations, Zarco remained anonymous. The subjects he'd investigated did not recognize his face, they weren't even aware of his existence. He was invisible and, as a result, he was immune. But the investigation into these murders had forced him to face the world head-on, with all of its human malice, stupidity, and selfishness. The males with whom he'd recently had contact had denigrated and belittled him starting with Sergeant Ferrando, an old school copper; then Ana's ex, that pompous idiot, Fran; then Dr. Roberto Gomis, an arrogant and disdainful surgeon.

Zarco was also bothered by Ballesteros' condescending attitude, behaving as if he were a step above him. They were a pack of homophobes and narcissists.

Unfortunately, his investigation and subsequent failed attempt to solve the case hadn't helped him. He would have imposed his own vengeance: throw the stuck-up surgeon in jail and solve the case that Sergeant Ferrando and his entire police team had failed to do, despite having the full backing of the judicial branch—where the attorney had also failed. But things never work out as well in real life as they do in our imagination. Zarco attempted to remember the fundamentals of Buddhist philosophy that had provided him with peace and serenity on so many occasions. Now he was upset on account of his own ego. If he didn't take himself so seriously, his feelings of shame and humiliation would disappear. After all, Álex Zarco was no more important to the cosmos than a mosquito or a microbe. And yet, even his self-reflection did not bring him the tranquility he was searching for. At times he had come close to the level of wisdom that implies acceptance of everything as it exists, including oneself; a higher plane in which happiness can be found. However, those instances in which he had nearly reached the summit had been unsuccessful. He had allowed himself to be trapped by the mundane trivialities that create negative feelings: the neighbor that doesn't say hello when you walk by him on the stairs; the driver that has no respect for crosswalks; the person who doesn't recycle his garbage; the innumerable cases of political corruption that he read about daily in newspapers ... All of these aroused feelings of anger, hate, and impotence, which made Zarco roll downward and away from spiritual peace. He felt like Sisyphus pushing the rock uphill, only to have it roll back down again. During those moments he wanted to destroy, attack, tell the person who wouldn't recycle garbage that he was a thoughtless and intransigent moron; and yell out *dim-witted asshole!* to the neighbor that rudely turned his head away whenever Zarco courteously said *good morning.* Later, when he was calmer, he tried to dispel those negative feelings. And during this pendular motion between his search for Buddhist serenity and his aggressive outbursts, the detective's daily life passed by. Zarco remembered his hospitalization in a mental facility ten years prior, due to a nervous breakdown. On his first day there, he was locked in a padded cell to insure he wouldn't harm himself, and in the days that followed they loaded him up with tranquilizers that kept him lethargic.

However, as the optimists say, every unpleasant experience has a positive side. And in that facility full of tormented souls who spent their days sedated, Zarco had discovered a new passion: reading crime novels. It was there he conceived the idea of becoming a private investigator. That future project—combined with Agatha Christie—helped him to sustain his hope, his dream, and his sanity during the six months he was hospitalized. He had remained sane since his discharge thanks to his karate practice and his daily medication which, together with his work, constituted the three pillars of his life. He remembered something his psychiatrist had said a few days before he was discharged: *If human beings expressed all the thoughts out loud that go through their minds every day, the vast majority of them would be hospitalized in a mental institution. We all have strange ideas, fears, fantasies, and phobias. What sets the sane people apart is that they keep those demons in check.* In fact, Zarco battled daily with wraiths and internal voices that struggled to emerge. He had not yet vanquished his own demons, but he had learned to live with them. Every night, before going to sleep, he checked under the bed and opened closet doors to confirm no one had hidden there while he was out. And every morning, before leaving the house, he carefully scrutinized the street from behind his window curtains, to assure himself that no one was waiting for him outside. These paranoid habits had become routine and he performed them daily, automatically. He didn't attach much importance to them; it was like the people who count stairs or steps from their doorway to the car.

Zarco walked to the bathroom, took a brown glass bottle out of the closet, twisted off the lid and opened it. He took out two pills, put them in his mouth, and swallowed them with some water. As he looked at himself in the bathroom mirror he saw an unkempt man with messy and slightly oily hair, bags under his eyes, and a 3-day stubble beard. Zarco shaved and took a shower, then dried himself next to the heater and put on some clean clothes. He was beginning to feel better, as if the hot water in the shower had peeled off the dirt that clung to his skin, allowing him to breathe more easily. Or perhaps it was the effect of the extra pill he'd just taken. The point was that, after three days of being submerged in the turbid waters of depression, he seemed to be floating to the surface. He was not giving up. He hadn't had the last word yet. He would investigate Dr. Gomis extensively. He still needed to confirm whether the doctor owned a white vehicle like the one that had followed him and Raquel. And he also could confirm the other patients that had benefited from Cañas' donor organs.

The kitchen clock indicated 11:30 a.m. Zarco took another look at his whiteboard. He had two options: he could visit Dr. Gomis again and blackmail him by threatening to tell his wife about the affair with Ana López, or he could visit Isabel González, Santiago Cañas' widow. Next to her name on the board, he noticed he'd written and circled two words with a red sharpie: *hiding something*. He opened the nightstand drawer and took out his Glock, placing it in his inside coat pocket. He walked outside to his motorbike, put on his helmet and gloves, and drove the bike to the street where Cañas' widow lived. At least she was the only person, besides Raquel, that had treated him kindly over the past few weeks.

36

At the Ses Bote Bar, where Ballesteros usually had breakfast, he unexpectedly ran into another regular patron. Sergeant Ferrando was sitting on a stool reading the Ibizan newspaper, *Diario*, which he'd spread out on the counter. Ballesteros pretended to not see the Civil Guard officer, and proceeded to order his usual orange-carrot juice, coffee with milk, and toast with butter and marmalade. He picked up his order and took it to a table.

"Can I speak with you a moment?"

Ballesteros looked up upon hearing the voice and saw Sergeant Ferrando holding a cup of coffee.

"What do you want?" the attorney asked with hostility. He didn't harbor resentment toward the sergeant for their previous quarrels, his arrogant treatment at command headquarters during Eduardo Riba's interrogation, or the possible blackmail he had subjected his client to in order to obtain a confession. Those were occupational hazards. Everyone had his own role to play in the theater of justice, whether it was the police, judge, prosecutor, or attorney. What did bother Ballesteros was someone interrupting his calm morning interlude during which he started planning his workday while savoring his coffee and breakfast.

"Can I sit? This is important."

"Sit, but I have to leave for the office in a minute. I have appointments with clients," answered Ballesteros, who was becoming mildly intrigued by the officer's behavior.

"What I'm going to tell you is not at all pleasant. It's about your detective."

"You're referring to Zarco?"

"Yes. I'm referring to Álex Zarco. He told me you'd hired

him to investigate the murder of Ana López. It appears you were not satisfied with the results of the trial, which I can understand. Why did you hire him? Did you know him previously?"

"He was hired by Ana López' sister. They knew each other in school. But according to what you told me, you're here to provide information, not interrogate me, right?"

"Yes. Don't be impatient. A few days ago, Mr. Zarco came to see me at my office in Santa Eulalia. The truth is I'm not really sure what he wanted. I don't know if he came to share information regarding the Santiago Cañas' shooting, or to see if I could provide information, or why he was there. The fact is I didn't feel good about it. You know what they say about police instinct, that sixth sense we develop after years of associating with psychopaths, murderers, and compulsive liars. I made some inquiries, and it turns out Mr. Álex Zarco suffers from schizophrenia. He was hospitalized for more than six months in a psychiatric hospital in Palma."

"He's definitely a strange guy, but I don't believe he's dangerous. I don't know if Raquel knew he'd spent time in a facility. How long ago was he hospitalized?"

"It's been a few years. After he finished university and before he started playing detective."

"What you're telling me is surprising, but I don't see where you're going with this. Zarco could have suffered from this illness and recovered. He could now be living a normal, or almost normal life, trying to keep his head above water, as the majority of us do."

"This disease cannot be cured. It's chronic and it's also serious. And symptoms include delusions, hallucinations, and behavioral changes."

Ballesteros remembered the theory the detective had proposed a few days before, accusing the doctor of having committed the murders. However, he didn't express his thoughts aloud and preferred to let the officer speak.

"I still don't understand what you're suggesting, "said Ballesteros.

"Don't you see? Zarco murdered Cañas and, possibly, Teresa. He suffers from a type of schizophrenia characterized by a split personality. He is Dr. Jekyll and Mr. Hyde. In his case, he is the detective *and* the murderer. Look, his ambition was to be a great private investigator, not to spy on unfaithful husbands. To that end, there needed to be a murderer to pursue. And if there was no murderer, he had to invent one."

"You mean he killed Cañas in a fit of insanity?"

"Yes, although, more than a fit, I would say that with Zarco it's a state of insanity, of derangement. I believe he's responsible for both Santiago Cañas' death and the nurse that was stabbed a few days ago. This morning, I'm going to ask the judge for a search and seizure warrant for the detective's home. I don't know if we'll find anything. He may have destroyed the gun he used to shoot Cañas, but there's a chance he kept it. These types of mental patients can be very astute, but their behavior, at times, does not adhere to logical patterns. They see reality through a different prism."

"I appreciate that you're confiding in me, Sergeant. However, Zarco seems harmless, incapable of swatting a fly, much less a human being."

"Don't trust appearances. They committed him to a psychiatric hospital for assaulting his parents. He practices martial arts and holds a black belt in karate." Ferrando paused and, fixing a hard stare at the attorney, continued, "I haven't told you all of this just to keep you informed. I want you to watch Mr. Zarco and, if you notice something strange, call me immediately. On the other hand, be on your guard. He is extremely dangerous, and it wouldn't be at all farfetched for him to kill again."

"And what about the murder of Ana López Demichellis? You don't think that could also have been Zarco? It seems that the three crimes are all connected with the Can Misses Hospital."

"The Ana López murder has already been solved. The killer, as you well know, was tried and convicted. Perhaps that murder inspired Zarco to kill the second nurse. I imagine the psychiatrists will have to explain that to us."

Ballesteros watched as the sergeant swaggered out of the bar and the door closed behind him. He called his office and told his secretary to postpone the appointments he had scheduled for the morning. The attorney urgently needed to speak with Raquel. He was not convinced that the officer had solid evidence against Zarco, but it wouldn't be a bad idea to let Raquel know about the sergeant's conjectures. He called her and they made an appointment to meet at a café in the Plaza del Parque, a popular square in Ibiza town.

Although businesses were open at that early morning hour, there were few patrons. Ballesteros informed Raquel of the sergeant's suspicions, attempting to faithfully reproduce the officer's words without providing any judgment of his own. As the attorney's account progressed, Raquel looked at him with growing apprehension. Ballesteros finished his narrative with one question:

"Did you know that Zarco had been hospitalized in a mental health facility?"

"Yes, I knew ..."

"Shit!" interrupted Ballesteros. "And you didn't tell me?"

"It was many years ago. I knew he'd been hospitalized. I certainly didn't know he was schizophrenic. I thought the problem was anxiety attacks or something like that," she paused. "Zarco was always special, for want of a better word. When we were studying psychology at the university, he was the weird guy in the class. I was his only friend. I don't know if you've noticed that he has difficulty communicating with people but, on the other hand, I find him to be an honest and affectionate man, incapable of committing a crime. I know he was hospitalized shortly after obtaining his degree. Still, he has an exceptionally analytic mind, and, despite his peculiarities, he was able to arrive at a profession that he loves. How many people you know can tell you they love their work?"

"A pyromaniac can also enjoy burning down a forest. The problem may be that his work is only the product of his imagination or of his schizophrenic delusions. Do you remember the first day you brought him to my office when he started to exaggerate about his high level cases?"

"He may be a bit of a bragger, I'll acknowledge that," conceded Raquel. "But still, Raúl, to what point are you willing to trust that Civil Guard sergeant? At my sister's murder trial, you yourself accused him of having blackmailed the man he arrested so he would confess to the crime."

"Excessive zeal may lead some cops to take certain liberties. That doesn't mean he may not be right in this case."

"It's paradoxical that an excess of zeal, as you say, can lead them to break the law. I wouldn't completely trust him. According to his version, Álex shot a man three times, and seven months later he stabbed Teresa."

"Just when we were starting to investigate your sister's murder."

"And who killed my sister? The man they convicted?"

"Maybe Zarco also killed your sister. He knew you and he might have imagined that you would hire him. Or, if you hadn't contacted him, perhaps he would have shown up to offer you his services."

"I can't believe that Álex would be at all connected to Ana's death." Raquel's face reflected both incredulity and concern. "We have to clear this up, and the only way to do it is for you and I to meet with Álex. We don't even know for certain if he was in Ibiza when the first two murders occurred."

"You're right. But I'll take precautions, just to be on the safe side. If Ferrando is correct, Zarco may be dangerous. Do you have a gun or something to defend yourself with?"

"It's not the norm to carry a gun in this country! The only thing I have is pepper spray which I bought a few years ago. I don't even know if it's expired."

"If I were you, I'd check it." The attorney thought for an instant, remembering a detail that was circling around his head. "Did you actually see the car that was following you a few days ago?"

"I didn't get to see it. Zarco told me a car was following us and I didn't dare turn around to look. I didn't want the pursuers to know we were onto them."

"So basically, you didn't see it," murmured Ballesteros.

"What are you insinuating?"

"It seems obvious, Raquel. Zarco was the only one who saw the car. Who's to say it wasn't a fabrication to deflect suspicion, or one of his delusions."

37

Álex Zarco parked his motorbike between two cars across from the entrance to Isabel González' home. He pulled off his helmet, identified himself through the intercom as he had a few days earlier, and walked up the stairs to where Santiago Cañas' widow lived. The home looked cleaner and more organized than on the detective's prior visit. Only a single ashtray with a few cigarette butts and a half glass of wine suggested the owner's ongoing decline.

"Did you discover something new?" she asked. She appeared more sober, which could also be attributed to the early noon hour.

"Something. Have you been watching the news these past few days?"

"Are you referring to the nurse's death?" she responded with another question.

"Yes."

"And what does that have to do with Santi's death? I don't see the connection."

"Clearly there has to be one, though to be honest I haven't found it yet." The detective thought that for every question he asked her, she responded with two of her own. And it was obvious she had a slight accent that seemed to suggest she was originally from Galicia. He remembered someone saying that with all generalizations there are often large errors. But, apparently, there are also large truths. "Are you from Galicia?"

"Yes. I was born in Ourense, but as a child I came to Ibiza. Are you asking because of my accent?"

Zarco had actually noticed it because of her penchant for answering his question with another question. "Yes. It's not very noticeable, but there's a certain something. Was your husband also from Galicia?"

"No. He was born in Ibiza. His family was from Úbeda, in Andalucía."

"You told me your husband was an organ donor ..."

"Yes, he was."

"Do you know who the recipients of his organs were?"

"I signed the necessary paperwork and that's all. I think it's morbid to try and meet the person who received one of my husband's organs. It doesn't fit into my mindset." Zarco sensed that she trusted him and wanted to get something off her chest. He had the impression that she'd isolated herself from the world and she needed to make a connection. He detected a distinct rush of sympathy toward him and thought it had to do with a relaxed feeling she experienced when she observed some of the detective's mannerisms; the ones that made him appear uneasy or self-conscious, such as when he looked down at the floor. Perhaps it made her feel she had the upper hand, or at least, that she was not being threatened. Zarco was aware that he sometimes evoked compassion, and it didn't bother him when he was in the company of women. It was completely different when the person treating him with benevolence was an alpha male, a neanderthal, or a dimwit—terms he considered synonymous.

"Do you know a doctor named Gomis?"

"No. I think the doctor who operated on my husband was named Arroyo, though I'm not completely sure. Would you like a drink? Some wine, beer, a glass of water?" she asked.

"A glass of water would be good."

"Do you mind if I smoke?" Isabel asked the question as she walked toward the kitchen. She picked up a bottle of water and a glass and brought it to the table where they were sitting.

"Obviously, this is your home and you can smoke as much as you want."

"And I can also understand that the smoke might be bothersome," she said as she filled the glass with water and offered it to him.

"Thank you. May I ask you a personal question?" asked

Zarco.

"Ask. If I think it's offensive, I won't answer," she said, as she poured some white wine in a glass and brought it to her lips.

"It's about something you said that got into my head. I keep going around it and I can't puzzle it out. The last time I was here, you said something about every person having to pay for their sins, but that your husband, in fact, didn't have any sins. What did you mean exactly?"

Isabel was silent for a moment. Her face grew sad and her gaze was indiscernible. She took a long swallow from her glass of wine.

"That's all I was trying to say, that Santi was a good person, that he'd never hurt anyone, at least deliberately." Her response sounded false to the detective's ears, like a half-truth, which could also be a half-lie. Isabel nervously lit a cigarette and took a long drag from it. She appeared about to break down.

"Are you sure that's all you meant? I'm not trying to be rude or annoying, but please allow me to insist. It was my impression from what you said that your husband's death was payment for a sin. If it wasn't his …"

"Have you never done anything that you regretted? Something that eats away at your conscience?" she asked. She slurred her words slightly while hinting at a forced smile that ended in a strange grimace.

"Of course. One of my wishes, which I imagine will not come true, is to live another life so that I can correct all the errors I have committed in this one. Some of them have been voluntary, others not so voluntary."

She gave him a sidelong glance, trying to assess this person that was at once stirring compassion in her while at the same time showing acute observational skills. She'd felt destroyed since the death of her husband and had spent several months on a daily diet of cigarettes and alcohol which had only increased with the passage of time. She was on the verge of a collapse. Perhaps she needed to purge her venom, confess the guilt that consumed her and didn't spare her a moment of peace.

"Yes, I have several sins. I am a despicable and cowardly woman. You know, your idea of living another life doesn't sound at all bad. I would be happy with just reliving the past two years …"

"I'm sure you're exaggerating. We don't know each other well, but I think I'm a good judge of character and I believe you to be a sensitive, honest woman, "said Zarco, knowing that flattery always paid off.

"Even honest women can be dishonest sometimes."

"It can't be that serious."

"Would you believe that I was unfaithful to my husband?"

"Well, I would have bet against it. However, experience has taught me that anyone can be unfaithful under certain circumstances. I mean if someone meets the right person at the right time …"

"He was not the right person," she interrupted. "I was. Santi and I had been together a lifetime, since we were in grade school. We started going steady and we swore eternal love for each other. Then we grew up and got married. He was the only man in my life. When I turned thirty-three, I got this idea that I was starting to get old. I began to notice some gray in my hair which, thank goodness, I was able to dye. But then there were a few wrinkles. I met a man at work. Like I said, looking back he was no great thing. He was, however, very good-looking, athletic, the type of guy who women always tried to chat with wherever he went. And the funny thing is he was the one who noticed me, he flattered me, he complimented me. Also, after fifteen years of living with Santi, our sex life was virtually nonexistent. I felt the need to experience new things. And, like I said, he was very attractive."

"Up to this point, your story seems quite understandable. You shouldn't blame yourself for being human and having desires."

"Perhaps you're right. But then things got complicated. One weekend, I went to the Peninsula with two girlfriends. They were going shopping, and I used that opportunity to see my lover."

Zarco noted that Isabel omitted the man's name. Questions arose in the detective's mind: did her lover have something to do with her husband's death? After all, apart from money, passionate impulses are one of the most common motives for committing a crime. Had she spoken to the police about her lover? But Zarco refrained from asking questions and allowed her to continue speaking.

"The night before we returned to Ibiza, he and I went out to dinner in Denia. We drank a lot of wine and were headed back to the hotel in the car. I was driving carelessly because of the wine, and because I was thinking about my lover's body and getting excited. Suddenly when I turned a corner, I hit a woman who was crossing the street at a crosswalk. I couldn't react in time, and I hit her hard. She laid there with her legs on the road and her upper body on the sidewalk. I panicked. I thought that if I stopped, I'd have to take a sobriety test and I would fail it. And then Santi would find out that I was with another man. How could I explain that to him? My lover said we had to leave right away, that we would stop and call an ambulance to come quickly and help her. The truth was we'd already run her over and we weren't doctors, so there was nothing we could do. Well, obviously, we could have faced the consequences, which is what a decent person would have done. But we got scared and we fled. We did stop at the first pay phone we found and reported an accident so an ambulance would go," Isabel paused briefly to sip her wine and take a drag from her cigarette. "We thought the best thing to do was to park the car and take a taxi to the hotel, but then my lover noticed there was a slight dent on the corner of my fender and one of the blinkers was broken. What would we say if we were stopped by the police? Besides, the car was my husband's ATV, and I would have to explain the dent to him. So we decided to fake a fender bender with another car. But what if the other driver decided to call the police? We wanted everything to stay under the radar, so we opted to lightly bump a parked car, just enough to create a small dent, and we left our contact information on their windshield wiper. We wanted to have an excuse in the event that the following morning, when we boarded the ferry back to Ibiza, the police or Civil Guard might be investigating the accident. The dent with that parked car was our alibi.

The next morning, I drove my husband's ATV to the ferry. I was scared to death. Every signal from ferry employees while directing the vehicles to parking areas on the boat seemed suspicious to me. But nothing happened. When I returned to Ibiza, I told my husband I'd had a small accident. He said if there hadn't been any personal injuries, it wasn't a problem. And our car was fully insured. The owner of the parked vehicle called me. He thanked me for my courtesy by not taking off without leaving a note, and we exchanged insurance information."

"Do you know what happened to the woman you hit?"

"I didn't want to know. I didn't watch TV or read newspapers for a few days, in case something was reported. I wanted to pretend nothing had happened; at least, that nothing had happened to me. But I was fooling myself. And I never saw my lover again. I wanted to erase anything that would make me remember the worst thing I'd ever done in my life. I kept thinking that if I hadn't wanted to screw a handsome guy, none of this would have happened. He tried to contact me to meet up again but I refused. The truth is he didn't insist, and I was relieved." She paused again to drink some more wine and light a cigarette. "Want to know what the strange thing is? My husband found out anyway."

"That you had a lover?"

"No. He discovered that the actual accident was nothing like the version I gave him. A few days before he was killed, he came home with a serious expression and asked me what had really happened that day with the car. He didn't speak in a reproachful tone or ask me who I was with. He just wanted to know what really happened. And I told him the truth, I mean, I told him everything I told you except for the fact that I was in the company of another man. Santi didn't get angry. He tried to get me to calm down; told me that nothing would happen. At that moment I was so shocked that I simply explained everything that had occurred, at least in an effort to mitigate the mountain of lies that had come between us. But afterwards I kept going over all of it in my head and I couldn't understand how he'd found out about it several months after the accident. The only explanation I could come up with was that my lover had told him about it, since no one else knew about the hit-and-run. But that was a farfetched idea. It made no sense that he would talk to Santi to tell him he'd had an affair with me, and that we ran over a woman and then ran away like cowards. I've been going over and over it since then, and I still don't understand how he found out."

"Why didn't you ask him?"

"I didn't want to bring it up. I felt so guilty about it, and I wasn't really sure if Santi knew there had been another man. I thought it would be less risky if I just didn't talk about it, and it would also be easier to forget the whole thing."

"Did you tell the Civil Guards that investigated your husband's death that you'd had an affair?" asked Zarco.

"No. I can assure you he had nothing to do with Santi's death. In order to kill someone you have to be in love, and neither of us was in love with the other. We enjoyed sex and little else. I didn't tell them about him. I didn't want my shit to stain the memory of my husband."

"When did the accident occur?"

"A little more than a year ago. It was in early December of 2011, around the Constitution Day long holiday weekend."

"Don't worry about what happened. After all, it was an accident."

"You're a good person, Álex."

"Take care of yourself."

Zarco got up slowly despite being in a hurry to return to his office. He needed to confirm some facts and compare dates. If his suspicions were correct once he'd finished verifying everything, he would know who the killer was. After his first failure, however, he had to proceed with caution. It would be unprofessional to keep hurling accusations at different people every day, and besides, he didn't want to put his foot in it again. If he made another false move, he'd have to drop the case. He couldn't handle a second mistake. But if Sergeant Ferrando's wife had been hit by a car during the Constitution Day weekend in 2011, then all the pieces would finally fit.

38

Raquel stepped out of the elevator, turned on the stairwell light, and headed toward her apartment. She searched her purse for the keys. A slight noise alerted her to the presence of another person on the stair landing. She looked up and saw the unmistakable silhouette of Álex Zarco near the end of the hall. He was sitting on the second step of the stairway leading to the upper floor with his feet flat on the landing and his forearms resting on his knees.

"I've got it, Raquel!" he said as he stood up and approached her.

Raquel gave a sudden start. Without taking her hand out of her purse, she dropped the keys and her fingers searched for the pepper spray. Although she had defended her friend's innocence during her conversation with Ballesteros, Zarco was behaving strangely. His pupils were dilated and his eyes sparkled, as if he were under the influence of some drug. And why had he shown up at her house without letting her know? She felt the small cylindrical bottle in her hand and, with an imperceptible movement of her fingers, she unhooked the cap. She pressed it against the palm of her hand and placed her index finger on the pepper spray nozzle.

"What does that mean? What is it you have?" she asked, trying to sound calm.

"I know who killed your sister and committed the other two murders. I was wrong, it wasn't Dr. Gomis ..."

"Álex, forgive me if I seem skeptical, but just a few days ago you accused the doctor. What made you change your mind?"

"I did a bit more investigating and now all the details fit. I know why Cañas was shot. The murders of your sister and Teresa were collateral damage ..."

"And according to your new information, who is responsible for the crimes?" asked Raquel, amazed by her calm tone despite feeling a bundle of nerves due to her overwhelming fear.

"Sergeant Ferrando!"

"You mean the Civil Guard officer in charge of the investigations?"

"Yes. I know it sounds absurd, but please let me explain. Why don't we go inside your home?"

Raquel hesitated for a moment. The pepper spray was her defense, her protective shield. If she let go of it to pick up her keys, the burly detective might surprise her with a sudden attack and she wouldn't be able to defend herself. She was tired of the tension and uncertainty and decided to confront her friend.

"Why did you show up here instead of just calling me on the phone?" she blurted out harshly.

"Our phones might be bugged," Zarco answered, confused by the violent tone in her voice. "He's a police officer, Raquel. Don't you get it? What's the matter with you anyway? You're acting as if you don't trust me, almost as if you're afraid of me."

Raquel thought Zarco's excuse was not unfounded, but she didn't want to back down. If she found herself forced to use the pepper spray or run for her life, she preferred to do it soon. She noticed that the hand holding the spray container had become moist from sweat, so she decided to show her cards and force a reaction from the detective.

"Ferrando went to speak with Ballesteros and told him you were their prime suspect in the murders of Cañas and Teresa. He also said you had been hospitalized in a mental facility for assaulting your parents."

Zarco felt paralyzed for an instant, trying to take in the flurry of accusations in Raquel's words.

"It didn't happen like that. I didn't attack my parents." Zarco looked at his friend, his eyes were pleading. "My parents tried to stop me from leaving the house—I suppose they had good reason—and I pushed them away, which led to a slight injury. But it was never my intention to hurt them."

"That's not the most relevant concern here. What about the murder charges?"

Raquel felt her sweaty hand clinging to the spray with clenched fingers. She didn't know if she would be able to react fast enough and remembered the instructions provided by the spray salesperson: while you point the nozzle at the attacker, take a step back and stretch out your arm to avoid the spray reaching your own face.

"Do you not understand what's going on here, Raquel? He's trying to incriminate me just as he did to Eduardo Ribas! Listen, the day Teresa was murdered, you came to my house and told me you'd just spoken to her on the phone. How long did it take you to get to my house? According to you, it was about fifteen minutes. Do you think I had enough time to kill her, return to my apartment, and pretend nothing happened?"

Raquel stared at her friend and remembered the afternoon that Teresa was killed. She remembered the nurse's telephone call and how it had been cut off abruptly, her own subsequent and unsuccessful attempts to call back, and her decision to go find Zarco. The time lapse from the moment her call to Teresa was disconnected to her arrival at the detective's house wasn't even twenty minutes. Zarco hadn't had time to go to the nurse's house, stab her, and return home. In that exact instant, Raquel saw the events from another perspective, and she relaxed. Ferrando's accusations and the sudden appearance of Álex in the stairwell had set off all her alarms. Now she understood the reason for the police officer's accusations: her friend was the perfect scapegoat. His psychiatric history and his emotional frailty had made him an easy target. She took her hand out of her purse, moved toward her friend, and hugged him tightly. Zarco wasn't socially adept and his behavior around other people was awkward and often inappropriate. He had lots of eccentricities, such as fixating on the number 4 when looking at license plates, and exhibited other compulsions that might be classified as paranoid. However, Raquel did not think he was capable of shooting a man in cold blood, let alone strangling her sister and stabbing Teresa. Her fear had made her irrational. And if Ferrando's accusations were false, it would confirm Zarco's suspicions and point to the police sergeant as their prime suspect.

"Álex, I still don't understand Ferrando's motive in killing my sister and Teresa."

"I already told you they weren't his primary targets. I'll tell you everything in detail. Right now, we need to go see Ballesteros and come up with a strategy. It won't be easy to implicate a Civil Guard officer."

"Ferrando told Ballesteros he was going to request a search warrant for your house. Do you think he's trying to incriminate you?"

"It certainly looks that way," replied Zarco. "He may try to plant evidence in my house that could implicate me, such as the murder weapon he used to shoot Cañas."

"And what can we do about it?"

"I have surveillance cameras in every room. If they go unnoticed during the search and Ferrando tries to plant evidence, his move could backfire on him."

"That seems like a remote possibility. We need to get ahead of him. We should go see Ballesteros," she said. "You can explain everything in detail and we can ask him for advice on how to stop the warrant, or at least to be there and keep an eye on Ferrando."

They went outside and started walking at a brisk pace. By the time they arrived at Ballesteros house they were nearly out of breath. Zarco's face held a serious expression. He dropped his small backpack on a table and asked the attorney for a glass of water, which he drank while quickly downing a pill he'd taken out of his coat pocket. On their way there, Raquel had called Ballesteros and briefly informed him of the situation. She told him it would have been entirely impossible for Zarco to have killed Teresa and, without providing details, she suggested that he'd made some new and surprising discoveries.

"Alright, explain yourself!" insisted Ballesteros, without hiding the irritation in his voice. Although Raquel had assured him that Zarco was not responsible for the murders, the attorney remained skeptical about the detective's professionality and his ability to uncover the person or persons behind the crimes. He had even begun to doubt whether the facts proven during the trial in which his client was convicted corresponded with what had actually occurred. There were certainly small contradictions, details that didn't square, but then life was not a perfect puzzle. Not everything could be explained or understood.

"As you both know," Zarco slowly began to explain while trying to stay calm and not become flustered, "I was operating on the assumption that these three murders had to be connected. Ibiza is an island where few crimes are committed, and two murders in a row are too much of a coincidence. And if we count the nurse's recent murder, that makes three victims. The disconcerting part was the method used: each of the murders had been different. The first was a shooting. The second, a strangulation after anesthetizing the victim with chloroform to make it appear like a robbery. And the third victim was stabbed repeatedly. In short, I began to theorize that this didn't involve a normal individual but had to be a gang, or a perhaps a professional killer. I wasn't completely off the mark there, but not in the way you think."

"On the other hand," the detective continued, "there was a single common location that we knew of where all three victims had been: Can Misses Hospital."

"Zarco," interrupted Ballesteros impatiently, "just tell us who your suspect is and then explain the course of your investigation."

"Patience," responded Zarco, ignoring the attorney's growing irritation. "As I was saying, we have a common location. That's why I initially suspected Gomis, the doctor. But there was also another person that was connected to at least the first two crimes: the Civil Guard officer that investigated both murders and had been in charge of investigating the burglaries in the Cap Martinet area: Sergeant Ferrando."

"Zarco, I'm missing something here," said Ballesteros

vehemently.

"Raúl, please, let him explain," pleaded Raquel.

"Perhaps my explanation is too convoluted," continued the detective, unfazed, "I'll try to explain things chronologically, as the events occurred. A little over a year ago in 2011, during the long holiday weekend for Constitution Day, Ferrando's wife was run over by a white ATV. The driver fled the scene. In theory, they never found the driver of the car, but Ferrando did discover the identity of the vehicle owner. It couldn't have been very difficult for a judicial police agent like him to make inquiries in local body shops or even to figure out the make and model of the vehicle by using fragments from the broken blinker that were found at the scene of the accident. The owner of the vehicle that caused the accident was none other than Santiago Cañas, and he lived in Ibiza. Ferrando requested a work transfer and arrived on the island one month before Cañas' death. According to Ferrando's co-workers, he was transferred due to pressure from higher ups because of an incident that had occurred with a judge. But I believe he came here looking for Cañas."

"And why not arrest him?" asked the attorney.

"You, better than anyone else, know what can happen with some crimes. There really had been a hit-and-run accident due to reckless driving, and possibly failure to call for an ambulance—though that part would be difficult to prove since the guilty party did call 911 later from a pay phone. In any case, the sentence they could get for this crime wouldn't be greater than two years in prison and, without any priors, they wouldn't set foot in jail. That would've been too little for Ferrando, who had to watch his wife wasting away in a wheelchair. So, he makes an appointment to see Cañas and, without giving him time to explain, shoots him three times."

"And the 50,000 euros Cañas took out of the bank that morning?" asked Ballesteros.

"That was very shrewd. To a certain extent, I think I've figured out how the sergeant's mind works. He had two reasons to ask for the money: the first, to deflect the investigation; the second, to obtain 50,000 euros. In fact, shortly after Cañas' murder, the sergeant purchased a handicap accessible vehicle that cost him a large part of that amount. Ferrando got in touch with Cañas and pretended that he wanted compensation for the hit-and-run accident. What's interesting is that Cañas hadn't been driving the vehicle the night of the accident. It had been his wife. Cañas had remembered that, after that trip, she had told him about an insignificant accident. So being the clever businessman that he was, before telling the sergeant to go to hell, he spoke to his wife who confirmed that the sergeant's allegations were true. Cañas didn't tell his wife about the blackmail, nor did he tell Ferrando that he hadn't been the one driving the ATV the night of the accident. He thought that by paying 50,000 euros the issue would be forgotten. Perhaps he thought he owed some compensation to the sergeant and his wife."

"And being a good businessman, he thought that proper compensation would fix everything," corroborated Ballesteros. "That would explain the first murder, but not the two girls."

"The thing is that, by some miracle, Santiago Cañas didn't die from the gunshot wounds. He successfully survived the surgery. Cañas had seen his killer face to face, and Ferrando could not allow him to recover. Using the investigation as an excuse, he went to the hospital. Cañas' widow informed me that she had spoken to Ferrando and that he'd appeared worried about her husband's condition. Of course, he was worried, but not in the way that she thought. In a moment of carelessness, he must've entered the unit where Cañas, who was still under the effects of the anesthesia, was located. It would have been easy to put a pillow over his face and smother him without leaving visible marks. Who would even think that Cañas had been suffocated in the hospital after being admitted with three gunshots in his body? The cardiac arrest would be attributed to the bullet wounds."

"And here's where Ana comes in. She was in charge of the patient's care. She must've seen Ferrando near Cañas' bed and walked over to say something. He thought he had been discovered and saw his whole plan falling apart, so he decided to forge ahead. He could have threatened Ana with his gun, or even identified himself as a police officer and asked her to accompany him. The fact is they walked out of the hospital together."

"Teresa told us that she'd seen Ana accompanied by a doctor with a serious face. She assumed he was a doctor because they were in a hospital, or perhaps Ferrando was wearing a doctor's coat to slip by undetected. Either way, the person she saw was the sergeant."

"Around that time, Ferrando was investigating burglaries in the Cap Martinet area, and he'd run some experiments with chloroform. He knew the burglar's modus operandi, and he knew how he entered the victim's homes. There would be nothing easier than to anesthetize the girl, strangle her, and then rig the scene of the crime to make it seem like another robbery in the series he was already investigating."

"Ferrando gave an order to increase monitoring in the Cap Martinet area and they arrested the man that had been committing the robberies. You are the ones who explained to me how he'd forced the poor drug addict that had been arrested to confess."

"It also seemed strange that there had been such little investigation for these two crimes. The victims' families were barely questioned, even if simply to rule out close relatives who often tend to be the initial suspects. Ferrando was heading the investigations, and wanted them to fizzle out so he could close them as soon as possible. One of the cases had a trumped up suspect; the other would remain unsolved and open to much speculation regarding a hypothetical settling of scores or gambling debts. His best move was to avoid stirring the pot, and let things wind down as soon as possible to avoid any possible risks."

"Then there was the third murder, Teresa. To a certain extent, I'm responsible for that. Why did he kill her eight months after the first two murders? Simply because, at first, I didn't know that someone had seen him leave the hospital with Ana López. A few days ago, I was feeling immensely proud of myself and went to see the sergeant. I told him there was a witness that had seen Ana the morning of her disappearance accompanied by a man, and I revealed Teresa's identity to him. He must have been afraid that he'd be found out. He had come too far to turn back and decided to kill the only person that could give him away. And just a few days before, a picture of Ferrando had been in the Ibizan *Diario*, with an article about how he rescued an English tourist. There was a possibility that the nurse had recognized him when she saw the newspaper, and that appears to have been what happened. The afternoon she was killed, Teresa called Raquel. I believe she wanted to tell her that she'd recognized the man she saw with Ana the day she'd disappeared, but she never got the chance. What I don't know is if we'll have enough evidence to charge him. The sergeant knows well how police investigations work and I'm sure he was very savvy. There are probably no fingerprints and, even if there are, he could say they were left during the murder investigations."

"If they know who to investigate," interrupted Ballesteros, "they can always find something. Ferrando was quite sure of himself and may not have taken enough precautions. A ballistics test of his regulation firearm should be performed. His bank accounts can also be searched to confirm where he got the money to purchase the handicap accessible vehicle. I can present the facts to a prosecutor I know and ask him to request a search warrant for Ferrando's home. If he is the killer, as everything seems to indicate, we'll prove it."

"And that's why he wanted to blame you for the crimes!" exclaimed Raquel looking directly at her friend. "To get the monkey off his back! What we absolutely need to avoid is the search warrant for Álex's house. God only knows what machinations that cop's twisted mind can come up with!"

A familiar voice made Raquel, Ballesteros, and Zarco stop in horror.

"Very clever, Mr. Private Detective." The three of them turned and fixed their eyes on a shadowy silhouette backlit in the doorway. They recognized him instantly. The figure took a step forward and was illuminated by the light of the room, making Sergeant Ferrando's distinctive features completely visible to them. He held a gun in each hand, with barrels pointed right at them. The first question in Ballesteros' mind was how long Ferrando had been standing there listening, and whether he'd heard the entire conversation or just the end. Zarco remembered that his Glock was in the inside pocket of his coat, which was resting on the back of a chair, and he debated how complicated it would be to access it. If he didn't come up with something, this might be the last night of his life.

"As you can all see, Mr. Detective is not the only one who knows how to open a door with a credit card," continued the sergeant in a hoarse voice. "But the truth is I underestimated him. I didn't think he was capable of figuring anything out. You, "he said, looking at Zarco, "would have been a good addition to our judicial police team."

"What do you intend to do? Kill all three of us?" asked Ballesteros calmly. His own lack of fear surprised him. In truth, he gave two shits if he got shot. His only regret would be not seeing his daughter again. The rest of his life, at present, wasn't worth much.

"There's no other way out for me," said Ferrando, closing in on the two men while holding the guns casually, as if he were talking to three friends. Raquel remained on the couch, petrified. "Believe me when I say I'm sorry, just as I was sorry about the two girls. But I have to take care of a disabled wife, and spending years in prison is out of the question. All I wanted was to kill the son of a bitch that ran over my wife and left her lying there like a dog. You know: if he'd only stopped, my wife wouldn't be crippled. But he left her lying there on the road and then another car ran over her legs causing a spinal injury."

"It's certainly a tragic story, but you're slaughtering many innocent victims," interrupted Raquel.

"My wife was also an innocent victim," said Ferrando impassively, as if he'd already made a decision from which there was no turning back.

"Do you think she'd approve of all these deaths?" asked Raquel.

"She will never know. You three are the only loose ends left, and I've already taken necessary measures. Tomorrow, the police will have a warrant to search the detective's office and they might find something. Perhaps what's left of the 50,000 euros. The gun I'm carrying is the same one I used to shoot Cañas. When my fellow officers arrive, they'll find you two have been shot with this gun," he said, waiving it at Raquel and Ballesteros, "and the detective will have a couple of shots in him from my own service weapon. I'll say I arrived too late to stop him from killing you, and I had no choice but to kill him myself. I don't think anyone will doubt me."

"You had it planned all along. That's why you were seeding suspicions about Zarco," said Ballesteros.

"You're a shrewd attorney. But you should have just left well enough alone."

"Do you want to know what's so funny about this, if you can even use that word after so many crimes?" asked Zarco, and kept talking without waiting for a response, "that all of this started because of a mistake you made. The man you killed wasn't even driving the car that ran over your wife."

"You're trying to use a cheap trick to confuse me. I think you've been watching too many B movies. Cañas owned the ATV, and when I told him he had to pay me 50,000 euros as compensation for damages so I'd forget the incident, he didn't even blink."

Zarco remembered that Santiago Cañas' widow told him that her husband had found out the truth about the accident. Ferrando had blackmailed him, and Cañas hadn't denied being the person who caused the accident because he'd wanted to protect his wife. The tragedy of this woeful paradox was that, after so many deaths, the sergeant didn't even know who the author of the hit-and-run accident was. The person who triggered this tide of violence had actually been Cañas' widow.

Just then, they heard the clear metallic sound of a key in

the latch, unlocking the door. Ballesteros' brain was the first to react, alerted by the danger. The person opening the door was his daughter, Julieta. She had agreed to come over to have that talk about smoking joints. Ballesteros stopped thinking coherently and could only feel terror. Up until a moment ago, he'd only thought about retaining his dignity in the face of almost certain death. He had already lived enough, however; his daughter's life was just beginning. He could care less if she smoked joints or if she wanted to be a writer or whatever. At that moment, all he wanted was for her to stay alive. Perhaps he hadn't always shown his daughter how much he loved her, he was often so guarded in their daily interactions, and he knew full well that Julieta wasn't fond of displays of affection. Nevertheless, he knew he would make every effort or sacrifice for his daughter's wellbeing. Without even thinking about it, he suddenly pounced on Sergeant Ferrando while yelling at the top of his lungs, "Run, Julieta. Run!"

Ferrando was two meters away from both the attorney and Zarco, and had both guns pointed at a spot halfway between them. Although Ballesteros' reaction had surprised him, Ferrando's response was swift and agile. He took a half step backward and struck Ballesteros in the face with the butt of the gun he held in his right hand. Blood began to abundantly flow from the attorney's nose as he collapsed onto the carpet. Raquel was terror-stricken. She couldn't move. Zarco saw an opportunity to try to grab his own gun, but couldn't remember if he'd taken off the safety nor was he confident in his own ability to handle the weapon. He was, however, certain of one thing: if he was going to do something, now was the time. He wouldn't get a second chance. In a flash, Zarco took a short step and, despite his excess weight, he nimbly positioned himself to stand in profile to the sergeant. He lifted his bent leg, poised to deliver a *yoko geri* kick to the sergeant's head. This lateral kick was Zarco's favorite. He'd practiced it more than any other and excelled at the technique, having mastered the ability to focus all of his weight and body strength to his leg. Ferrando, after having inflicted a butt-stroke to Ballesteros that had left him semiconscious with blood spewing from his face, noticed from the corner of his eye that the detective had made some kind of leap, but couldn't second-guess his intention. He pointed the gun at Zarco and fired at the same time that the detective's leg hurtled toward him. What occurred in a split second in real time played out in slow motion in Zarco's mind: he saw the bullet approach his head and then felt a part of his skull crack. He thought he would only have a short time left to live. He focused all of his mental strength on the kick. It was the type of strength that erupts from the deepest part of a human being and makes us transcend ourselves—find strength when we had none left. He immediately knew that for the first and only time in his life, he had found that thing his sensei had talked about throughout his years of training: his *Chi*, his energy, his inner strength. Zarco's leg unfurled like a whip, while the edge of his foot delivered a strike to the sergeant's throat, crushing his trachea.

39

The police arrived fifteen minutes later. Julieta had distinctly heard her father's voice yelling for her to leave, followed by furniture falling and a loud boom that sounded like a shot. She ran down the stairs and called 911 to report that she'd heard gunshots in her father's home. Then she hid in a nearby doorway. Just a few minutes later, a National Police car arrived with its roof lights spinning and flashing. She directed them to the floor her father was on, and the two officers went upstairs with their guns drawn. They found the apartment door open. Everything was quiet. They walked through the foyer toward the living room where the lights were on and found three men on the floor. Raquel had managed to bandage Álex Zarco's head wound to slow the blood loss, and she had also placed a pillow under Ballesteros' head. Although he was still groggy, Ballesteros was able to emit pitiful moans indicating he was still among the living. The third man appeared dead.

40

Ballesteros awoke in a bed at Can Misses Hospital, but didn't know where he was. He half-opened his eyes and soon realized he wasn't at home. The first rays of daybreak were filtering through the slatted window blinds and he slowly became aware that he was in a hospital, though he didn't remember how he'd arrived there. He pushed the call button that sat on a small table. His head ached and he was disoriented. He began to remember fragments of what had occurred: Ferrando pointing a gun at him and at Zarco; his daughter opening the door. And that was all he remembered. He desperately needed to know what had happened to Julieta.

A nurse appeared wearing white scrubs and a light blue tee-shirt. Ballesteros spoke hurriedly.

"Excuse me, nurse! Do you know where my things are? I need my phone!"

"Sir, when you came in, you didn't have a phone," replied the nurse.

"Yes, but I need to call my daughter. I don't know if something has happened to her."

"Your daughter was here with your wife. They left last night while you slept."

Ballesteros relaxed. If Julieta was safe and unharmed, everything else was insignificant. She's probably in class, he thought. And he must not be in serious condition.

"What happened to me?"

"You received a sharp blow to the head and have a mild concussion. You lost consciousness and have a fracture in your nasal septum. That's why there is a splint on your nose."

Ballesteros touched his face with his hand and felt a bandage and some pieces of metal on both sides of his nose.

"Don't touch it," admonished the nurse.
"Can I look in the mirror?"

41

A few hours later, Ballesteros was fully conscious. A stabbing pain located in some undefined area of his head reminded him of the wallop he had received, although he couldn't recall the details. What had happened? How did he escape what he had thought was certain death? And where were Raquel, and Zarco, and Ferrando?

Two men with decidedly serious demeanors walked into his room. One had on a well-tailored suit while the other wore the unmistakable green uniform exclusive to the Civil Guard.

"It looks like you've recovered. My name is Joaquín Cardona, Commissioner of the National Police," the man in the suit introduced himself. He turned and gave the floor to the man in uniform.

"I am Leandro Villanueva, Lieutenant-Commander with the Civil Guard. We'd like to ask you a few questions."

"I don't understand," responded Ballesteros, slightly confused. He also thought it strange to find the Civil Guard and the National Police working together. Although both officers were members of law enforcement agencies, they belonged to different organizations that rarely collaborated, as each had well defined territorial jurisdictions. "I don't know what happened. I don't remember."

"Goddammit! One man is dead and it seems nobody is going to tell us anything!" barked the commissioner.

"Look, we know you have a good reputation in the lawyer's guild," the lieutenant-commander said in a calmer tone. Ballesteros asked himself if they'd rehearsed their good cop–bad cop routine or if it just came naturally to them. Didn't they know that everybody was familiar with that strategy by now? Were they trying to con him? "Tell us what you remember."

"Yes, gladly. But I just heard you mention a dead body. Who died? Zarco?"

"No," the commissioner intervened again. "Mr. Zarco remains unconscious. He's critically injured, but alive. However, a Civil Guard officer has died and we don't understand what the hell the two of you and the woman from the Treasury Department were doing, and how all of you became involved in this deadly brawl. The young lady told us a story that was difficult to believe and, don't take this the wrong way, but we wanted to corroborate with you before you had a chance to speak with her."

Ballesteros explained everything from the beginning, when Eduardo Ribas was arrested, tried, and convicted for the murder of Ana López Demichellis, undeniably prompted by the confession obtained by Sergeant Ferrando. While relating the story, Ballesteros furtively glanced back and forth at the officers' faces, trying to discern to what extent his account surprised or alarmed them. He told them how Raquel, feeling unsatisfied with the results of the trial, decided to investigate her sister's death with assistance from Zarco and from Ballesteros himself. He continued to relay the events, telling them how Zarco had found a connection between Ana's murder and the man who'd been shot and subsequently operated on at Can Misses Hospital, how Ferrando had carried out a series of crimes including the murder of another nurse (who was a co-worker of Ana López') fearing that she would recognize him, and finally, how the sergeant had burst into Ballesteros' home, guns in hands, intent on eliminating loose ends. Both law enforcement officials remained stone-faced as they listened to the attorney's account. They were evaluating the veracity of his statement and the narrator's credibility.

"The last thing I remember," concluded Ballesteros, "is the sergeant pointing two guns at us and then hearing my daughter begin to open the door to the house."

"Ever since his wife's accident, Ferrando lost his way," commented the lieutenant-commander. "Poor woman. Disabled, widowed, and now her husband's memory sullied."

"I suppose you have evidence to back up what you're saying," the commissioner leveled this question at Ballesteros in the form of a statement.

"The main evidence is that he tried to kill us."

"But all we have is your word and the girl's statement to determine if things happened as you say. The sergeant cannot defend himself."

"The sergeant pointed two guns at us and, according to what he told us, he used one of them to shoot Cañas. I imagine you can find the sergeant's fingerprints on both weapons, and then verify that I'm telling the truth," rebutted Ballesteros.

"Indeed, two weapons were found, and the fingerprints are being examined," interrupted the Civil Guard officer. "Let's leave this man alone." He looked at the commissioner. "I think he's already gone through enough emotional turmoil. As you already know, you'll have to make a statement to the judge." He paused briefly, as if he was having difficulty finding the right words. "I would prefer it if the press did not find out about Ferrando's dirty laundry. I don't want to add any more suffering to his widow."

"They won't hear anything from me. But keep in mind that you'll have to reopen Eduardo Ribas' case, the man who was convicted of Ana López' murder. And apart from us, there are a multitude of people who have access to this information: police officers, the judge, prosecutor, officers of the court. Even my neighbors may have seen something. Basically, it's a lengthy list. Can I go home now? I have an incredible urge to take a shower and lie down on the couch."

"If the doctors approve, we don't have a problem with it."

42

Ballesteros was discharged at noon. Before he left the hospital he tried to visit Zarco but the nurses wouldn't allow it. They told him Álex had been admitted to the ICU and was in a coma. Ballesteros left Can Misses and went home. He took a long shower while trying to keep the bandage dry that was covering his nose. He put on his pajamas and laid down on the couch. At 2:00 o'clock, he started to prepare a stir-fry with peppers, onions, leeks, and an artichoke, so he could make a vegetable *fideuá*. As he stirred the vegetables with a wooden spoon, he realized his daughter would already be out of school, and he dialed her phone. They had a brief conversation. She told him she'd visit him later in the day.

Immediately afterwards, he called Raquel, who summarized what had occurred after he'd pounced on Ferrando and how Zarco had risked his own life to save theirs. They agreed to meet the following morning. He added broth from a carton to the pan, covered the vegetables and, when the liquid began to boil, he added the noodles. He let it boil for about 15 minutes, until the noodles absorbed the broth, removed the pan from the fire and covered it with newspaper. While the *fideuá* rested, he turned on the TV and lit a cigarette. At that hour, most channels were broadcasting news programs, but he didn't like any of them. They were all quick to show their political leanings either in favor of or against the current government. Although Ballesteros' particular leaning was conservative, he had lost faith in the political stratum, on one side as well as the other. There was no good or bad: they were all bad. No political party was immune from the taint of corruption. He continued changing channels until an attractive woman appeared on the screen discussing the day's news with a serious demeanor and apparent sincerity.

He heard the familiar droning that was repeated at least once a week: "*another new victim of sexist violence...*" He broke away from that segment though he left the news channel on. Ballesteros was heading for the kitchen when one word caught his attention: Ibiza. The commentator had mentioned the island of Ibiza. He turned toward the TV and confirmed the images were of central Ibiza. At that moment, the reporter was interviewing a neighbor who confirmed that: the husband was a genuinely nice person, and it simply wasn't possible that he could do what he'd done. The presumed offender, thusly identified by the reporter, was a German national. Ballesteros pushed the red button on the remote and turned the TV off. He didn't want to hear the name of the man who had allegedly killed his wife. He hoped the man's name was not Derek Neumann and indeed, Ballesteros assumed that Neumann would already have called him if he'd been arrested. Once again, too many coincidences. He imagined the German strangling his wife or throwing her out the window. Ballesteros hadn't listened to the details, but one thing was indisputable: life was fucking hell.

That's why he envied Paco. It often seemed as though the problems, worries, and depression we mortals face simply didn't exist for him. He lived in a state of happiness that was, frankly, insulting. It was perplexing that Paco could escape everyday problems that torment and frequently overwhelm us. And yet, as perplexing as it was, he still cared for his friend and was happy that Paco had that protective armor. He thought that, as much as we all struggle and endeavor, perhaps happiness is really all about luck, or what the ancient mystics referred to as divine gift. Paco was simply born lucky. Where did luck hide? Could you just find it one day and it would stay with you for the rest of your life like a faithful lover? He checked his phone for missed calls. There were none from his friend.

Ballesteros covered the *fideuá* with aluminum foil and sat out on the terrace, looking out at the street. He'd lost his appetite. He turned off his cell phone to avoid a possible call from Derek Neumann, though he hadn't actually heard Derek's name mentioned on television and wasn't sure he was the wife killer. 'The presumed wife killer,' he corrected himself with a cynical smile.

He had decided to take a few days off and the broken nose provided a perfect excuse. He could travel to Menorca and relax on an island that still preserved its natural beauty and wasn't yet as overdeveloped as Ibiza, nor had it been overrun with superhighways. He could go fishing at an unspoiled inlet and, if he had time, lie in the sun for a while. He could fish, take a walk, or go into town at night for dinner. Perhaps he'd meet a beautiful woman. Or he could catch the car ferry to Denia and aimlessly cruise around the Peninsula driving north or perhaps south, stopping to eat or sleep in some small, quaint town. The only thing he knew for certain was that he needed a rest and, in order to get it, he had to leave Ibiza. The island tied him to his work and to numerous complications. And he could now add the shooting he had been involved in to his ongoing daily worries. Ballesteros knew it wouldn't be long before the media got its hands on all the gory details. He felt that, although his appearance hadn't changed much, his personality had evolved. Twenty years ago, he would have believed that getting thrust into the media spotlight would be his career trampoline. Now it just seemed like a hassle and a nuisance. He preferred anonymity to fame; his ambition had turned into a desire for solitude. Someone, he couldn't remember who, once said that the worst thing about wishes is that they sometimes come true. Ballesteros had always considered that to be pretentious horseshit. Now he was beginning to understand the meaning of that sentence: as long as our dreams remain unfulfilled we can keep up the illusion; but the moment they come true, the fantasy train stops and we find ourselves alone in an empty station, waiting for a new wish to replace the old one and give us the motivation and strength to go on. During his years as a student, Ballesteros' dream was to be a great attorney and he had dedicated his time and energy to that end. There were interminable days of studying and working diligently, days that extended into the dawn. Now he relished prestige among his colleagues and among judges and magistrates and yet, he longed for that obsession that had consumed him from the moment he awoke and continued to fuel his energy all day long. Now he realized that he preferred the inexperienced and enthusiastic attorney he used to be, to the smugly complacent lawyer he had become.

The ringing of the intercom interrupted his self-critical, almost self-destructive thoughts. It seemed strange that Julieta would arrive so early, although she was the person he most longed to see right at that moment. However, it wasn't his daughter who had pressed the call button.

Ballesteros opened the door, left it ajar and waited in the doorway. He listened to the sounds of the elevator motor and grinding gears until it stopped at his floor. The elevator door opened automatically and there was his friend, or rather ex-friend, Paco. He walked toward Ballesteros with a half-smile that the attorney couldn't really discern. Paco lazily extended his hand and Ballesteros impassively held out his own. Neither man wanted to show any pleasure.

"How are you feeling?" asked Paco. "I tried calling your phone but it was either off or out of service."

"Yes, I turned it off. I wanted to rest a bit. And regarding how I feel: I suppose that given the circumstances, I'm good."

"From what I read in the newspaper, you were almost dead."

"The press always exaggerates just to sell papers."

"Is it true that the private detective is in a coma?"

"Yes, so it seems. He just underwent a complicated surgery. He had a bullet in his head. I suppose we'll have to wait and see. They say the next twenty-four hours are key, but it's certainly not looking good. Do you want a drink?" Ballesteros offered. "If you haven't eaten yet, I just finished making a *fideuá*. But after I made it, I lost my appetite."

"I've already eaten. But I'd take some tea," replied Paco.

"Perfect. But I have a mild headache so, if you don't mind, make it yourself. You already know where to find the cups and water. The teabags are in the cupboard on the right. Make me one as well, please."

Paco Marín walked into the kitchen. He put some water in a pot and set it on the stove to heat, grabbed a couple of cups and placed a bag of red tea in each.

"If you're tired, I can go," he said loudly so his friend could hear him from the living room.

"No. I'm glad you came. Look, I'm sorry about what I did. You know, Paco, I've been re-examining my life and I believe I've squandered so much of it. I've made so many mistakes!"

"We all make mistakes," responded Paco, as he placed the cups on the living room table and sat on a couch across from of Ballesteros. "The fact that you've realized it says a lot in your favor. It's much harder to acknowledge having made a blunder than it is to actually make it."

"You spend your whole life learning, and it doesn't seem to be enough."

"Alright, now tell me this whole story."

"Do you remember when I told you we were investigating the case for my client, Eduardo Ribas, and that we'd hired a private detective who was a little weird? Well, that was only the beginning."

Ballesteros explained the entire investigation from the beginning, leaving nothing out. His description of Raquel López Demichellis betrayed the attraction he felt for her.

"And the pisser is," continued the attorney, "that we argued on our first date—and it was about bullshit. And, well, she has some foibles of her own, I mean, she drinks Diet Coke with her *Jabugo* ham and *Cabrales* cheese?! But I think I could almost forgive her that."

"You argued with her on your first date? What were you thinking?"

"You know, we somehow got on the topic of domestic violence laws," said Ballesteros.

"I know you think the laws are terrible, but I don't understand how you could end up arguing about them with an attractive woman."

"Yeah. It was not my intention to argue, but if you criticize the law, you come across like a chauvinist in favor of abuse. Politicians are more interested in what is politically correct than the truth. And, unfortunately, we're at their mercy. There was a new case in Ibiza today which just adds fuel to the fire. And as if that weren't enough, I think he might be my client. I'm not sure it was him because I didn't finish listening to the news. If I could, I'd leave Spain and move to a more civilized country. Like Switzerland, for example."

"It's the same everywhere," said Paco, using one of those trite phrases that can be adapted for any occasion. "And do you think there will be a review of that man's case, the one who was convicted for the nurse's murder?"

"It's complicated, but possible. He was unjustly convicted."

"The truth is you could write a novel with this story."

EPILOGUE

And that's where the idea emerged for this chronicle which I'm about to finish. After my visit with Raúl, several relevant events occurred that affected some of this story's protagonists which I should make known before finishing this narrative. The most noteworthy of these was the private investigator's recovery. After several days in a coma, Álex Zarco opened his eyes one morning and rejoined the world of the living. He did not suffer any serious brain damage and was able to regain his speech and motor skills which, considering the gravity of his injury, surpassed the doctors' expectations.

Although law enforcement agencies, particularly the Civil Guard, tried to keep Sergeant Ferrando's involvement in the three murders that took place in Ibiza over the past year from becoming known, all the particulars of the case were brought to light, which inadvertently provided unexpected publicity to the Zarco and Cía. detective agency, and extolled its only employee. The detective had to convalesce for several months before completely regaining his strength. During that time, his phone never stopped ringing. He got calls from reporters, who wanted to learn about the investigation firsthand; from curious acquaintances and strangers; and from people who wanted to retain the services of Zarco and Cía. Given his debilitated condition, he decided to employ a couple of assistants to help him manage the avalanche of new clients. The demands for his services came not only from Ibiza but also Madrid, Barcelona, and other Spanish cities. In light of his agency's resounding success, he established his headquarters in a location outside of his home, in an office building in the center of Ibiza, and hired a handsome male secretary to answer the phone and greet clients. He also hired Xicu, the hacker, on a full-time basis. That way, Zarco could ensure that the "genius" would always be available to him, and make it impossible for other detective agencies to contract his services. Xicu, initially too unaspiring to want a salaried position, eventually acquiesced after he reviewed the pros and cons: mainly that he would lose his freedom but was assured a significant monthly income, and he thought that, after the age of thirty, security is just as valuable a commodity in life as freedom. On the other hand, he continued to independently dedicate himself to activities he enjoyed (hacking). Now it was Zarco and Cía, in the fullest sense of the name.

The appeal that Ballesteros presented to the court for the review of Eduardo Ribas' conviction was heard and his expectations were realized. And, despite the characteristically slow turning of judicial cogs, Ribas was finally set free. Ballesteros also sought compensation of half a million euros for his client, for damages caused by the unlawful administration of justice. This petition was denied in the first appeal, on the understanding that the trial had been carried out with all available constitutional guarantees, and that any failures had been consistent with the information that was available at that time. Finally, when legal resources had been exhausted, the Supreme Court upheld the complaint but reduced the damages awarded to six thousand euros in compensation paid to Mr. Ribas by the state for having spent one year and twenty-two days in prison.

The relationship between Raúl Ballesteros and his daughter, Julieta, improved at an astonishing speed. It may have been attributed to Julieta who, having experienced firsthand the near possibility of losing her father, became aware of her strong affection for him. Perhaps she was moved by how her father had risked his life to save hers, or perhaps she was just shedding the non-conformity and defiance of youth. It seems unimportant and even senseless to seek out the origins of feelings, even for this dilettante author who is addressing you now. Julieta became open and friendly with her father, and he felt the love of a daughter whom he thought he had irremissibly lost. Julieta had dropped her aspirations of becoming a writer and sustained continuous conversations with her father about her future profession. Ballesteros counseled her about going to university and choosing a career that really interested her, since we often dedicate more of our time to work life than to our family, friends, and hobbies. The only career he advised against, based on his own experience, was that of attorney and especially, a criminal attorney. A few weeks later, Julieta told her dad she'd decided to study law, and specialize in criminal law.

One evening, Ballesteros invited Tanya and I to dinner at his home. Tanya didn't know that Raúl had hired an agency to investigate her, and I was never going to tell her. Raquel was also invited. It was a pleasant meal. Raquel was a lovely young woman, though her demeanor was rather serious, which I identified as arrogant. Perhaps she would be a good match for Raúl after all. For a moment, I looked at both ladies and thought how lucky Raúl and I had been. Who would have told us, when we were young students and could barely get dates, that at forty-five years old we'd be sharing a meal with two striking and sensuous ladies. If we'd been able to see our future selves sitting at that dinner table, we might have been more patient. Tanya and Raquel hit it off instantly and their conversations seemed effortless. Raquel's frosty exterior melted, and she became chatty and affable. When we finished dinner we were all a little tipsy, and Tanya and I said our goodbyes so they could be alone and because we had our own plans for the evening. At least, I did.

"I don't understand anything," Raúl told me the following day. "We were doing so well, and I thought there was an attraction between us. I took her home and we kissed goodbye. But I called her today and she didn't pick up the phone. And later I sent her a text, and she didn't answer. I confirmed that she read it."

"I don't know Raúl, maybe she wants to be alone."

"Paco, I understand that she may want to be alone or maybe she's meeting someone, but the least she could do is respond. That's just my opinion. I don't know what to think. Maybe

I disappointed her last night because I didn't insist."

"I don't think so. If she really likes you, she may even have thought it was novel."

"You mean weird?"

"No, not at all. I would say almost elegant."

"You're just saying that so I'll stop brooding about it," said Ballesteros.

"I'm being serious, "I responded.

Three days later, Raúl and Raquel got together again. This time, it had been Raquel who'd called Raúl. He was still annoyed with her for not having picked up the phone even though she'd sent a message apologizing the next day. Despite his displeasure, Raúl was still very attracted to her and had decided to see her again. They had dinner at Cana María restaurant, and when he walked her home they kissed again. This time, Raúl insisted on staying with her. After all, they weren't kids anymore. She gently refused, and he went home smiling.

Raúl didn't want to appear impatient and waited a few days before contacting her again. She didn't answer the call. Raquel's behavior unsettled him. He didn't understand her attitude, and was not the right age or personality for these types of silly games. If she wasn't going to reply to his calls or texts, he wasn't going to try a second time. Maybe she was looking for more persistence from him, or maybe she was just off her rocker.

Tanya liked Raquel and they had become great friends in no time at all. They saw each other several times a week. I didn't tell Raúl about it to avoid stoking his obsession, nor did I make any comments to Tanya about her new friend's quirkiness.

One evening, Tanya returned home after having spent the afternoon with Raquel. She looked at me with a serious expression and said we 'had to talk'. That preamble gave me an uneasy feeling. It only took a few seconds for several dark misgivings to cross my mind. However, Tanya's outward appearance was serene and calmed me for a moment. Then I understood: she must be ill.

"Paco, I have to tell you something," she repeated.

"Okay then, tell me. You're making me nervous," I answered, trying not to be too curt.

"I'm sorry. It's just that it's not easy." She paused. "I'm leaving."

"You're leaving? What does that mean? Where? Are you going to Russia? Are you leaving this house?" Now I was irritated.

"The second one. I want some time apart ..."

"In my experience, that sentence really means it's over. I don't understand. I thought we loved each other." One possible explanation crossed my mind like a sudden jolt. "Is there someone else?"

"Yes, there's someone else."

"I suppose he's younger than me," I replied hurtfully, feeling the victim.

"Yes, younger, but age has nothing to do with it. You and I have been great together, our age difference has never bothered me. The only one who was ever bothered by it was you."

I thought she was choosing words that wouldn't hurt me. Her theory about our age was very romantic but, at the end of the day, she was leaving with a thirty-something.

"Do I know him? Will you tell me who he is?"

"Yes, you know her. It's Raquel. We are in love. We both knew it the minute we first saw each other at dinner at Raúl's house. Paco, I have loved you and, to a certain extent, I always will. But my feelings for Raquel are much stronger."

We stood there in silence. I tried to assimilate the news. Tanya had hinted at her sexual leanings, and I hadn't known how to interpret them because bisexuality was hard for me to understand. My egocentric mindset, thinking that other humans live and feel the same as me, had led me to huge mistakes throughout my life. This was one of them.

"I'm going to grab some clothes and my toothbrush and a few cosmetics," she said. "Tomorrow, I'll come back to get the rest of my things. Do you want me to give you the key now?"

"No. Take it. If I'm not here when you come to get your

things, leave it on the table and lock the door behind you."

"We're going to live in Madrid. If you travel there one day, I hope you'll come visit us." She kissed me on the cheek and slowly walked toward the bedroom.

Nothing is permanent. Life is a series of sensations. We aren't even the same people from one year to the next, or one day to the next. I had loved Tanya, just as I had previously loved other women. Still I knew that, given time, I would forget Tanya the same way I'd overcome other heartaches over the course of my existence. I walked out onto the terrace and pondered the clear evening stars. A warm breeze enveloped me. I remembered fragments of Antonio Machado's poetry: *"everything goes and everything stays"* ... *"Traveler, there is no road. You make your own path as you walk"*... *"and when you look back you see the path you will never travel again."*

Tanya's voice got my attention from inside the house. "Paco, I'm leaving." I went back inside. She was standing by the door with a small suitcase.

"Tomorrow I'll come and get my things," she reminded me.

"Whenever you want," I replied.

She approached me and gave me a hug. We remained in an embrace for a few seconds. Then she left. I gazed at her from the doorway. She got into her car, started the engine, and drove off without looking back at me.

"I told you that the proposal for a threesome was not normal," Raúl Ballesteros reminded me while we ate on the terrace of Ibiza's Club Náutico. It was May and the sun was shining. "On the bright side, it turns out she wasn't after you for the money."

"Right. And actually, I'm glad she left me for another woman and not for a man. I'm also glad they're going to live in Madrid; I think it will make it easier to forget her. They make a good couple: two young and beautiful women. And we're two old geezers. More than we care to admit."

"So true," acknowledged Raúl. "We're getting left behind. And, changing the subject, are you still writing that novel?"

"I'm almost finished."

ACKNOWLEDGMENTS

My decision to send this novel to a publisher was, in large part, motivated by friends and family who read it and encouraged me to do so. To that end, I want to thank: my sisters (Bárbara, Carolina, Patricia, and Pilar), María Alzira Abad, Pedro Basurko, Maica Delgado, Luis Garcia, Antonio Martín, Alberto Prats, Maglo Ripoll, María Paz Samper, Marta Terán, Josu M. Zulaika and, especially, Rita and Milena Prats, for the many happy moments we have shared over the years.

Milton Keynes UK
Ingram Content Group UK Ltd.
UKHW011415200624
444507UK00025B/108